DARK MAGE RISES

Star Mage Saga

Book Two

J.J. Green

INFINITE.BOOK

PREQUEL

Sign up to my reader group for a free copy of the *Star Mage Saga* prequel, *Daughter of Discord*, discounts on new releases, review crew invitations and other interesting stuff:

https://jjgreenauthor.com/free-books/

BOOKS OF STAR MAGE SAGA

Prequel: Star Mage Exile

Book 1: Star Mage Quest

Book 2: Dark Mage Rises

Book 3: Wildfire and Steel

Book 4: Mercenary Mage

Book 5: Accursed Space

Book 6: Flight from Sanctuary

Book 7: Fatal Star

Book 8: Galactic Rift

Book 9: Never War

ONE

As Carina Lin returned to consciousness, she struggled. Her wrists and ankles were tied and a gag was wrapped tightly around her face.

The hard floor she lay upon was vibrating ever so slightly, indicating she was aboard a starship. Wriggling around and pushing with her elbows and knees, she maneuvered herself to a sitting position. The room she found herself in wasn't much larger than a clothes closet and it was entirely bare. The door was smooth and featureless with no way to open it from the inside. She'd clearly been put in some kind of holding cell for prisoners, so the vessel was a military craft. Was that preferable to a criminal outfit, like human traffickers? She didn't think so.

Though she hadn't been able to get a good look at the attackers who had boarded the shuttle she'd stolen, she had a strong feeling they were the very last people she wanted to meet.

The last people she ever wanted to see again were the Sherrerrs. After her mother's experiences at the hands of those arrogant, aggressive meatheads, Carina was certain that if she encountered another Sherrerr before she died it would be far too soon. She doubted they would say the same about her. The clan would be very happy to have their shuttle back and a family of mages returned to their control. Yet there was another faction in that galactic sector that posed an even greater threat.

She had no idea how much time had passed since she'd been stunned. Perhaps an hour or longer, judging by how stiff and sore she was from lying on the hard floor. She recalled a brief battle, during which she'd managed to wound three of the shuttle's boarders. It was the last thing she remembered before waking up.

She waited, leaning against the wall with her knees drawn up, reflecting that her captors' decision to gag her seemed a particularly stupid move. What did they think she was going to do, shout her way to freedom? Then she recalled that time she'd bitten Stefan Sherrerr's neck. If she'd only managed to sink her teeth a little deeper, she might have killed her mother's rapist and torturer. She smiled grimly. Perhaps a gag was a good idea after all.

She twisted her hands and feet, attempting to improve the blood flow to her extremities. When would her kidnappers come for her and what would they do? Her thoughts turned to her half-siblings. She'd managed to Transport them all to the planet surface, using up the last of the elixir. Little Darius would be safe with Parthenia, her oldest half-sister. The twins, Ferne and Oriana, were together too. And nasty Castiel, who was a couple of years younger than Parthenia, was with his sister-acolyte Nahla.

She recalled Castiel's claims that he possessed mage powers, and shuddered. Parthenia, Ferne, Oriana, and Darius could be trusted to uphold the mage philosophy of never intentionally hurting anyone, but Castiel could not. If he was telling the truth, she dreaded what he might do. He was as evil as his father had been.

She'd been forced to Transport her friend, Bryce, alone to the surface, but he would be okay. He would find a way to return to his family on Ithiya. She was more worried about her mage brothers and sisters. They'd been brought up in sheltered luxury and hadn't developed the skills required to survive in a harsh environment. Even more dangerous to them was the fact that they didn't have any practice at concealing their mage skills. Ma had known all about the dangers of revealing her abilities to strangers, yet she'd still been captured and subjected to a life of enslavement and misery. What chance did the woman's naive offspring have?

If Carina escaped she had to protect them, but it would be hard to find them. Parthenia had given Carina one of her bracelets to help Locate her, but the kidnappers had taken it. Everything had been taken from her except her clothes. Parthenia had also given one of her bracelets to the twins, so at least they would be able to reunite with her. Maybe with the four of them working together they might remain safe.

As well as worrying about them, Carina already missed her brothers and sisters. In the few weeks she'd spent with Parthenia and her other mage siblings, she'd grown to love them. Only a few months ago, she hadn't even known she had a family.

If they ever got the chance to be together again, she would take them on a journey to find Earth, the planet where mages were rumored to have originated. In that remote place they might create a sanctuary where all mages could live openly without fear of capture. For the moment, however, that was all a dream.

Carina sighed and tried to clear her mind of gloomy thoughts. Escape was what she needed to focus on. There was a slim chance she was wrong about whose ship she was on. If she wasn't wrong, there was an even slimmer chance her captors wouldn't discover she'd crossed them in the past. She was in need of a lot of luck.

A metallic click sounded, and the door slid open. A man in uniform entered. His head was shaved, making it difficult to tell his age, though from his bearing he appeared to be a high-ranking officer. As he stepped closer, she saw the starburst insignia on his collar. Her luck was all out. He was working for the Dirksens.

The guard who entered behind him was carrying a chair. After she set the chair down, the officer waved her away. The door closed and the man sat, crossing his legs. As far as Carina could see, he wasn't armed. He was alone with a prisoner but carried nothing to defend himself. That didn't seem very smart, but before making a move, she waited to hear what he had to say.

The officer leaned forward, resting his elbows on his knees. He said nothing, only gazed at her. She returned his gaze. She wasn't cowed, if that was his intention. She had endured plenty of intimidation and beatings in her eighteen years. She could endure some more, and she would take her revenge if she got the chance.

The officer held eye contact for a while, not blinking.

"Eeeeennnnnooooor-e?" she asked through her gag.

He got to his feet, took two steps over to her and pulled it off. He then returned to his seat. "What did you say?"

"I said, is this a new torture method?" She worked her mouth to ease its dryness. "Because it isn't very effective."

A corner of the man's mouth lifted but then his eyes turned serious again. "I know your kind. We could go through the usual steps: I could ask you what you were doing aboard a Sherrerr shuttle, days from the site of a recent battle, yet not wearing a Sherrerr uniform. You'll stoically refuse to answer me. I'll tell the guard to rough you up a bit. You'll still refuse to respond. I'll threaten more pain and humiliation but after the guard does her job again, your lips will remain sealed. And so on and on. All very messy and distasteful and ultimately unlikely to bring either of us any satisfaction."

He tilted his head before continuing, "I know *you*. Where do I know you from?"

Carina's stomach clenched. This was it. She was going to be

identified, and then everything would be over. It was a shame she wouldn't see her family again.

The officer leaned forward and peered at her. "I'm right, aren't I? I do know you."

Damn. He'd read her reaction to his words in her face. Carina fought to calm herself and clear her mind as Nai Nai had taught her. This interrogation was turning out to be harder than she'd expected. Pain, she could withstand. This officer's methods were subtler.

"Hmm... Shut down your emotional response, have you?" he asked. "So you've been trained to do that. Perhaps you rank highly in the Sherrerr forces. Maybe you're a spy. That might explain some anomalies." His gaze roamed her features closely. "Yet you're too young to be a high-ranking officer. You're even younger than you look, I think."

Carina watched him defiantly yet didn't trust herself to respond, not knowing what he might interpret from her words. She wasn't going to hand answers to him on a plate.

His dark eyes were thoughtful. "Don't have anything to say? You were quite talkative a moment ago, trying to speak even though you were gagged. Do you find my observations unsettling? I've caught you unprepared, haven't I? You were expecting something quite different, and I've shocked you into silence. Not so cocky now, huh?"

The officer stood and straightened his pants. "You're quite the enigma, but that's fine. I enjoy a puzzle. I'll figure you out." He rapped the door with a knuckle and was let out.

As the door closed she cursed. It was childish, she knew, but she wished she'd thought up a smart comeback to the smug bastard's assertions. He'd been right about nearly everything. Though he hadn't raised a hand to her, she felt defeated somehow. Even his lack of a weapon had been an attack, she realized, and he'd won. He'd been demonstrating that she posed no threat to him. He'd been right. His words had disarmed her.

Had he seen a vid of the attack at Orrana? Was that how he knew her? It had to be. The Dirksens never forgave anyone who opposed them. Carina had known that when she'd agreed to take on the job with her merc band. Though she would never for a second regret what she'd done, her past was catching up to her.

The Dirksen officer was clever. He would discover what she'd done sooner or later, though what would happen then depended on what else piqued his curiosity. He reminded her a little of Calvaley, a Sherrerr commander who had deluded himself into believing he was fighting an ethical war for the betterment of human civilization.

The smart ones were the worst enemies, not those who were naturally aggressive, belligerent, and evil. People like Calvaley and the Dirksen officer were intelligent enough to weigh up the pros and cons of what they were doing, yet do it anyway.

She shivered. She was sunk.

———

Hours of boredom took the edge off her tension, and eventually she dozed. Some time later—she didn't know exactly how much time had passed—the door opened again. The shaven-headed, dark-eyed Dirksen officer came in carrying an interface and looking pleased with himself.

She eyed the screen with dread. She knew exactly what he was about to show her. How should she respond? She had no idea how to react to make things go better for her. She didn't think there was a reaction that might have that effect.

"I knew I'd seen you before," the officer said. "I have a good memory for faces, but even so, I wouldn't have recognized you if you hadn't taken off your helmet."

Taken off your helmet?

"No need to fake looking puzzled," said the officer. "Or maybe you aren't faking. It doesn't matter. The resemblance is unmistakable."

Her stomach dropped as she remembered the moment she'd removed her helmet. This was looking worse than she'd hoped.

The officer dragged his chair over and sat down before holding the screen in front of her face. "Does this look familiar?"

The scene was indeed familiar. The interface showed the interior of the smelting plant on Orrana. Her merc band had been tasked with rescuing a kidnapping victim from there—the Dirksens had abducted a Sherrerr child.

She had thought the Dirksens might have vids of the first attack on the plant, when her band had gone in through the reception, but this scene was from the second attack after the first had failed. She was looking at the room where the Dirksens had held the child, the boy she'd later come to know was her half-brother, Darius.

A soldier burst in. It was herself, wearing merc armor.

She watched calmly, trying not to betray any emotion. In the vid, the soldier squatted down, and as the camera tracked her movement the kidnapping victim came into view. Little Darius looked even more terrified than she remembered, and it was no wonder. The Dirksen thugs had tortured him to try to make him confess his mage powers—unsuccessfully. Her brother was a tough young man.

But at that moment, he'd been frozen with fear. So to show him she wasn't as scary as she looked, she'd... There it was. The soldier took off her helmet.

The Dirksen officer paused the vid. He was smiling. "Those

helmet visors make it impossible to identify faces. Thanks for making it easier for me. So you aren't a Sherrerr. You're a merc, though why you were aboard a Sherrerr shuttle remains to be revealed."

She didn't reply. She couldn't stand the man's gloating, and she shrank from what was probably coming next along with all its repercussions.

"But that isn't all, is it?" said the officer. "You aren't just a merc who took on a bad job. You know, that's what I like about you. You're so interesting. Right. I'll show you what I mean. I won't bore you with the slow bits." He forwarded the vid, skipping over the part where Carina persuaded Darius to come with her and they left the room. "Here it is." He slowed the vid to normal speed. "You carry the boy to a vent. Smart move. He would have been hurt if you'd tried to take him through the fire fight going on at the stairs. Your band's shuttle was up on the roof, and you figured you could climb through the network to reach it, didn't you? Only things were getting heated. You had a limited amount of time to reach the roof or your companions might have died waiting for you. One of them did die, in fact, I think."

Her heart ached. Poor Captain Speidel.

"Sorry," said the officer, "I didn't mean to bring back bad memories."

"Get to the point," she said between her teeth.

"I'm getting there, my young conundrum. No need to rush me. So, let's see. This is the time stamp for when you took the kid into the vent. Then here you are on the roof, only seconds later. You didn't have time to climb through the vent tunnels, especially with a kid encumbering you. So how did you manage it?"

She didn't reply. She'd Cast Transport in order to get Darius and herself up to the roof before the shuttle left.

"What a pity we didn't have surveillance cameras inside the vent system, huh?" the officer asked. "I would have loved to see exactly what you did. We had the boy because we guessed the Sherrerrs were pulling some weird shit. It looks like we were right, and that whatever it is, you can do it too. Is that why you were running from the Sherrerrs? Did you get tired of meeting their demands?"

When she remained silent, he went on, "Thanks for not insulting my intelligence by claiming ignorance. I appreciate it. I wish I could extend you some mercy in gratitude. Unfortunately, that isn't going to be possible. We lost the Sherrerr boy, but now we have you instead. And after that attack on our shipyard, my superiors are keener than ever to find out what this strange ability is. I can assure you they'll be expecting you to use it in their favor."

Two

The vibrations coming through the floor ceased. It had been several long hours since the Dirksen officer had left Carina's holding cell, but it looked like something was about to happen, and probably to her.

She wasn't certain where the ship was. So much time had elapsed since she'd been captured that it might not be at Ostillon, where she'd Transported her siblings and Bryce. The Dirksen vessel could have traveled to another planet or even to another system. Or it might only have been in orbit all the time.

What were the Dirksens even doing on Ostillon, if that was where the ship had stopped? According to the scant information she had managed to discover, the planet was one of two inhabited worlds in the Floria System, which was way off the main routes. As far as she'd been able to tell the system wasn't under Dirksen or Sherrerr control. Neither clan had taken an interest in the place, so it was officially 'disputed territory.'

Whatever the reason was for Dirksens to be lurking there, she guessed she might soon find out. Once more, her powers had placed her in a dangerous position. After witnessing what had happened to her mother after her abilities were discovered, she was prepared to fight to the death to avoid the same fate.

She waited tensely for what seemed an age before the door to her holding cell finally opened. This time, she didn't see the dark-eyed Dirksen officer. Two guards had arrived. One of them unfastened her ankle restraints and pulled her roughly to her feet. He grabbed her upper arm and pushed her forward. A hard metal edge was pushed into her head from behind. It was the muzzle of the other guard's gun.

"I understand, you know, language," she said as they forced her through the cell doorway. Her remark earned her a knock on her skull from the muzzle. It wasn't hard enough to daze her but she felt a trickle of blood run down her neck. Before another smart remark could slip out, Carina bit her tongue. Bravado wasn't going to help her escape and it wouldn't ease her tension either.

As the guard's hand fastened tightly around her bicep, he urged her along a corridor so fast she was almost running. The vessel was, as she'd guessed, a modestly sized military craft. The interior was bare, featureless metal, and she could hear the tramp of booted feet. She was probably inside a patrol ship. The Dirksens had been surveying the system for unscheduled arrivals of suspicious spacecraft. The stolen Sherrerr shuttle had been an obvious target.

A bright light shone ahead, and as they rounded a corner she saw it was daylight. They'd arrived at an exit ramp that led out onto the planet surface. The patrol ship was even smaller than she'd thought. Few space worthy ships could land and take off through a planet's atmosphere. She must have paused in surprise because the guard grunted, "Move," and pushed her down the ramp.

She caught a glimpse of a spaceport and a city before she was forced into the back of a ground transport. The door slammed, leaving her in total darkness on the floor of the vehicle. It lifted off the ground and then accelerated fast. She had been half-crouching. The sudden movement made her stumble. Her wrists remained tied, preventing her from saving herself. She hit the floor.

She was about to sit up when an idea occurred to her. It was a long shot but worth trying. Though she couldn't see a thing, she remembered where the door was. Lying on her back, she lifted both her legs and drove them hard against it. The door held firm, however.

Having nothing better to do as the journey progressed, she kicked the door again and again until a voice from the front of the vehicle growled, "Cut it out or I'll come back there and stun you."

She gave the door a final, defiant kick but then lay still, panting with exertion. She was uncomfortable lying on her tied arms so she turned onto her front. Where was she being taken? What Dirksen figure of importance was she about to meet? Would he be like Stefan Sherrerr, more monster than human being? What would the Dirksens do to her when they attempted to force her to reveal her mage powers?

She knew only one thing for sure: she would never admit to her ability to Cast. The minute she did that, her life would be over. The Dirksens would never rest until they compelled her to do what they wanted, by whatever means necessary. She recalled the time Stefan Sherrerr had forced her to raise a tidal wave against Dirksen troops, killing who knew how many of them. A clean fight was different. Mage powers were not supposed to be destructive.

She refused to live a life of shame and dishonor.

While waiting for the journey to end, she tried to recall what she'd seen of the city outside the spaceport before she'd been pushed into the transport. The metropolis had looked surprisingly high tech for a backwater place. Her home planet had also been in the middle of nowhere and life there had barely been above subsistence level. Other out-of-the-way locations she'd visited when working as a merc had been similar. Even the Sherrerr stronghold, Ithiya, had been provincial. She'd heard of highly developed places toward the center of the galactic sector, but she hadn't ever visited one.

Her glimpse of the cityscape had revealed tall blocks in many complex designs. Some had been decorated with vegetation and walkways linked the sections. She'd also seen small private transports flying between the blocks.

The vehicle turned a corner quickly, throwing her across the floor, and then a short while later it halted. A door at the front opened and slammed. The one she'd been kicking also opened. She looked past her feet, squinting in the sudden light. A burly man stood outside. She guessed he was the owner of the growly voice. Beyond him hovered an expensively dressed woman. Her expression reminded Carina of a type of bug she used to keep as a child. The beady-eyed insects had always been ready to pounce on whatever prey happened by, and the woman looked the same. Carina didn't relish the idea of being her prey.

The burly man reached in and grabbed her tied wrists before pulling her out of the vehicle in one smooth motion. She landed on her knees on the dusty ground and blinked in the piercing sunlight.

"Now then, Harmon," the woman said. "Not so rough, please. Help the girl up."

Harmon gripped her elbow and yanked her to her feet. They were under a wide awning outside a large residence. The city she'd seen at the spaceport had gone. The house seemed to be in the middle of nowhere, in fact. She was disheartened. If she managed to escape, she would have plenty of country to cross to reach an urban area.

"Come inside, dear," the woman said. "I do hope the guards haven't treated you too badly. They can be overzealous at times." She turned toward the entrance but then glanced back and said, "Remove her restraints, Harmon. How ridiculous."

Carina blinked again, though this time it wasn't due to the bright sunlight. The reception she was receiving wasn't at all what she'd expected. Harmon unfastened her wrist ties and, now that his mistress's back was turned, shoved Carina toward the door.

After another glance around—noting she wouldn't get five meters before Harmon could stun her—Carina followed the bug-like woman into the mansion. Harmon remained one step behind all the way to a lounge, where the woman invited Carina to sit. He hovered at her side until he was ordered, rather shrilly, to step back and "give the poor girl room to breathe."

"You must be exhausted," the woman continued. "I'll order some refreshments then Harmon will show you up to your apartment. I insist that you rest a while, for as long as you need. We can talk business later."

Carina was beginning to wonder if she was unconscious and dreaming. Perhaps she hadn't come around yet from being stunned on the Sherrerr shuttle. Perhaps the dark-eyed officer didn't exist. Or maybe she was still asleep on the Dirksen patrol ship.

"You seem confused," said the woman. "That's entirely understandable. Let me introduce myself. I am Langley Dirksen."

Perhaps Carina wasn't going mad after all.

"And it's my intention to make your life as comfortable as possible."

On the other hand...

Langley Dirksen lifted a comm to her lips and spoke softly,

ordering food and drinks. When she finished she looked up at Carina and said, "And you are…?"

Carina was so taken aback at the situation, she almost gave her name as a reflex. But instead she clamped her lips shut.

"Of course," Langley Dirksen said, "I understand." Her tone carried a hint of iciness that betrayed the politeness of her words. She folded her hands in her lap, resting them on the fine, pale-green, silky fabric of her dress. After a moment, she said, "Well, this is awkward, isn't it? I hope that we can be friendlier over the coming days. I'm sure we will be. Oh, here we are."

A maid trolley had arrived carrying snacks and glasses of drink. It trundled to Carina first. While she was tempted to kick the thing over and make a run for it, she knew that was pointless. Besides, she was famished and thirsty. She seized several plates, piling them on her lap before grabbing two full glasses. After downing one glass of a syrupy but refreshing juice, she bit into a pink confection and swallowed it in two mouthfuls.

Carina was dimly aware of Langley's gaze upon her. The Dirksen woman probably disapproved of her lack of manners, but then from the look of her Langley hadn't ever starved. Carina wasted little time with concerns about what impression she was giving. After quickly finishing the snacks on her lap, she retrieved the remaining ones from the trolley. Carina wasn't waiting for Langley to help herself. She'd had her chance.

The snacks were light and not intended to supply much energy, Carina guessed. Then she abruptly stopped eating. What if the food was drugged?

"Aren't you going to eat anything?" she asked Langley.

"I'm not hungry," Langley replied, looking gratified that Carina had finally spoken.

"Eat something," said Carina. "Or make him." She looked at Harmon, who still hung around like a bad smell.

Langley sighed. "Harmon, have a snack."

Harmon reached into the trolley and picked out a pale yellow cake in the shape of a flower. He popped the entire thing into his mouth and chewed solemnly. After observing him, Carina proceeded to eat the rest of the snacks. When she'd finished, she burped.

"Well, you certainly were hungry, weren't you?" said Langley.

Carina drank her second drink and returned the empty glass to the trolley. "I don't know why you've brought me here, but I take it if I try to leave, Harmon might have something to say about it."

"He might indeed, and so may the many other Harmons who patrol my estate. But we're starting off on the wrong foot. As I see it, there's no need for us to be on opposite sides. We can have a mutually beneficial relationship."

"If that's the case," Carina replied, "I suggest that, as a gesture of good faith, you allow me the freedom to leave."

"Hmm... Not just yet. You're tired and you've been treated badly no doubt by those military types who picked you up. Please, rest for a while. When you've recovered, we can talk business. Harmon, show our friend to her apartment."

Carina didn't have much choice except to do as Langley Dirksen directed, though she distrusted the woman's fine words. Even if Langley's intentions were currently noble and she really did want to strike up a fair deal in exchange for Carina using her mage powers—which Carina doubted—the woman's attitude would soon change. That was what knowledge of a mage's abilities did to people. It turned them into envious, exploitative, evil monsters like Stefan Sherrerr.

Whatever good treatment she received, Carina would never admit she was a mage. And when Langley Dirksen finally realized she wasn't going to get anything, her reaction would show just how well-intentioned she really was.

Meanwhile, Carina worried what would happen to Parthenia and the others. How were they going to survive? She hoped they would have the sense to never let anyone know they could Cast.

THREE

"Can we Cast Transport to bring us some food?" Darius asked.

He'd asked the same question twice already, but Parthenia guessed her little brother didn't remember. She couldn't expect a six year old to have a good memory. And he was probably as hungry as she was, if not hungrier, and very tired. "Well, we don't have any elixir, and we would need to see the food, or at least know exactly where it was. You know that. And it would be stealing."

She pushed aside a low branch of a tree that stood in their way and let Darius go ahead of her. They were following some kind of track through the forest. She wasn't sure what had made the track, but she hoped it was human.

"Would it be stealing?"

"Yes, it would because it would be taking something that doesn't belong to us. I know that when we went into town the store owners would let us take whatever we wanted, but that was because Father made them. Most people can't do that. Most people have to pay for food with money. We don't have any money."

"Oh. How do we get money?"

"I don't know yet. Maybe we can work. That's how most people get money." The truth was, Parthenia didn't know what they were going to do. Somehow, they would have to make a new life and it would very different from the one they'd been used to. She didn't even know how to begin. All she knew was that the first step was to reunite with their mage siblings since Carina had been forced to Transport them all separately from the shuttle to the planet surface. They had to find each other again.

She'd been waiting for hours to hear from Carina or perhaps Ferne or Oriana. She'd given one of her bracelets to her older sister and another to her twin siblings. They should be able to use a bracelet of hers to Locate her and then Send a message. Then they could all meet up and together they could decide what to do. She guessed Oriana and Ferne were having the same difficulty as her with creating elixir in the middle of nowhere, but Carina was resourceful and smart. She would have made contact sooner.

Darius hadn't spoken for a while, which was unusual. He was looking worried. She gripped her youngest brother's hand tighter. "Don't fret. Carina will Cast Send soon. I'm sure she will. Until then, we'll keep on walking and trying to find our way out of this place, okay? Carina wouldn't want us to just sit around waiting to be rescued, would she?"

Darius said, "No, I don't think so. But what if she doesn't Cast Send? What do we do then?"

"Carina would never abandon us, Darius. I mean, she wouldn't forget about us if she knew we needed her."

The little boy nodded. "When the bad men took me, she came and found me."

"That's right. She'll find us too, but it might take a while. So let's see how brave we can be and find out all the things we can do without her help." Her skirt caught on a thorn and ripped. "Oh, wait a minute." As she carefully pulled the cloth away the back of her hand brushed another thorn, receiving a scratch. "Ow!" Parthenia sucked on the drops of blood oozing from the wound.

"Does it hurt?" Darius asked, standing on his tiptoes to try to see her hand. "I could Cast Heal. Oh no, I can't. Are you sure you don't know how to make elixir?"

"I do know. I just don't know how to make it out here. I don't know how to start a fire, for one thing."

Darius came down from his tiptoes and hung his head. "I miss Carina."

"I do too." Parthenia took her brother's hand again and they continued walking. The barely visible thread of worn ground wound through the undergrowth. Sunlight slanted through the tree branches. Parthenia guessed it would be several hours before the sun set. She hoped Carina would find them before then. She didn't want to spend the night alone in the forest. They hadn't seen or heard anything except bugs and some kind of arboreal creature that had swung away as they approached, and then climbed high and flew. Maybe animals that preyed on humans lived here.

It had been hours since they'd arrived on the planet, and they'd been walking ever since. Parthenia's legs were aching. Darius was probably even more tired, though he hadn't mentioned anything except his empty stomach. Deciding it was time to call a halt and let her brother rest, she said, "Hey, let's stop for a while. Let's find somewhere to sit down." She led Darius off the track and over to a gap between two tall trees where nothing else grew. She sat him down on a root that protruded from the ground.

"I'm thirsty, Parthenia." Darius squashed his little body into the scant remaining space on the root.

She sighed. "Me too." If only Carina would Send soon. Perhaps she might even Transport herself here and then take them both to a safe place. Her talk about showing her sister how brave they could be had been just that—talk. She didn't feel at all brave. She'd begun to realize how ill-prepared they were to live an ordinary life in the real world.

As she'd been growing up, Parthenia had gradually come to understand she led an unusual life. It was only through reading books and during brief visits to the local town and even briefer visits to the capital she'd realized other people didn't live in large estates and have everything they needed given to them. Although her father had been very controlling and had treated her mother worse than an animal, Parthenia had never been hungry or deprived of material things. She'd slept in a comfortable bed every night and the only work she'd had to do was schoolwork, making elixir, and Casting.

If she was ever sick a splicer would come to the house to treat her, and she'd always worn expensive dresses and had all the toys, paints, interfaces, and other playthings she wanted. She'd even had her own pet. Thinking back to the tarsul she'd left behind on Ithiya, Parthenia suddenly felt so sad she wanted to cry. But she didn't want to upset Darius with her tears so she swallowed and bit her lip.

"What's wrong?" her brother asked. He climbed into her lap, though he barely fit there anymore.

"Nothing. I'm all right," Parthenia replied.

Darius wrapped his arms around her neck and rested his head on her shoulder. "No, you aren't."

There had never been much point in trying to hide emotions from Darius, Parthenia reflected. He always knew what you were feeling, whether you admitted it or not.

Now they'd stopped walking for a while, she was growing

cold. They were wearing the thin clothes they'd worn aboard the battleship, and they'd left the shuttle so quickly Parthenia hadn't even thought to grab the emergency blankets they'd been using to stay warm on the chilly ship.

"It's time we started walking again," Parthenia said. "Have you rested enough?"

"I guess so," Darius replied, getting up, though Parthenia heard the tiredness in his voice. "But where are we going? Are we nearly there?" They set off again.

"I was hoping we might find a way out of these woods," said Parthenia. "If we can find a house or a small town, maybe someone will give us some money for my bracelet." She hadn't thought of the idea until she said it. She'd only been intending to make something up to distract Darius from his hunger and thirst for a while. But it was actually a good plan.

Carina might take a long time to find them. They might even have to wait until tomorrow. Parthenia had one bracelet left. She wasn't sure how much it was worth, but she guessed it might be a lot of money. Father had always insisted his family had the finest of everything.

If they found other people, maybe she could sell them her bracelet for enough money to last them for days. But then the idea of encountering other people got her worrying. "Darius, if we do see anybody, we must remember what Mother told us."

"I know," her brother replied. "I won't tell them about Casting. I won't tell them we're—oh!" His foot had caught on a vine lying across the path. He fell hard into a patch of thorny plants and squealed as he tried to get up.

"Don't move," Parthenia exclaimed, fearing he was going to scratch himself some more.

Darius obediently stopped wriggling and lay still, looking up at his sister with tears running down his face.

"Keep still and I'll untangle you."

It took Parthenia several minutes to detach the thorns from Darius's clothes and skin, and she received plenty of scratches during the process. Eventually, however, she could finally stand the boy on his feet. His mouth was turned down and his chin trembled, though he'd finally stopped crying. He looked like he was at the end of his strength, yet he'd walked for hours with Parthenia without complaint.

"Would you like me to carry you?" she asked him.

Darius gave two firm nods and a small smile.

"Okay." Parthenia turned around and squatted down. "Climb aboard."

With her brother's legs tucked under her arms she continued down the track. She could feel him resting his head on her back and guessed he might soon fall asleep. She was tempted to stop so they could both lie down, but fear of what might happen while they were sleeping would probably keep her awake.

Parthenia pushed on through the undergrowth. She was beginning to think the track must have been made by animals. What would be the point of people walking so far in the forest? With her gaze focused on the vegetation ahead, she desperately hoped to see some sign of an end to it, but there was nothing visible except leaves, branches, and vines.

In fact, that part of the forest looked familiar. Had they come this way before? It was so hard to tell. Surely the track led some-where, or had they been going in circles?

"Parthenia," said Darius, "what if Carina didn't Transport out of the shuttle? What if the people who were coming aboard caught her?"

"Don't be silly," Parthenia replied. "Of course that didn't happen. Carina wouldn't let them capture her." It was a possi-bility Parthenia wasn't willing to entertain. The idea they might have to survive without their oldest sister's help on a world where they knew no one was horrifying. Even if Ferne and Oriana managed to find them, the four of them wouldn't be much better off together than apart.

How would they get money? After she sold her bracelet, Parthenia didn't know what else she could do. She didn't know how to work at a job. Everything she'd learned in her classes had been academic or oratorical. She didn't have any simple skills like cooking or cleaning or fixing broken tech. All she could do was Cast, and doing that would extremely risky. From what she could understand, that was why Father had treated Mother so badly. He'd used her because she was a mage. She hadn't wanted to marry him. Mother must have been married before because Carina had a different father. Parthenia had never found out what had happened to him.

"Are you sure Carina Transported off the shuttle?" Darius asked. "She wasn't caught?"

"I'm sure. I don't know how long it'll take her to find us, but she will. So don't worry about it, okay?"

"Okay. I won't."

Parthenia pushed the prospect of trying to survive without Carina's help far from her mind. Her sister would come. She had to. Parthenia couldn't look after Darius all by herself. She couldn't keep them both safe on her own.

Darius said, "I wish we could Cast Transport to bring some food."

FOUR

Carina waited five minutes before trying to open the door from the suite in the Dirksen mansion. Predictably, it was locked. Harmon was probably outside too, she guessed. She was standing in the lounge of the suite, which also contained a bedroom and a bathroom. The first thing she'd done was to quickly search the rooms for ingredients to make elixir, but she was out of luck. Though there was plenty of wood and metal and she could get water by pretending she wanted a drink, there was no earth in the rooms or any way for her to make a fire.

She went to the lounge window. It was also locked and the square frames that held the panes were too small for her to squeeze through, assuming she could break the glass without someone hearing it. Outside, the grounds of the estate stretched to the horizon. No fences or walls broke the wide, flat parkland landscape. If she tried to cross it in daylight she would be spotted easily, and at night infrared sensors would pick up her body heat.

Carina wasn't about to let those facts stop her from trying to escape. The estate probably had a shuttle pad and a few private shuttles, or perhaps she could steal one of the hover vehicles used for transportation on this world. Turning from the window, she skimmed the room with her gaze.

She walked over to an internal wall and touched it, running her hands over the surface to find out how it was constructed. If the wall was only made of board, she might be able to break through it, though then she would have the problem of getting out of the house. On the other hand, she was only on the second floor. Perhaps she could make a hole in the external wall? Or maybe she could remove the entire window frame?

She peeled back the fabric wall covering and found plaster underneath. Using the metal base of an ornament to dig through plaster, she discovered the internal walls were made of bricks. She could chip away the mortar and remove the bricks, but it would take time. And she would have to choose a wall that didn't adjoin the main corridor or her efforts might be noticed. Perhaps she could make a hole into the room next to her bedroom. That room's window might be unlocked.

Carina continued through the suite, trying to figure out how she could slip away. But after half an hour's investigation she hadn't managed to find a quick escape route, though she'd thought up several plans. All of them would take time to execute, however. After her long confinement on the patrol ship and the journey to the Dirksen estate, she was exhausted. Carina lay down on the sumptuous bed. Worrying about her mage sisters and brothers, she fell asleep.

———

She woke to the sensation of someone gripping her shoulder. Reflexively, she punched where she guessed the person's head might be. Her fist connected with a skull. As she opened her eyes, she rose up and grabbed for the person's throat. It was muscly and thick—too thick for a proper grip with one hand. She grabbed it with her other hand too, though it ached from the punch.

Harmon's very surprised face swam into focus. He brought up his arms between hers and broke her grip before shoving her onto the bed. "Calm down, huh? I just wanted to wake you for dinner. You didn't answer when I knocked." As he turned away, he rubbed his head where she'd punched him. "I'll wait for you outside." He walked out of the bedroom, still rubbing his head.

Carina nursed her sore knuckles. She'd been deeply asleep and dreaming when Harmon had woken her. The threads of the dream were already slipping from her mind, but she recalled a large monster leaning over Darius. Somehow, she'd known the monster was her brother's father, Stefan Sherrerr, and he was taking him to whatever dark place he'd gone after he died.

She rubbed her upper arms, chilled even though the room was warm. Stefan Sherrerr had died a terrible death, and though he would never hurt Darius again she was concerned about how the little boy was faring. Parthenia would do her best to look after him but Carina still worried. None of her mage brothers and sisters would adapt easily to their new lives.

When she went into the lounge, Carina saw that night had fallen. She'd slept for hours. Clothes had been spread across the sofa: fine dresses, pants, and shirts, all her size. They were intended for her, no doubt. Was she supposed to change her clothes before going down to dinner? Carina sighed. She wasn't a doll for Langley Dirksen to dress up.

When she tried the door, it opened. Harmon was waiting in the corridor, his hands clasped in front of him. He looked her up and down. "You have to—"

"I go down like this or not at all," said Carina.

Harmon sneered and wordlessly gestured for her to go first.

As he followed her, she said, "Is this your usual job around here, Harmon? Locking up young women? Your family must be proud." She smirked at him over her shoulder.

The burly man pushed her, forcing her to face forward. "You better shut up or I'll hurt you where it won't show."

When they reached the first floor, he guided her to a room for dining. Langley Dirksen was sitting at one end of a table and a man was sitting at the other. Carina thought this had to be Mr. Dirksen but then the man stood and turned to face her and she saw he was much younger than Langley. Though he was tall, he was an adolescent.

Langley's gaze drifted briefly down Carina's clothes and back up again before she forced a smile. "Thank you for joining us. I hope you slept well."

"No need to thank me," Carina replied. "I didn't have any choice about it. Harmon here woke me up with a slap and dragged me downstairs."

"Harmon!"

"Not true, ma'am. I believe our guest is trying to cause trouble."

Langley looked concerned. The young man stifled a small grin. He was her son, judging by the resemblance between the two.

"Please, join us," said Langley.

Carina pulled out a chair and sat down. She began piling food on her plate. "Tell me, is it normal around here to lock your guests in their rooms? I've never encountered that before and I was wondering if it's a local custom." She dug a fork into a pile of some kind of starchy vegetable and filled her mouth.

At this, Langley's son gave a brief snort of laughter before putting a hand over his grin. His mother glared at him before turning to Carina and saying, "Please believe me, I would not be doing this unless I felt it was necessary and beneficial to both of us in the long run."

Carina raised her eyebrows, chewed, and swallowed before lifting up another forkful of food. She wasn't going to allow this woman the satisfaction of thinking she was doing her a favor by locking her up. But Carina was hungry again. There was no point in passing up the opportunity to fill her belly while her future was so uncertain.

"Let me introduce you to my son," Langley said brightly. "This is Reyes."

Reyes nodded at Carina. His gaze briefly slipped back to his mother before turning down to his plate.

"Reyes is an inventor," said Langley. "Isn't that right, dear?" Reyes didn't look up but he gave a small nod. "He's so smart. I don't know where he gets it from."

Carina wondered what had happened to Reyes' father. No fourth place was set at the table. She didn't ask. Indulging in small talk would send the wrong signal. It would give Langley the impression that her behavior was acceptable.

A serving dish piled with meaty ribs sat in front of Carina. She picked one up and began to gnaw it.

Langley took a drink, appearing to attempt to quell anger or anxiety or perhaps both. "Shall we get down to business?" When Carina continued to ignore her she put down her glass and went on, "I will be entirely frank with you and I hope that in return you will show me the same respect.

"Firstly, I know something of what you can do, so there's no point in hiding it. I'm sure you're aware of the rivalry between the Dirksens and the Sherrerrs. In recent years, my clan has lost considerable ground to our competitors—business dealings, allegiances, military technology development, and so on. In many areas, the Sherrerrs have overwhelmed our interests. Some movement back and forth is to be expected, of course. We can't expect to win all the time. But certain events have been very odd. Businesses that had been loyal to us for generations suddenly made deals with the Sherrerrs—deals that were to their disadvantage. Secret military installations have been attacked and weapon prototypes stolen. These events were so remarkable, we paid one arms trader a lot of money to allow us to send a spy as his representative in a business deal.

"Obviously we couldn't implant any kind of bug on our spy. The Sherrerrs would have detected any tech immediately. All we had to go on was his report on the meeting after it took place on the Sherrerr stronghold on Ithiya. Interestingly, during the meeting he agreed to a deal that would eventually put the actual arms supplier out of business. Something odd had happened. The spy reported that the only abnormal thing he remembered was that a young woman had sat in on the meeting for no apparent reason. It was almost too preposterous to countenance, but we were forced to conclude that this young lady had done something to influence our spy's decision-making, causing him to sign up to an agreement no one in their right minds would accept."

Carina continued to eat, not allowing her expression to betray the thoughts whirring through her mind. She had a good idea of what had gone on in that meeting.

"Further reconnaissance efforts revealed the young woman lived on a country estate with her family," Langley said. "We watched the estate, curious about what it was the girl had done to influence our spy. When another child in the family left the estate's grounds, we took him for questioning."

You took him and tortured him. Carina fought to keep her features neutral. It was possible that Langley wasn't aware of what Dirksen thugs had done to Darius. Not that it was an excuse.

"Reyes, be quiet," Langley snapped.

The young man, who hadn't been making very much noise at all, put down his knife and fork.

"My dear," Langley said to her, "I know you rescued the boy. I've seen the vid. I also know that you have some kind of special ability too, and you became caught up with the Sherrerrs somehow. None of that matters to us. I don't want to be unreasonable about this, but we need your help. We're prepared to reward you handsomely if you will perform similar services to those the Sherrerr girl provided for her clan. That's all we're asking. And what you see around you is only a taste of the benefits you could enjoy if you agree."

All the while Langley Dirksen had been speaking, Carina had been eating. She was now full. She finally lifted her gaze to the older woman. "*If* I knew what the hell you were talking about, which I don't, do you really think it's reasonable to lock me up? Do you actually think someone you *kidnapped* is going to help you? That's got to be the craziest thing I ever heard. You Dirksens hauled me off my ship, locked me up, pushed me around, and forced me somewhere I didn't want to go.

"If you're as nice and reasonable as you make out, prove it. Let me go. You might as well, because it won't matter how long you keep me here, how much nice food you feed me, or how much fun Harmon has with me while your back's turned, I can't do whatever the hell it is you're asking me to do. You'll be wasting both our time if you don't let me walk out of here."

Langley smiled resignedly. "I can see it's going to take longer to persuade you than I thought. That's okay. I'm a patient woman. And when you finally do make the right choice, you'll see how sensible you've been."

FIVE

Carina had expected to spend the rest of the evening in her room and she'd been looking forward to using the time trying to figure out how to get out of here. But Langley Dirksen had other plans. After dinner was eaten, in silence—Reyes hadn't yet spoken—Langley announced they would be attending "Mech Battle."

Reyes punched the air. "Yes!" He paused and added, "I *can* go too, right?"

"You may," Langley replied graciously. "It will be good for you and our guest to get to know each other better."

Carina nearly dropped her glass. She darted a look at the young man, who seemed embarrassed by his mother's remark. Did Langley really imagine the two of them might strike up a romance? The idea was insane. Even if Reyes wasn't the son of her kidnapper, he was just a kid.

"You're joking, right?" she asked Langley. "And anyway, I don't want to go to your stupid event. I demand you release me. I haven't done anything wrong. I haven't committed any crimes and you have no right to hold me like this."

"Not committed any crimes?" Langley asked. "Well, maybe you aren't a criminal, but your situation might be better if you were. My dear, you were captured aboard a Sherrerr shuttle. You're worse than a criminal. You're an enemy prisoner." Her polite expression transformed to hostility. "You *have* no rights." Then the mask of politeness fell over her features again. "But let's not squabble. I'm not so foolish as to believe that compelling you to work for us is the best solution in the circumstances. Whatever we managed to force you to do, you would exert the minimum effort, and no doubt you would try to secretly sabotage your results.

"It would be to both our benefits if we can come to a mutually agreeable arrangement. I know you don't believe so at the moment, but it's true. As hard as it may be for you to accept, I don't want you to work under duress. And so, as an enticement, I would like you to see the kind of lifestyle you could live and the things you could have if you agree to use your abilities to help us." She looked again at Carina's worn, dirty clothes. "I take it you won't agree to change before we go?"

"No, I won't."

"Very well. We'll leave in five minutes or so. Reyes, please keep our guest entertained until then." Langley rose and left the room.

Carina picked up a gnawed rib and nibbled at the remnants of meat that clung to it, speculating what the kid might do. Harmon still hovered in the background, so Reyes would probably have to follow his mother's order. It looked like Langley ran the show and if Reyes didn't do as he was told the matriarch would soon hear about it.

Reyes looked about as uncomfortable as Carina had ever seen anyone look. After a few moments, he said, "She isn't as bad as she comes across, you know."

Carina put down her rib bone and gave a short laugh. "You

mean your mom? That's some compliment. *Not as bad as she comes across.* I hope someone says that about me one day." She pushed back her chair and stood up, wiping her greasy hands on her pants. She glanced at the kid, who seemed to be chewing over her words. She'd been planning on ignoring the spoiled brat, but she reasoned that it wouldn't hurt to have a young, impressionable ally. "So, what's this Mech Battle we're going to? Mechs battling, I guess?"

Reyes's eyes lit up, either due to the mention of the event or Carina's willingness to speak to him. "It isn't exactly mechs. That would be boring. It's new inventions especially for fighting."

"You mean like weaponized armor?" Carina had heard of armor that was more like an exoskeleton and had weapons attached. Equipment like that had a place in some battles, but it wasn't generally used in the military. It was too bulky and it had marginally slower reaction times. A soldier in a mech suit was slower than a soldier in regular armor.

"Sometimes it's kind of like that," Reyes replied, "but you never know what it'll be until the competitors come into the pit. That's the fun of it. They can wear almost whatever they like. There are only a few rules. They can't use anything that might be dangerous to the audience, like explosives or projectiles. But that's about it."

Carina's interest was no longer feigned. She'd been in plenty of engagements. The idea of watching newly invented mechs fighting sounded interesting. "So who controls them?"

"I don't know to be honest. Men and women. That isn't important, is it? There are a few major sponsors of the battles. I guess they pay the fighters to compete."

"How dangerous is it?" Carina asked, imagining the fighters were probably ex-soldiers or mercs.

"Oh, pretty dangerous. People have died. It's rare that a fighter doesn't have to retire from the match due to injury."

Carina doubted the competitors were only paid a set fee. She'd encountered similar arrangements on other worlds. Usually, the fighters received a percentage of the house's take, and there was always gambling at such events. The fighters would be betting on themselves too. "How do they tell who's won?"

"That's easy. You know the winner when the first mech is incapacitated. As soon as a competitor can't fight back, the match is over."

"Should be interesting," Carina said, giving Reyes a conspiratorial wink. He grinned. It looked like she might have made a friend.

———

For her second journey by hover transport, Carina was allowed to sit up front. Her short conversation with Reyes had persuaded her to ditch her oppositional stance. Her defiance would only work against her. If Langley Dirksen believed she was on the verge of joining the Dirksens, she might become less vigilant.

A woman Carina hadn't seen before sat at the front of the vehicle, controlling it. Behind her sat Langley and her son. Harmon sat next to Carina in the back seat.

"I never heard of Dirksens living on this planet," Carina remarked. "I thought it was neutral territory."

"We were forced to move here after the Sherrerrs began to expand their range," Langley replied. "As far as I know, they aren't aware we've taken control of Ostillon, and that's how we'd like to keep it."

What had she meant by "taken control of Ostillon"? If the Dirksens' methods were like the Sherrerrs,' they'd probably enacted a military coup of the planet's government or governments, imposed harsh taxes on businesses and individuals, and recruiting local thugs into a militia, turning them against their own people and encouraging them to support themselves with protection money. She shuddered. There was no way she wanted to help the Dirksens, even to get back at the Sherrerrs who had allowed her mother's evil treatment. However, she didn't mention her feelings to Langley. "What's your role in the Dirksen clan, if you don't mind me asking?"

"My, what a polite question," Langley replied. "I thought you could be nice if you tried. Well, I guess you might call me one of the inner circle. I'm responsible for many of our larger businesses, which is why I was very interested to hear about you." She turned in her seat to look Carina in the eyes. "Believe me, you could have received much worse treatment from some of my associates. Some would want revenge for the offenses we've suffered at the hands of the Sherrerrs in recent times. They would love the opportunity for someone to bear they brunt of their anger. Luckily for you, and I think for the rest of my clan too, you fell into my hands. Others might not understand how valuable you are to us unharmed and compliant. You would be wise to remember that if you aren't agreeable I won't be able to protect you from the rest of my clan forever."

Carina broke eye contact with the matriarch to look out the transport's window. Already she was under the threat of violence, torture, and whatever else the Dirksens had in store. So much for Langley's fine words.

The lights of the towers of the metropolis rose in the distance, a multicolored kaleidoscope. Hover transports moved across the city, shifting the pattern. "Has Ostillon always been this high tech? Or has it developed since the Dirksens' arrival?"

Langley had turned to face forward once more. "Ostillon has

changed almost beyond recognition over the last few cycles. My clan generally hate to live in backward places without modern conveniences. Of course, some aspects of the older culture cling on. You'll see one example of it tonight. On our other stronghold worlds, the Mech Battle would never be allowed. It's far too uncivilized. But it's such a popular sport in Ostillon, it would have been counter-productive to outlaw it. Besides, it allows the population to vent some of the natural aggression they feel in response to our takeover."

By the time they arrived at the Mech Battle stadium, Carina's curiosity had risen further. If the contest was as riotous as Langley implied, she might have an opportunity to slip away. A crowd was a good place to hide. She was glad she hadn't changed into the fine clothes offered to her, which would have made her easier to spot.

They went through a private entrance in the back of the stadium directly to a small, empty box that overlooked a wide, dusty, very deep pit. The stadium was split into halves, with two tall walls separating the sides. Some of the audience was in the pit, though they were being rapidly evacuated, and the side shows set up at the edges were being dismantled. Though no fighting was yet taking place, the noise of the crowd was deafening. Twenty to thirty thousand people were present.

Harmon shut the door to the box and stood in front of it, his bulk almost covering its entire frame. The woman who had controlled the transport also remained in the box, sitting next to Carina. Langley had taken out an interface she was consulting, and Reyes sat at the front of the box, peering into the pit.

A compere spoke from somewhere Carina couldn't see, announcing that the first battle would commence in five minutes. Reyes asked his mother, shouting over the hubbub, "Who are you betting on tonight?"

"Spearcorps," she replied. "They did very well last time."

"Go Spearcorps," exclaimed Reyes, returning his gaze to the pit.

The ground shook, and what Carina had taken to be walls on each side of the stadium split down the center. The walls were massive gates, and through both strode the most amazing mech fighting machines she had ever seen.

SIX

Parthenia was so tired she could barely stay upright. Darius had fallen asleep long ago as she carried him. He was resting against her back and she struggled to hold onto his relaxed body. He seemed ready to slip off at any moment.

It was so dark she could only just make out the shapes of the vegetation, yet she'd continued walking long after sunset, too frightened to stop and lie down to sleep. The narrow track they'd been following had disappeared in the darkness and she was going wherever she could pass between the trees. As dusk had fallen the noises of the forest had grown louder. *Things* were moving around her. Were they following her? Nothing had drawn close— yet. Were the night creatures only waiting for her to stop before they pounced? Her legs felt like they were on the verge of collapsing. She'd passed what she'd thought was the end of her strength hours ago. It was pure fear that kept her putting one foot in front of the other.

Thorns had torn her dress to rags. Whenever her clothing caught on one, she no longer stopped to remove it. She pulled herself free roughly, heedless of tears. She'd walked tens of kilometers, she guessed, farther than she'd ever walked. The forest had to be huge, unless she'd only walked in circles. She shook her head. She had to stop thinking about that and concentrate on reaching the end of the woods.

Why hadn't Carina Sent to her? She couldn't understand it. Had her sister decided to abandon her family? Parthenia knew that she and her siblings were a lot of bother. They weren't tough like Carina. They'd been coddled all their lives and didn't know how to do hardly anything for themselves. Perhaps Carina had decided she would be better off without them. It was true. She *would* be better off without them.

Parthenia had promised herself she wouldn't cry. Her arms were so tired from holding Darius's legs they trembled. Her back ached from bending over to prevent him from falling. Her leg muscles throbbed. She was also painfully hungry and thirsty. She'd wanted to be brave, but as she accepted that Carina might never come for them, tears spilled down her cheeks.

It seemed so unfair. She couldn't believe that after all their efforts to escape—from their dash through the corridors of the flagship *Nightfall* under fire, through the long chilly days aboard the shuttle, to being suddenly Transported to the middle of nowhere on a remote planet—everything would end for her and Darius on their first night by themselves. She wished they'd been able to stay with the others. She wouldn't have minded so much if she'd been with her family. But wishing wasn't going to change anything.

Parthenia had reached her limit. She was now walking so slowly she was barely moving. Whether she stopped or not, the night creatures could catch them if they wanted. She might as well stop, she guessed.

"Don't worry, Parthenia," said Darius sleepily. "Carina will come soon."

"I didn't know you were awake," Parthenia replied, comforted by the sound of her brother's voice close to her ear.

"Yes, I woke up. I want to get down now."

Parthenia bent her knees and Darius slipped off her back. The relief was wonderful. She stretched her arms.

"It's dark," said Darius. He moved closer and wrapped his arms around her.

"It's still night time," Parthenia replied. "Can you walk now? We should keep moving."

"Do we have some water yet?"

"No. But we've walked a long way. We must be nearly out of the forest now. If we carry on walking, we might find a house soon, and we can ask the people who live there for a drink." It was odd how trying to be positive for Darius's sake made her feel better. She thought she could manage to go a little farther now she was relieved of her brother's weight.

"Hmm..." The little boy looked around. "Okay." He took her hand and they set off again.

Darius's hand was cold. Parthenia was cold too, despite her physical exertion. That was another reason to keep going. If they stopped moving they might become dangerously chilled.

"What's that?" Darius asked. He was pointing off to his left.

Parthenia looked in the same direction but all she could see was the black shadows of trees. "I don't know what you're looking at. What can you see?"

"There's a light over there. Is it the house where we can get water?"

"A light! Where?"

"Right there," the little boy replied pedantically as if his sister were stupid.

"I can't..." Parthenia squatted down to her brother's level and followed the direction of his gaze. He was right. Through a gap in the vegetation a small blue light shined steadily in the distance. She hadn't been able to see it, but Darius was short enough to see the space. She gripped her brother's arms tightly. "It *is* a light. Good job, Darius. Good job. Let's go there, shall we?"

"Yes, let's get some water."

Traveling in the direction of the light proved hard, however. The trees were clumped together more tightly that way than any other, and they lost sight of the light several times as they went along. Trying to head toward the blue glow involved pushing past thick ferns and bushes, resulting in many scratches for both of them. At one point, they lost sight of the tiny light entirely and Parthenia almost gave up hope of ever finding it again. They were forced to double back a long way and try a different route. Eventually, though, the tree trunks and undergrowth thinned out and the blue spot grew nearer. As the wider landscape became more visible, Parthenia realized the beam was shining from the top of a tower and the base of the tower was somewhere below the level of the forest.

In his eagerness to reach the light and the water he desperately wanted, Darius let go of her hand and ran ahead.

"Darius," Parthenia called. "Stop! Wait for me." Her brother didn't answer. "Darius! Darius! Stop!"

"Wh—" Her brother gave a gasp and cried out.

"Darius!" Parthenia rushed forward. Somewhere in front of her, vegetation was being smashed by a falling body. It was as she'd feared. They'd reached a ridge and her brother had run right over the edge.

"Darius," she called down. All she could see was the dark shadows of trees.

"Parthenia! Help!"

"Where are you?" She stepped gingerly down the steep slope,

holding a branch to prevent herself from sliding on the loose, dry leaves.

"I'm here!"

"Hold on. Don't move. I'm coming to get you." Parthenia eased down the incline, heading toward her brother's voice. "Keep talking so I can find you."

"I'm here, here, here!"

Despite the dire circumstances, Parthenia almost smiled. "That's good. Don't stop."

"Here I am. Here I am. Here I am." Darius echoed his own words several more times, his tone becoming more sing-song as he went on.

Parthenia finally saw her brother clinging to some tree roots. The spot he was at was particularly steep. She wasn't sure how to reach him, and if he let go of the roots to try to climb up to her he would probably slide away.

"You found me," he exclaimed.

"Yes, but don't move, okay? Don't let go."

"Okay."

"Are you all right? Have you hurt anything?"

"I bumped my leg. It hurts a bit."

"Okay. Just hold on. I'm going to try to get down to you. But don't let go until I say so."

Parthenia had an idea. If she went on all fours and crawled backward down the slope, she thought she could reach her brother and he could climb onto her. Then she could carry on moving slowly downward until they hopefully encountered an area that was less steep.

Her plan worked at first. She reached Darius, though the rough ground hurt her knees and hands. But as soon as her brother let go of the root he was holding and tried to climb onto her, he fell again. Parthenia shouted and tried to grab him, and then suddenly she was falling too. She slithered down the coarse surface, hitting bushes and vines, bouncing from tree trunks until finally, mercifully, all her motion ceased.

Dazed, it took Parthenia a moment to take in her surroundings. She was at the bottom of a muddy ditch and the slope she'd come down was dark and shadowy above her. For the first time that night, she could also see the wide, starry sky.

"Parthenia," Darius called. "Where are you?"

"Here," she replied. "Where are you?" To her amazement, Darius came walking along the bottom of the ditch toward her. He didn't seem to have been seriously harmed by his rapid descent.

"We fell," he said. "Are you hurt?"

Parthenia moved her arms and legs. She hadn't broken anything as far as she could tell, but when she tried to stand, she gave a small scream and fell over. She'd done something to her right ankle. "I think I did hurt myself, Darius. Can you help me?"

Her brother came closer and she put her arm over his shoulders. They were both coated in evil-smelling mud from the ditch. Parthenia hoped there was someone at the tower who would help them. Neither of them were in a position to go any farther tonight, and if they didn't get water or food soon, things would look very bad.

The smooth, black silhouette of the tower and its blue light were easy to spot against the stars but not so easy to reach. They walked—or rather, Parthenia hopped—along the ditch but there didn't seem to be any way out of it. They were forced to scale its slippery side. Parthenia pushed Darius up to the top of the edge, putting her weight on her good leg, so he could climb over onto the ground above. Then after several tries she managed to climb out too.

She stood on one leg, leaning on her brother's shoulder.

Behind them, the forest overshadowed the sky. Parthenia could just make out black shapes flying above it. She shivered and turned in the other direction. The land was flatter though still quite wild. The tower was the only building she could see and it displayed the only artificial light for kilometers around. She wondered what purpose it served. They were very lucky Darius had seen it.

"Let's go ask the people for some water," Darius urged.

Parthenia partly walked, partly hopped beside him as they made their way through rough scrub to the base of the tower. The building was about as wide as a house but stood seven or eight stories tall. She couldn't see an entrance. Her heart sank, but then she realized she was being stupid. Propping herself up with one hand on the cold, polished stone of the tower wall, she hopped around it to the other side, Darius trailing.

There was the entrance. A metal door was flush with the wall, following its curve. A small light shined above the door but otherwise there was no other ornament save a security pad.

Her throat tight, Parthenia pressed the key on the pad. She feared there might be no answer, and yet she also feared who might answer if there was.

SEVEN

The mechs strode powerfully into the pit, their steps shaking the floor of the box where Carina sat. She'd never before seen anything even resembling the mechanical fighting machines that were about to do battle.

She could just make out their human operators ensconced in control centers in the mechs' chests. Thick metal walls protected the chambers, and the windows were narrow slits, allowing the operators limited real life visuals of their surroundings. Carina guessed the control centers held interface screens that relayed data from sensors as well as feedback from the mechs' systems. The windows were a last resort if the mechs' sensors were destroyed.

The machines stood roughly two stories tall. If it hadn't been for their massive size and power, they might almost have been caricatures of the kinds of mechs Carina knew. As a merc, she'd operated the exoskeletons aboard her band's ship, the *Duchess*. But their machines had been antiquated and mostly used for handling supplies. Though they were fitted with weapons, no one would have dared to fight in them. That had been one of the disadvantages of fighting for a commercial outfit: making do with outdated equipment.

Remembering her life as a merc, Carina looked forward to the day she never had to fight again. She would be happy if she could only reunite her little family and keep them safe. Yet these two metal monsters interested her. It was easy to see why the crowd was wild with anticipation: the battle would be spectacular. Even Langley was flushed with excitement. Her eyes were bright as she gazed at the mechs.

Langley's fingers quickly skimmed her interface, placing her bets. Carina wondered how much ill-gotten credit the Dirksen matriarch was frittering away. It was no wonder the clan had decided not to stamp out the Mech Battles. The contest was a gambler's dream. The chances of winning a bet were probably around fifty percent—it wouldn't make sense to stage battles where the opponents weren't evenly matched. Of course, the chances of losing were around fifty percent too, but that part of the equation was rarely considered.

Also, the outcome might not be clear until the final moment. Bets probably continued throughout the battle, odds rising and lowering according to the performance of each mech. Once more, Carina wondered who those barely visible faces inside the great mechanical beasts belonged to. It was possible a successful fighter could retire on his or her winnings from one battle. Though the arena only seated a few tens of thousands of people, the spectacle was no doubt being broadcast and the betting could be planet-wide.

The mechs were moving their various parts, apparently checking all their systems were working before the battle commenced. It was all for show, of course. No fighter in their right minds would enter the pit without performing extensive checks. No, the motions were all intended to bring the crowd to a frenzy and prompt them to lay out even more money. The preparations were having their desired effect too. The audience was so loud Carina could barely hear herself think. The stadium seemed to vibrate with the noise of shouting. And the battle hadn't even begun.

The mechs began to circle the pit.

Carina had been expecting Langley to check on her reaction to the event. Langley probably wanted her to appreciate the older woman's generosity in bringing her. But the matriarch was so intent on the battle, she ignored her. Langley's gaze only switched from her interface to the pit and back again.

Harmon wasn't equally entranced. As he stood at the back of the box in front of its exit, he stared at Carina, his hands folded in front of him, formidable. She scowled at the burly thug. He was definitely going to be the biggest obstacle to her escape. On her right sat the transport driver, looking bored.

A great metallic crash sounded from the pit. She had missed the beginning of the battle. The gigantic mechs were gripping each other with their enormous pincer-like grabbers. They grappled, their massive gears straining with the effort. Hisses and screeches and the noise of bending metal sounded through the stadium, and the crowd roared.

One mech was slowly overpowering the other, forcing it over to one side. Carina guessed that a way to win was to force the opponent to fall over. Then, gravity would confer a big advantage, allowing the still-standing mech to crush the other. A prone position might expose vulnerable areas too.

But in this case, the mech that seemed to be losing didn't fall. It managed to disengage and twisted away so fast its attacker nearly overbalanced. The mech's bending to one side had been a feint and it had nearly worked. But the attacking mech pulled back in time to remain upright.

"Oh," exclaimed Langley. Her fingers moved over her interface. Had she bet on the duped mech? When Carina peered more closely at the machines in the pit, she could make out SPEARCORPS across the faux "head" of the attacking mech. Out of curiosity, she spied out the name of its opponent: PYRECO. It was another name that was meaningless to her. The two were probably major conglomerates on the planet and perhaps the territory.

The Pyreco mech swung its pincer up at the Spearcorps mech's head and connected with such force it bent backward. The crowd gave a massive *Ohhhh!* Despite the whirring of gears and sounds of protesting metal the Spearcorps operator couldn't straighten the head. It wasn't serious damage, Carina guessed. A mech rarely used its head for fighting. But the effect would be to unbalance the machine. Now the Spearcorps mech was much more vulnerable to toppling over.

It responded by immediately grabbing the Pyreco mech in a fierce clinch. At close quarters, it was much more difficult to overbalance your opponent. Spearcorps drove Pyreco against the wall of the stadium. The audience in that section surged in a panic to get away from the gigantic machines, though the pit was beneath their feet.

By this time, Reyes was leaning over the edge of the box and yelling at the top of his voice. If he leaned much farther, he would be in danger of falling out.

A cataclysmic crash came from the pit. Pyreco was down. Spearcorps, its head bent weirdly backward, rained blows on its opponent. Pyreco tried repeatedly to rise, but each time Spearcorps was too fast and beat the mech down again. It was painful to watch the fallen mech's movements. Though it was just a machine and its operator wasn't in a lot of danger, its desperate efforts to escape were almost pitiful.

"Yes," exclaimed Langley, clutching her interface in sweaty palms. "Yes! Hit it. Hit it. Hit it."

"Go Spearcorps," roared Reyes, now on standing upright, his fists beating the air. "Spearcorps are the best!"

Pyreco didn't give up even though it was clearly beaten. Carina wondered if there was a cost to losing other than humiliation. The operator might have overextended themselves financially with their bets. Another explanation for Pyreco's tenacity was the battle was staged and the outcome preordained. If Pyreco was being paid to take a dive, its defeat had to look convincing or the punters would suspect.

Spearcorps ceased hitting the prone mech. After a moment's checking that there really was no more life in its opponent, the mech raised its pincers to the sky. This time, the response from the crowd was so loud, Carina actually covered her ears. The stadium gates opened and Spearcorps strode triumphantly out. Pyreco was in no condition to leave so easily. Transports zoomed through the other gate and hovered around the fallen mech.

People in overalls jumped out onto the massive limbs and torso of the mechanical monster and walked over it, assessing the damage. It would take a while to remove the machine from the pit now it was immobile. Carina asked Langley's driver, "Do we leave soon?"

"Leave?" the woman replied. "That was only the first match. There's another four to go yet."

"Four more?" Carina said. "We'll be here all night."

"Exactly." The driver rolled her eyes and yawned, covering her mouth.

Although the Mech Battle had been somewhat interesting, Carina didn't relish the idea of sitting through another four. She looked at Harmon, who didn't seem to have taken his eyes off her the entire time. She sighed. It was going to be a long night.

———

The battles that followed weren't very much different from the first. Spearcorps fought in two of them. The winner of the first battle had to face newcomers until it lost. From what Carina could understand, if a mech won all five battles, it received an additional pay out. By the time the third engagement arrived, however, Spearcorps was too battered to put up much of a fight. Its unbalanced head proved its undoing when it was toppled within a minute of the battle's beginning.

Langley looked crestfallen at the result, but she wanted to stay and watch the remaining two battles nevertheless. Reyes quickly switched allegiance to the winning mech as soon as it looked like it was all over for Spearcorps.

To Carina's relief, the end of the fifth battle finally arrived. The mechanics entered on their transports to see to the removal of the losing mech. Carina expected that Langley would finally be ready to leave, but the Dirksen woman remained in her seat.

Reyes turned around and said, "Can't we go now, Mother? No one will notice."

"Don't be ridiculous," Langley snapped. "Of course they'll notice. When will you ever learn the importance of appearances in these matters?"

"What's happening?" Carina asked the driver. "What are we waiting for?"

"Urgh, just some stupid Ostillonian ritual," she replied. "It only takes a few minutes."

Carina watched with mild interest to see what the ritual entailed. The fallen mech was being dismantled on the field as it couldn't be repaired sufficiently to make its own way out. During the times she'd visited new worlds in her travels as a merc, she only ever spent brief episodes planetside. Her band, the Black Dogs, would do their job and leave as quickly as they'd arrived. So Carina had never been allowed time to learn about the worlds and their people. She'd heard of various religions over the years but she'd never gotten to know much about them.

When a young woman wearing ceremonial robes walked out to the center of the pit, Carina stood up for a better view. The woman squatted down and took some items out from a bag. First, she piled up sticks as if to make a fire, and then she took out a metal bowl. After pouring clear liquid into the bowl from a bottle, she grabbed a little soil from the ground and sprinkled it in.

Carina frowned, wondering what the woman was doing. Was she going to cook something? She looked again. Although she was watching from a great height, Carina could swear the woman was filing something made of metal so the particles also fell into the bowl.

Her heart seemed to stop. Could it be possible? It couldn't be. She had to be mistaken.

But then the priestess took a fragment of dry twig and also filed it over the bowl. She was adding sawdust to the liquid too. It was all Carina could do to remain upright and not allow Langley or Reyes to see her shock as the woman in the pit lit the fire.

She was making elixir. Right there in front of the entire crowd. Was it possible no one knew what she was doing? Was the woman herself aware?

After making the elixir, the woman lifted the bowl with tongs and held it up to the crowd. They murmured some kind of prayer Carina couldn't make out. Langley and Reyes said nothing. Then the woman tipped out the elixir onto the ground of the pit.

Mech Battle was over, and Carina was left with a mystery the likes of which she'd never known.

EIGHT

The man said he was a ranger. Parthenia wasn't exactly sure what a ranger did, but she assumed he worked in the land that lay around the tower. When the man had opened the tower door she'd taken a step back. He was so tall and his hair and beard were so black and shaggy, he looked for a moment like a big, black wild animal. Of course, it had only been the darkness and her exhaustion that made her think so. When he'd spoken, his voice had been gentle after his initial surprise.

He'd noticed her limping and offered to carry her up the stairs that wound around the tower's interior wall, apologizing for the lack of an elevator. "I'm alone out here. If I lost power, I'd be stuck," he'd explained.

Parthenia had declined his offer and made her way up the spiral staircase with Darius' help. Now, sitting in the round room the ranger had brought them to, she could finally relax. Or could she? It suddenly occurred to her that the man would want to know why she and Darius were by themselves in the middle of nowhere.

All the time they'd been wandering through the forest, she'd only thought about the danger they were in and wondered what had happened to Carina and the others, or what might happen if they didn't get to safety. She hadn't thought up a story to explain their presence here if they found someone they could ask for help.

Parthenia had no idea what the clan allegiance of the planet was. If Ostillon were under the hegemony of the Sherrerrs, there was no way she could let it be known she was a member of that family. If she did, their rescuer's first move would be to return her and Darius to their clan as soon as possible, regardless of anything she said. Although she was nearly an adult, Darius was still a child, but, more pertinently, the ranger would want to avoid upsetting the rulers of that world.

He wasn't pressing for answers just yet, thankfully. He was bringing them food. "I'll turn on the heating," he said. "You two look frozen." The drinks he'd placed in front of them steamed. When Darius made a grab for his, the ranger cautioned, "Not yet, little one. Let it cool down first."

"Oh, please," Darius said, his big brown eyes pleading. "Can I have some water?"

"Of course," the man replied. "I'll get you some right away. Just a moment." He went over to the small kitchen area and poured out a glass of water.

The circular room was multipurpose. Parthenia and Darius sat on a small sofa in the living area. The ranger had put down their food on a knee-high table in front of them. The rest of the room apart from the kitchenette was taken up with a range of equipment, most of which Parthenia didn't recognize. She guessed the ranger used it in his work.

While Darius was gulping down his water, the ranger went to a control panel near the staircase. "There," he said after pressing the screen. "It'll be toasty in here soon. You would like some water too, I guess?" he asked Parthenia.

"I would, please," she replied. She'd been thinking up and rejecting one story about their background after another. She had to make up something plausible and wished she had more time. If only she'd used the hours they'd been wandering in the forest more sensibly.

"Are you in pain?" the ranger asked, bringing her some water.

"I am," she replied, seizing the opportunity to delay his inevitable questions. "I hurt my ankle."

"Of course you did," said the man. "I was forgetting. I don't get many visitors out here. You two have taken me by surprise. Let me wash your leg then I can take a look."

Parthenia's legs and most of the rest of her were covered in mud. Darius also had a thick, brown, smelly coating. They were both disgusting, in fact.

The ranger filled a bowl with warm water and brought it over to the sofa along with a washcloth. He removed her mud-caked shoe. Her foot was grimy. As he washed away the dirt from her ankle the skin that emerged was puffy and purple. The ranger gently prodded it, causing her to wince. Now she could see her injury, it seemed to throb more painfully.

"Can you move your toes?" asked the ranger.

She tried. She managed to wiggle them all, though it hurt her to do it.

The ranger said, "How about your ankle? Can you move that?"

She gently lifted her foot upward. "Ow!"

"Okay. Don't try any more. I don't think it's broken. I have a treatment cell we can put your foot in overnight while you sleep. It'll detect any fractures and it'll speed up the healing process."

"Are you a splicer?" Darius asked. He was regarding the ranger over the rim of his mug of hot drink.

"No, or I don't think so," the man replied. "What's a splicer?"

Parthenia's stomach tightened. They were getting into dangerous territory. If Darius used words that weren't used in Ostillon, the man would know they were from offplanet.

"Someone who helps people when they're sick," Darius replied.

"You mean a medic," said the man.

"No," said Darius, "I mean a—"

"That's right," Parthenia interrupted and turned to Darius. "A medic. That's what you mean." She went on, "He's only six. He gets confused sometimes."

"No, I don't," Darius exclaimed indignantly. "I mean a—"

"Be quiet, Darius," Parthenia snapped.

"Darius," the ranger said. "That's a nice name."

Dammit. She cursed herself for making yet another stupid mistake. She should have thought up fake names for both of them. Her clan was searching everywhere for them. How many Dariuses traveling with Parthenias could there be? Yet she couldn't give the ranger a false name for herself now without Darius reacting and making it obvious she was lying. To avoid delaying the inevitable she said with a heavy heart, "I'm Parthenia."

"Another nice name," the ranger said.

He didn't show any signs of recognition, she noted with some relief. It was something to be grateful for, but she knew now the ranger knew their real names they had to leave as soon as they possibly could. They must also give no indication of where they were going. News of the missing Sherrerr children would probably arrive soon and then the ranger would be bound to remember them.

"I'm Jace," he said, still gently examining her ankle. "So, what are—"

"Ouch," Parthenia exclaimed, though Jace hadn't actually

hurt her. She'd only wanted to stall him a little longer. What could she tell him about what they were doing here?

"Oh, I'm sorry," he said. He stood and wiped dirt from his hands with the wet cloth. "Your ankle's clean enough now anyway. Would you two like to wash off the rest of that mud?"

She readily agreed to delaying the moment she would have to spin her tale. She also welcomed the opportunity to prep Darius so he wouldn't give away that she was lying.

"The bathroom is on the next level," Jace said apologetically.

"That's okay," Parthenia said. "I can manage." With Darius' help, she hopped over to the stairway, which continued to wind around the wall of the room before disappearing into a hole in the ceiling. Jace led them up the stairs to the next floor. This room was his bedroom, and above the kitchenette on the floor below was a bathroom.

He found two clean shirts for them to wear and told them he would wash their dirty clothes, though Parthenia wasn't sure her dress was worth the effort. It was mostly rags.

The ranger descended the stairs and she went with Darius into the bathroom. As she helped her brother to wash off all the mud, she quietly explained to him that she might have to tell Jace some things that weren't true.

"But it's wrong to lie," Darius protested.

"It is, usually," she replied. "But sometimes we have to lie. Like if telling a lie stops someone from being hurt. Then it's okay."

"Is it?"

"Yes, it is. You know you can't tell anyone about being a mage, don't you? If someone asked you if you could Cast, you would say no. That's lying, right? This is similar. We can't tell Jace who we are or where we're from. If we do, we might end up being hurt.

Or someone we love could be hurt. You wouldn't want that, would you?"

"No, I wouldn't," Darius replied emphatically.

"Then, if you hear me say something you know isn't true, you mustn't jump in and deny it, okay?"

"Okay."

Parthenia finished helping her brother dry himself and then put a shirt on him before sending him out to wait for her while she washed. She undressed and hopped into the shower. It was a very basic kind and it had no blower so you had to dry yourself with towels, but she didn't care. Washing away the disgusting mud was blissful, even though it made all her cuts and scrapes sting. She was bruised and scratched head to toe and when she washed her hair the rinse water ran brown.

She wondered what Mother would have made of her and her brother if she'd seen them as filthy and disheveled as the poorest village children. Then she cried, because she knew that her mother wouldn't have minded at all. It had been their father who would be driven to a rage by messy hair or a besmirched face. She missed Mother so much.

When she was clean and dry, she put on the shirt Jace had given her and hopped out of the bathroom. Darius had disappeared. Gripped by fear he was telling Jace their life histories she hopped in the direction of the stairs but in her haste she stumbled and fell. Then she noticed a stick propped against the bathroom wall that hadn't been there before. Thinking it was for her, she took it and used it to help her walk to the stairs.

"Darius," she called. "Are you down there?"

"He's eating," Jace replied. "Do you need some help coming down?"

"No, I'll be fine." Parthenia went carefully from step to step, the warm air of the living area wafting up to her welcomingly.

Darius watched as she came down. He didn't look troubled or guilty, so she guessed he hadn't said anything he shouldn't have. His cheeks were bulging with food.

"Feeling better?" Jace asked.

"Yes, lots," she replied. "Thank you for helping us. I don't know what we would have done if we hadn't found you."

"It's no problem. Though I have to say you're the first two young waifs who have ever walked out of the woods around here as far as I know."

"How did you know we came from the forest and not from the other direction?" Parthenia asked. This was it. She was going to have to tell Jace the story she'd made up while she was in the shower. She doubted it was very convincing but it was the best she had.

"I guessed that was where you got your scratches. Not many thorns in the scrub around here. You fell down the forest ridge into the ditch, right?"

"We did," she conceded. That part of her story was true. "I guess you must be wondering what we were doing there."

"I was, actually. The forest belongs to the Dirksens. It was lucky for you that you came here and found me before you were picked up by one of their gamekeepers. There are severe penalties for trespassing on Dirksen land. Or, worse still, you could have been mistaken for game and shot. How did you end up in there?"

The forest belonged to the Dirksens? So the Sherrerr rivals controlled Ostillon. Parthenia didn't know whether that was good or bad news for her and her mage siblings. "Well, we—"

Parthenia? Can you hear me?

Jace was looking at her expectantly.

Parthenia? It was Ferne. He was Sending, at just about the worst possible moment. She had to answer him.

"Is something wrong?" Jace asked.

Parthenia wailed and covered her face. She pretended to sob. It was the only thing she could think of to do that would give her space to reply. *I hear you. Are you okay? Is Oriana with you?*

We're all right. We only just managed to make some elixir. How are you and Darius?

We're okay but I don't know where we are. I can't speak right now.

Darius put an arm over her shoulders, consoling her, not knowing she was speaking to Ferne.

Okay. I'll Send again in an hour, Ferne said. Then he was gone.

er relief at hearing from her brother was so great she really did cry a little, which helped to maintain her subterfuge. She wiped her eyes. "Sorry. We had a terrible time today. I was explaining what we were doing in the forest, wasn't I? Well..."

Ferne was okay and so was Oriana. And they'd managed to make elixir. Parthenia felt a massive weight drop from her as she told Jace her story. With luck, she and Darius would be able to reunite with their siblings tonight. But what had happened to Carina? That was a mystery that remained to be solved.

NINE

Harmon woke Carina up by prodding her and stepping away as she came around. He was clearly trying to avoid being punched again. After the Mech Battle had ended and they returned to Langley's estate in the early hours of the morning, she spent couple of hours working toward her escape before finally falling, exhausted, into bed. She'd scraped away some of the mortar between the bricks in the wall, but it would take her several days to create a hole large enough for her to crawl through.

She had only slept a few hours before Harmon came in to wake her. Langley Dirksen was giving her no respite. She guessed the older woman didn't want to leave her to her own devices for too long, knowing she would be doing her utmost to leave. It was wise of Langley, but Carina was determined to get out soon nevertheless. The longer she remained here, the more agitated the Dirksen matriarch would become at her refusal to comply with her demands, and the temptation to force the issue would increase. Carina knew only too well what that might entail.

She also wanted to leave because she was worried about her

siblings. She couldn't stop wondering where they were and what they were doing. They could be in dire danger and there wasn't anything she could do about it, or at least not while Langley Dirksen had her locked up. She also wanted to find out more about the ritual she'd witnessed the previous evening. What it meant she had no idea, but it had to mean something.

After a breakfast during which neither Langley nor Reyes appeared—*they* were apparently free to sleep in after their late night—Harmon told Carina she had the freedom of the first floor of the house, though she was never to leave his sight.

So, her shadow in tow, Carina spent an hour wandering through the mansion's rooms. She didn't bother hiding the fact she was trying to find escape routes and relished the look of frustrated anger her behavior provoked in Harmon. She guessed he expected her to be more cowed by his presence.

Each room she entered, she checked the windows, examined the ceilings, and looked for secret doors. Though she'd never been inside such a luxurious residence before, she'd read that secret doors and passages were often found in such places.

The mansion contained rooms that appeared to have been unused for years: lounges full of dusty furniture, playrooms stocked with piles of toys, a holo room with twenty seats for viewing vids, and an expansive bare room that seemed to be for large gatherings like parties or dances. Most of the rooms had a stale, neglected air. Carina also wandered into the staff area. When she went into the kitchen, the man and woman working there were alarmed by her presence. She quickly checked the place over. Here, she would find something she could use to create a naked flame, she was sure. And the pot on the windowsill that held a plant would provide the soil she needed. Noting there was no lock on the door, she left.

"What about outside?" she asked Harmon as they reached the

end of the corridor that led to the entrance hall. "Can I go out into the grounds?"

"What do you think?" He cocked an eyebrow at her.

"There's only one way to find out." She strode toward the front doors. Harmon was quickly behind her. He grabbed her hair and yanked her back.

"Harmon," a voice admonished from the top of the double staircase. "Please don't treat our guest so roughly."

Langley Dirksen was wearing a loose gown of silky material, and her hair was down around her shoulders. She descended the staircase. "Good morning, Miss Whoever-You-Are." As she reached the bottom of the stairs, she said, "Really, I can't go on not knowing your name. Won't you tell me it? Just your first name, so that I have something I can call you."

"Oh, all right," Carina said. "I guess it won't hurt."

Langley smiled brightly at her small victory.

"You can call me... Prisoner," said Carina. Langley's expression fell. "Or maybe Captive? Detainee?" She put a finger to her lips and frowned. "I know! Just call me Caged One. That'll do. Or would you prefer Slave? It's up to you. I don't mind."

"That isn't funny," Langley Dirksen said. She looked as though she was about to stamp her foot. "Why can't you be reasonable? Believe me, you could have things a lot worse. I could give you over to others in my family. They're asking for you, you know. It's only because you happened to arrive within my jurisdiction that I've managed to hold on to you. But I can't protect you forever. If I don't show them some results soon they'll be demanding you. I won't have much choice but to give you to them and then you'll find the rest of my clan won't be as lenient with you as I have."

Carina didn't doubt that Langley was telling her the truth. The information didn't have its desired effect, however. She only resolved to work harder to escape as soon as she possibly could. "I don't even know what it is you expect me to do. I rescued some kid. So what? I was only doing my job. Nothing extraordinary about it. If you do hand me over to the rest of your evil family, they'll be just as disappointed in me as you are. So let me go."

Langley tutted. "So stubborn. I'm going to eat breakfast. Tonight I'm having a small dinner party. I want you to attend. Perhaps when you meet some of the people who would like you for themselves, you might change your mind. I really am your best option. I hope for your sake you realize that."

———

Langley insisted on Carina's presence while the older woman went about her daily business. Carina hated sitting around with nothing to do while Langley chatted with business colleagues over vidcalls or discussed the management of her estates. By the time evening arrived, she was simmering with barely controlled anger, partly fueled by plain boredom. Langley sent her up to her room to "get ready for the soiree."

It was the first time she'd been allowed to be alone in her room all day. A selection of fine dresses had been prepared for her. She took great pleasure in ripping them all to shreds and throwing them out into the hall. But taking out her frustration on the dresses did little to appease her feelings. She was furious at being forced to attend the coming social event like a performing animal, and she'd devised a plan that would result in her leaving at its earliest stages.

When Harmon witnessed her destruction of the dresses, he followed her into the suite, strode over, and stood in front of her, his fists clenched. He managed to restrain himself, however. He only pushed her down, marched out, and closed and locked the door.

She leapt up and ran into her bedroom. She had a short time before she would have to go down to the party. She closed the bedroom door and pulled the bed away from the wall. Taking up the base of the metal ornament she'd left there, she carried on scraping away at the mortar between the bricks. If she could escape into the next room, she might be able to go from there to the kitchen where she could create elixir.

As she worked, she thought of Langley's son, Reyes. The kid hadn't appeared all day. She guessed he usually avoided his mother's company. That's certainly what she would have done in his position. She doubted she would see him that evening either.

After ten minutes she heard the main door to the suite open. She jumped up and pushed her bed into position, throwing herself onto it just in time as Harmon opened her bedroom door. He frowned, seeming to sense she'd been doing something she shouldn't have. He looked around the room. When he couldn't locate any evidence of subversive behavior, he said, "Come with me."

She walked across to her guard. It was time for her to party. Her clothes were dirtier and smellier than ever. *Good,* she thought. Anything she could do to ruin Langley Dirksen's fun and reputation would be worth it.

When she arrived in the lounge where Langley was holding her gathering, several guests were already there, richly dressed and adorned with jewelry. Some of the women wore elaborate hairstyles that had probably taken hours for their hairdressers to craft. All the guests turned when Carina entered the room. Their eyes popped and silence fell like a death knell.

"Am I in the right place?" she announced loudly. "I was told there was a party here. I love parties." She marched to the nearest group, which consisted of a woman and two men standing together, drinks in hand. Their mouths gaped. "You don't mind, do you?" she asked the woman. Taking her drink from her hand, Carina drained it, wiped her mouth on her sleeve, and returned the empty glass. "Urgh. That tasted terrible. How could you drink it? What about yours?" She snatched a drink from one of the men and drank it down. "Not bad. Getting better." When she moved to take the other man's drink, he put his hand in front of it protectively and glared at Langley.

The matriarch was sitting with three women on a sofa and chairs. Her shock at Carina's behavior quickly turned to fury. She rose to her feet and said coldly to Harmon, "Take her away."

Harmon grabbed Carina's upper arm and tried to force her from the room but she dug her heels into the carpet and resisted. She wasn't going to miss out on the opportunity to get revenge by creating the biggest spectacle she could. "Oh surely the party isn't over yet. I'm having so much fun." She twisted from Harmon's grasp and dodged past him before running around the edge of the room. As she passed a table spread with food, she grabbed the tablecloth and dragged all the dishes onto the floor. "Whoops!"

Gasps came from the guests along with a few titters. Langley was crimson, Carina noted with great satisfaction. Then Harmon caught her.

Not making the same mistake twice, this time he picked her up and carried her over his shoulder. The man was just too large and strong for her to do much about it. But as she was carried from the room, she lifted her head and waved at the gawping party guests. "*So* nice to meet you all. Sorry I can't stay."

It was in that final glimpse that one of the partygoers caught Carina's eye. A woman who was sitting with Langley had an unusual hairstyle. Her hair was wound into a spiral above her head. It wasn't the style that caught Carina's attention so much as the fact that it looked familiar. She was sure she'd seen the woman somewhere before.

When they reached the stairs, Harmon climbed them still carrying her. He carried her down the hall to her suite where he threw her on the floor. He left and locked the door but a few minutes later he was back, a satisfied smirk on his face. "I want to thank you for your little performance. Mistress just gave me permission to teach you to behave better. I'm going to enjoy this."

Harmon moved closer, smiling as he reached for her.

"Not as much as I am," said Carina, punching toward his groin. Harmon caught her fist in his giant paw and twisted, causing her to spin around to avoid a broken wrist. He switched his grip to her forearm and dragged her to her feet. She flew at him, aiming a kick at his knee, but he chopped sideways, the edge of his hand whacking her ear and skull and sending her sprawling. Her ear hurt like a bitch and began to ring.

This time, she waited for him.

"What's wrong?" he taunted. "Not used to fighting with men?"

As he grabbed her arm and lifted his other hand to strike her, she drove an elbow into his thick neck. He dropped her like she was a stick on fire and coughed, nursing his throat. His eyes narrowed and his nostrils flared. Ferocity drove him toward her. She stood her ground, waiting for the last split second before he reached her, then stepped aside, ready to kick him down.

He had anticipated her move. Both his arms were stretched out and she couldn't avoid his grasp. He had her by the waist. In one smooth movement he scooped her up over his head and threw her down. When she was on the floor he proceeded to kick her over and over again, grunting with the effort. She curled into a ball and tried to protect herself as well as she could.

———

When Harmon had finished and gone away, she lay still for a while. She checked that none of her bones were broken and she still had all her teeth. Then she got up and went into the bedroom. She figured she would be left alone for the night now, which meant she had many hours to work on removing bricks from the wall.

TEN

Pale, pre-dawn light was softening the night sky outside her bedroom window by the time Carina wiggled the final brick free. She placed it softly on the rug with all the others. The hole she'd made in the wall that adjoined the next room was narrow, but she estimated it was now just wide enough for her to squeeze through. The room beyond was dark and she hadn't heard any noises from it, not even the steady breathing of someone asleep. She hoped it was empty and the door leading from it wasn't locked.

She gently rubbed dust from her sore, bleeding fingers and bent down to the hole before putting her arms through up to her shoulders. This part of passing through the gap would be the most difficult, except perhaps when it came to her hips. Her head low between her arms, she wriggled forward, twisting her body and easing her shoulders into the narrow space. The edges of the bricks caught on her. She pushed harder with her legs, hoping she wouldn't get stuck. She would hate for Harmon to find her in such a humiliating position.

The hard corners bit into her shoulders. She couldn't move

forward and neither could she move backward. She began to regret her impatience at trying to get through the hole. Maybe she should have removed another brick. But she couldn't afford the time it would have taken. If she was going to escape she had to do it now while the inhabitants of the estate were asleep.

Was Harmon asleep too? Or was he outside her door, wide awake? If he was out in the hall, he would be bound to see her escape from the next room. But he couldn't be. The man had to sleep.

If he was outside she couldn't help it. It was a chance she had to take. After her behavior at Langley's party, the woman was sure to hand her over to her even nastier cousins today. Perhaps Carina had gone too far the previous evening but her actions had given her the time she needed to break out of her room.

That was if she could break out of her room. She braced her knees against the carpet and pushed as hard as she could. The bricks scraped painfully against her shoulders, but the soreness was no worse than what she already felt due to Harmon's ministrations. The pressure built. She gasped. Her shoulders slipped through.

Now she only had to bring the rest of herself into the shadowy room next door. She crawled forward on her elbows until her hips reached the hole. Once more, she stuck against the sides. Pulling forward with her forearms and pushing with her toes, she dragged her hips through the gap, wincing as her hip bones ground against the hard surface.

She was in the next room. She lay on the floor for a moment, assessing her surroundings. The room was a bedroom like the one she'd just left. The door was in the same place too. She guessed she was in another suite similar to hers except in a mirrored layout.

She got to her feet and tiptoed to the door. After listening at it for a moment, she gently turned the handle and opened it a crack.

The next room was dark too and seemed empty. She walked softly into it and over to the door that led to the hall.

Her pulse loud in the quiet of the sleeping house, she slowly turned the door handle, thankful that Langley wasn't as in love with modern conveniences as her brethren. If the door had been automatic, it might only have responded to those who had security clearance on the estate's system. A plain mechanical handle suited her fine. As she turned the knob as far as it would go, the door moved. It wasn't locked.

Now all she had to do was to get downstairs to the kitchen. If she could just have five or ten minutes to herself in there, it would be enough to make elixir and she could finally set about finding her family. She pulled the door toward her until the gap gave her a narrow view of the hall.

Damn. She could see a man's legs sprawling out. He had to be sitting down. She took a closer look. The legs didn't belong to Harmon. This man was smaller and wearing different clothes and shoes. She opened the door wider until she could see the rest of the guard. A light-haired man she hadn't seen before was sitting directly in front of her door. He was asleep. His chin was on his chest and she could even make out a thin trail of drool.

She estimated that about twenty meters of hall lay between her and the stairway. She only had to walk twenty meters without waking the guard to reach the stairs. But she had to walk right past him.

There was no time like the present. Dawn was rapidly approaching, and so might Harmon in order to take over from his sub. She opened the door and stepped into the hallway. The rugs in the Dirksen mansion were soft, thick, and perfect for muffling footsteps. Her heart in her throat, she took a step toward the guard and then another, keeping close to the wall.

He woke up.

She froze. The guard sat upright and stretched. He noticed the drool on his chin and wiped it off. He crossed his arms.

She was a statue, waiting for him to look in her direction. Or hear her breathing, or the sound of her heart thumping. How come he couldn't hear her heart? It was loud as a drum in her ears.

The guard adjusted his position some more and crossed and uncrossed his legs. After a few moments, his eyes closed. A few moments later his head dropped forward. Slowly, one arm slipped down his chest. It was followed by the other until both his arms were hanging down his sides and he was asleep again.

She crept past him, forcing herself to go slowly and quietly when all she wanted to do was run. Without looking back, she walked to the top of the stairs. A glance down the hallway told her the guard was still asleep. At the bottom of the stairs all was dark.

She had to hurry. The kitchen staff would arrive at their jobs soon to prepare a fancy breakfast for Langley and her son. She trod lightly down the stairs. Moving quickly through the dark, silent house, she headed toward the kitchen.

Ten minutes. That was all she needed. Maybe five. She could probably make the elixir in five minutes if she found all she needed immediately.

The kitchen door came into sight. She was nearly there. It wouldn't be locked. The door had no lock.

"'Morning." A figure stepped out from a dark room into the corridor in front of her, barring her way. He walked into the scarce light. It was Reyes. Langley's son stood between her and her freedom.

"Couldn't sleep?" Reyes asked. "I suffer from insomnia a bit myself. Pain in the ass, isn't it?"

She stared at the young man. He looked different somehow. Perhaps it was due to the half-light, but he looked older, and much more sinister.

"Where were you going?" Reyes asked. He glanced over his shoulder. "The kitchen? Can't wait for breakfast, huh? I guess you must be hungry after you missed the party last night. Mother told me what you did. I wish I'd been there to see it. It sounds hilarious. I would have loved to see all their faces. Pompous, puffed-up lot, they are."

She was calculating if she could close the distance between them and knock Reyes out before he had time to shout and raise the household. Probably not, but she didn't have any other option except to try.

"Don't let me get in your way," Reyes said. "If you want to eat, eat." He stepped back and waved an arm, motioning for her to pass him.

That was when she saw the gun. He'd been holding it casually behind his back.

When he saw her look at his weapon, he said, "Oh, don't worry about this. I'm not planning to hurt you."

She was confused. If he didn't want to stop her, why was he armed inside his own home? And why didn't he want to stop her? She walked toward the young man, not taking her eyes off him. If he was going to allow her free passage she wasn't about to refuse it, but there was clearly a catch somewhere that she wasn't getting.

Cautiously, she walked past him. He had to know she wasn't going to the kitchen because she was hungry. He might not know how she planned to escape from there, given that there were no exit doors, but he had to know that was her intention.

As she reached the kitchen door, he said, "You never told us your name. I'd like to know your name."

"You don't have any more right to that than you did to lock me up here," she replied. She opened the door.

"You're right," Reyes said. "You're absolutely right. I told Mother that. But she's used to getting her way. They all are. I'm not like them, you know. I hate them. They're my family and they've given me everything I could want, but I still hate them. I wish I could come with you. Here, take this." He reached into his pocket and pulled out folded plaspaper.

When she looked at him distrustingly, wondering if it was a ruse to make her approach him, Reyes said, "It's cash. People use it when they don't want their purchases to be traced. You'll need it."

She stepped over to him and took the money.

"Good luck," said Reyes.

She took a final look at him. The gangly youth had lost his sinister aspect. He now looked forlorn. His arms drooped at his sides and his weapon dangled from his hand. Had his Mother made him patrol the house that night to prevent her escape? Was he defying the matriarch by letting her go?

She went into the kitchen and closed the door. Reyes Dirksen wasn't her problem. She began to search for what she needed.

ELEVEN

Ferne arrived in the early hours of the morning, just as Parthenia had asked him to when he Sent to her for the second time. She'd been terrified that her brother would get his Transport Cast wrong and appear in the room below hers. That was where Jace was sleeping after insisting that she and Darius take his bed. It was the only bed in the place, and Parthenia guessed that the ranger was sleeping on the floor in his living room. While she'd waited for Ferne to arrive at the agreed time, she'd imagined him Transporting himself directly on top of Jace's prone figure, giving him the fright of his life and ruining everything.

She needn't have worried. Ferne appeared right next to the large bed where she and Darius had lain for the last few hours. Darius was sleeping heavily, entirely unaware that Parthenia had been in contact with his brother. She hadn't dared to trust the six year old with the good news. He'd been keeping their secrets fairly well for his age but she didn't want to rely on him.

Parthenia hadn't slept at all. Exhausted though she was, she'd forced herself to stay awake. If they were to be successful at leaving the ranger's tower, they had to do everything correctly. Jace seemed like a nice, kind man, but Parthenia didn't really know him. She didn't know how he might react to a boy suddenly appearing from nowhere. If he were to take the elixir Ferne was bringing they would all be stuck here and Oriana would be left alone.

Ferne's arrival out of thin air filled her with happiness. She climbed out of bed and hugged him. He'd brought elixir as he'd said he would. They would both need to drink it to Transport themselves and Darius back to Oriana. The steps would be a little complicated but they could manage it.

Parthenia released Ferne from her arms and whispered, "You look terrible." He did. He was filthy and his hair was full of bits of dead plants.

"Thanks," her brother replied. "Have you got any food?"

"Just a little," said Parthenia. She'd asked Jace if they could keep some food with them that night in case they were hungry. It was an odd request considering the amount they'd already eaten —especially Darius, who had stuffed his face—but the ranger had good-naturedly agreed. She held up the remains of her dress which she'd wrapped around the nuts and bread Jace had given them.

"Great," Ferne said. "So, how are we going to do this?"

"You take Darius with you. If we get separated, it's better he's with someone who can make elixir. I'll Locate Oriana, then Transport myself there. Have you brought something from her?"

Ferne handed Parthenia a few strands of hair. "Who takes the elixir with them?"

"Oh, I didn't think of that. Wait a minute." She went into the bathroom and brought out a cup. "I wish I had another bottle but this will have to do." Ferne poured elixir into it.

"You take the rest," Parthenia said. "Even if I can't Locate Oriana, I'll be able to Transport myself out of here."

"Okay," said Ferne. "We better wake Darius."

Noises of someone moving around came from the room below. Parthenia stared at Ferne. Had they woken up Jace with their talking? She thought they'd been quiet, but the ranger's lonely situation probably made him sensitive to the sound of other voices.

"Quick," Parthenia urged Ferne. "Don't bother waking him. Just take his shoes with you and go."

Ferne sipped elixir and ran to Darius' side. Parthenia winced at the noise of her brother's quick footsteps on the wooden floor. Jace would hear them for sure. Ferne grabbed his sleeping brother's hand and closed his eyes. A few seconds later, they were gone.

Parthenia sighed with relief. Darius was safe. Now it was her turn. She took a mouthful of elixir. Delving into the dark of her mind, she Cast Locate, focusing on the strands of hair she held, seeking out Oriana.

Her sister was far away. Right across the continent. Carina had Transported her pairs of siblings a great distance apart, due to the speed of the Sherrerr shuttle as it passed overhead. But all Parthenia had to do was Transport herself to Oriana. Ferne and Darius would be there already and most of their family would be reunited.

She opened her eyes to take another drink of elixir to Cast again—and found herself looking directly at Jace. He was standing on the stairs, his body halfway into the room and halfway below it. His bushy eyebrows were raised.

"What are you doing? Can't you sleep?"

Parthenia gulped down the elixir. She had no choice about it. She would have to Cast right in front of the ranger. If she didn't do it now she might never get another chance. She'd drained the last of the elixir Ferne had given her. If she didn't Transport out of that place, she would also face some very awkward questions about where Darius had gone.

She closed her eyes and tried to write the character within her mind.

"Parthenia?" Jace's heavy footsteps invaded her thinking. He was coming up the stairs. He was walking over to her. "Are you having a bad dream?"

Please stop talking to me. Parthenia fought to concentrate on the character and the Cast. If she didn't make it soon the effect of the elixir would wear off and she would be stuck here, a continent's distance from her sister and brothers.

She felt a hand on her shoulder. *No!* If the ranger didn't remove his hand she was in danger of Transporting him with her. And *that* would require a whole lot of explaining. Parthenia stepped backward, breaking contact with Jace. With a huge effort of concentration, she finished writing the character. Now to leave. She had to go to her family.

"Where's your brother gone?" Jace asked. Then louder and angrily, he said, "What's going on?"

A shiver of sensation passed over her and she opened her eyes. The Cast had worked. She was far from the tower and in a new place, which was in near darkness. The air was warm and moist and strange sounds were coming from all around her, as well as a strong smell of—

"Parthenia," Darius exclaimed. He barreled into her, almost knocking her from her feet. "I thought you'd never come. What took you so long?"

He was hugging her so tightly around her waist he was crushing her. She gently pulled his arms away, only for them to be replaced by those of Ferne and Oriana. Laughing, crying,

Parthenia gave up. She stood in a huddle with her brothers and sister for a while, just being joyful they were together again.

When they had calmed down and stepped apart she asked, "Where are we? And what's that awful smell?"

Now she could focus on her surroundings, she found she was looking at rough, dirty walls made of wood.

"We're in a barn," said Oriana. "It was the only place we could find to hide. But everything we need to make elixir is in here. We even found an old bottle. But it took us hours and hours to get a fire started. And now it's gone out. I didn't want to make it bigger in case someone noticed, and I was worried I might burn the place down. The animals hated it too. I think they were frightened of it."

"Animals?" Parthenia asked.

"Yes," said Ferne. "Come out and meet them. That's what... well, they're responsible for what you can smell. They're big but they're quite friendly once they get to know you."

Darius took Parthenia's hand, and with Ferne and Oriana he led her out of the small enclosed space where she had arrived from her Transport. She hated to think what Jace would make of her disappearing before his eyes. Now not only did he know their names, he also knew what they could do. If he heard a report of missing children using their names and performing strange tricks he would have an interesting tale to tell.

She tried not to worry about it. They were on the other side of the country, far from the Dirksens' forest. If they were careful, they could stay out of danger long enough for Carina to find them. The whereabouts of her older sister was another thing Parthenia tried not to worry about.

They turned a corner into a wider space, and she halted in fear. Huge animals loomed in the semi-darkness. "You didn't say they were that big," she whispered fiercely at Ferne.

"Honestly," he replied, "they seem to be harmless. I quite like them."

The animals' bodies were as tall as she was, but their heads were half as high again at the end of their long necks. They were short haired except for longer hair that grew from the backs of their necks and hung down over their eyes. All the animals were tethered to a bar by straps that connected to a kind of cage of straps around their heads and faces.

They were eating some of the same dead plant bits that were tangled in Ferne's hair, and Parthenia noted that though the animals' teeth were large they weren't pointed like those of predators. Perhaps they weren't dangerous after all, but she was sure she wouldn't be going near one any time soon.

"I don't suppose you brought any more food?" Oriana asked hopefully. It was clearly wishful thinking on her sister's part. It was obvious Parthenia didn't have anything else with her except the ranger's shirt she was wearing. She'd even dropped the empty cup before she Transported.

"I'm sorry, Oriana," she said. "Haven't you or Ferne found anything to eat since we left the ship?"

"Here," said Ferne, "let's eat what we do have." He unwrapped the cloth parcel Parthenia had given him and handed Oriana some bread.

"Can I have some?" Darius asked.

"Let Oriana and Ferne have it all," said Parthenia. "We already ate, remember?"

"I remember," her little brother replied. "But I'm still hungry."

"Well, Ferne and Oriana are hungrier."

"Okay," said Darius. His young mind flitted to another subject. "It was a big surprise to wake up here. Did you say goodbye to Jace?"

"Hmm..." Parthenia said. "Yes, kind of."

"I'm glad we're all together again," Darius said, watching Oriana take another bite of bread. "But where's Carina?"

TWELVE

Carina had Transported herself to a spot outside the stadium where the Mech Battles were held. It was one of the few places she knew on Ostillon. As soon as she appeared, she checked all around her. The massive stadium stood to her right and spreading out between her and the town was the parking lot. A few hover vehicles dotted it, perhaps temporarily abandoned by owners too inebriated to find them in the crush at the end of the show. She also noticed for the first time the large workshops that jutted out from behind the stadium. She guessed that was where the giant mechs were built and repaired.

Then she recalled the odd ceremony she'd witnessed being held at the end of the Mech Battles. The origins and meaning of the ceremony were a mystery she would love to solve but she had other priorities.

Although she was exhausted from working through the night and ached all over due to Harmon's beatings, the earliness of the hour was counting in her favor. There was no sign of any movement nearby and she didn't think her sudden appearance had been observed.

She checked the bottle she'd taken from the estate kitchen and tucked inside her shirt. The hard, smooth shape felt comforting to the touch. It was full of elixir. She finally felt somewhat relieved and hopeful for the future. She'd escaped Langley Dirksen's estate and now she was free to find her mage siblings.

After following the stadium wall around, she hit the long road that led through the lot and into the metropolis. She set off down the road quickly. The sooner she reached the comparative anonymity of the city streets the better.

Somewhere on that large continent Parthenia, Darius, Ferne, and Oriana were probably struggling to survive. She had to find them before they did something that revealed their mage powers. Ma would have drilled it into them that they were never to reveal their abilities to strangers, but her sisters and brothers had virtually no experience of the outside world. She wouldn't have been surprised if one of them had already done something risky. If they were caught saving them would be a lot harder. Even if they were being very cautious, hunger, thirst, and exposure to the elements would tempt them to do things they shouldn't and there were always evil people waiting to take advantage of others.

At the thought of evil people, Castiel popped into her mind. She'd successfully avoided thinking about her other half-brother over the last few days, but now she wondered what had happened to him. As with Parthenia, Darius, Oriana, and Ferne, she had Transported Castiel and her other half-sister, Nahla, to the planet surface while the Sherrerr shuttle was being boarded. She'd Transported Castiel and Nahla first, in fact, glad to say goodbye to them.

She felt a twinge of guilt at sending Nahla down to the surface with Castiel. The little girl didn't seem to be naturally bad but she worshipped her older brother, and he enjoyed exerting his strong influence over her. Castiel was as malevolent and malicious as his father, Stefan Sherrerr. What concerned her even more was the fact that he had asserted strongly he could Cast. Like Nahla, no one thought he had inherited their mother's mage powers. But after reluctantly taking the pair of them with her when she escaped from the Sherrerrs, Castiel had boasted he could Cast if he were given elixir.

If he was right and by some quirk of nature his ability hadn't developed until he'd hit puberty, the prospect was terrifying. He'd watched his siblings' lessons on Casting. He probably knew all the characters and principles. All he would need was some practice. She didn't even want to think of what her oldest half-brother might do were he given the chance to act out his nastiest fantasies. What was worse, he hated her passionately and all his other siblings except Nahla. They were physical reminders of feelings of inadequacy he had experienced while growing up, unable to Cast as most of his brothers and sisters could. And if his ego and pride were anything approaching his father's, those feelings would be unbearable.

She hoped she had Transported him and his minion sister far from everyone else in her remaining family.

She was drawing close the thoroughfare that would lead her into the city. The sun was coming up, and the city was wakening along with it. Every so often a hover vehicle would pass along the road, usually high up and traveling very fast. The tall building complexes she had seen from the spaceport were in the distance. She was heading toward a low-rise part of town that seemed poorer and older. She guessed this was a part of the city the Dirksens hadn't gotten around to developing yet.

It was a good place for her to be. She would be able to pay for things using the plaspaper money Reyes had given to her. First on her list of things she needed were new clothes. The ones she was wearing were so dirty and stank so bad she disgusted even herself.

More importantly, she had to get rid of anything that identified her. Langley Dirksen would have the streets combed for her as soon as the matriarch knew she was missing. She should cut her hair too, she mused.

The obvious thing for her to do would be to get as far from the neighborhood of the Dirksen estate as quickly as she could. Yet she didn't want to leave the place just yet. The metropolis was probably the capital of that region if not the entire continent, so it would be here she would have the easiest access to useful information, news reports, and so on. Also, the Dirksens might have already put up road blocks, guessing she would try to escape the city.

She reached the thoroughfare that formed a T with the road from the stadium. She stepped into it and turned left. A few pedestrians were already walking the streets. As they passed the men and women threw looks she guessed were not only due to her disheveled state. Her clothes, which had been provided by the Sherrerrs, were not what was usually worn here. She had to blend in with the local population but she wasn't sure how to go about it.

Hover transports were beginning to fill the roadway. Though it was only two lanes wide, the lanes were three tiers high. The highest tier was the fast lane and slower vehicles occupied the lane just above the ground. The vehicles pulled off into parking spots at the road's edge when they wanted to stop. In one of the spots was a stall selling handmade artwork. She glanced at the items idly as she passed by. The objects were beautiful: multicolored opalescent containers and simple decorative plaques.

Catching her looking at the display, the stallholder said, "See something you like? Special discount for my first customer of the day."

She smiled, barely deciphering the man's thick accent. She

shook her head and walked on. But the encounter had sparked something. The elderly man running the stall reminded her of her grandmother. Nai Nai had collected pebbles in the wild lands around the slum settlement where Carina had grown up, polishing them to reveal their beautiful natural colors before offering them for sale. In truth, the stones were nearly worthless and the living Nai Nai had scraped had been meager, but it had been just about the only time Carina could remember being truly happy.

She turned around and went back to the stall. The short stallholder was gazing upward absently at the expensive vehicles flashing past in the fast lane overhead. When he noticed her return, he grinned and stood up so quickly he knocked over his stool. As he stooped to pick it up, he said, "Changed your mind? Something caught your eye? Which piece is it you're interested in. I can recommend—"

"Have you had breakfast?" she asked.

The stallholder's eyes grew so wide the whites showed all around. "Breakfast? I... why do you ask?"

"You remind me of someone. She's been dead a long time, but you would be doing me a favor if you ate breakfast with me."

"Oh, well," said the man. "I'm not going to turn down the offer of free food. Of course I'll eat breakfast with you."

"Thanks. Where can I buy it?"

The old man gave her directions to a shop down a nearby alley and in a few minutes she had returned with hot, filled buns and an opaque, smooth tea. The stallholder pulled out a second stool and after she sat down they ate.

She hardly knew the reason for her sudden impulse but she guessed it wouldn't hurt to speak to a local and learn something of how people lived on Ostillon. She might learn how to avoid sticking out and how she might be able to find her siblings.

"This person I remind you of," said the old man, "is it a grandparent?"

"Yes. My grandmother brought me up. She sold pretty things too. Pebbles, though. Not like what you have here. Did you make all these things yourself?"

"Me?" The stallholder laughed. "Oh no. I could never make anything like this. My son is the artist. He had an accident as a child and he can't walk."

"I'm sorry," said Carina. She guessed the man was too poor to pay a splicer to fix his son's legs, but it would have been rude to mention it. "Your son is very talented."

"Thank you. I'm proud of him. I can tell by your accent you aren't from around here. Are you visiting family in the city? Or perhaps looking for a job?"

The state of her clothes and the bruises Harmon had left on her face, told the old man she wasn't much better off than him. She decided to run with his impression of her—it wasn't that far from the truth after all, and she might learn something useful. "That's right. Do you know where I might find some work?"

"I guess you're looking for something off the books?" He winked at her.

"Yeah, I am. Do you have that kind of thing around here?" She knew exactly what the stallholder was alluding to. The situation was the same everywhere she went. The clan-affiliated upper classes jealously guarded their wealth and privilege, the aspiring middle classes held a firm allegiance to the system and clung to the false hope that they might one day move upward, and the semi-illegal, shady underclass didn't—or chose not to—fit in. Sometimes these lower-class individuals' birth details had never been registered, they'd angered a clan member, or they'd committed a crime and were wanted by the authorities. Whatever the reason for their position, they lived outside the system.

"Of course," the stallholder replied. "Isn't that kind of thing to be found everywhere? There's an agency that hires casual workers for all kinds of legitimate and less-than legitimate work about half a klick down this road. Just tell them you lost your ID. They'll understand what you mean. They'll give you a uniform and pay cash at the end of the day."

A uniform would be a great disguise. She doubted the Dirksen thugs Langley sent out to find her would be looking for someone wearing a local uniform. "Thanks. That sounds like exactly what I need."

"Thank you for the breakfast. I hope our little chat has brought back some happy memories for you."

She smiled. "It has." The stallholder didn't only remind her of her dear, sweet, quick-tempered Nai Nai because of his age and situation: he was also just as kind and considerate. It was nice to feel looked after, rather than being the one who was looking out for everyone else.

Their breakfast was finished, and she had to get off the street and change her appearance soon before people came looking for her. She thanked the old man for his time and wished him good luck with his sales before leaving.

Thirteen

Carina ran a hand through her newly shorn hair. She'd told the barber to cut it short. She had something resembling her merc's military cut. It felt good.

Her head seemed lighter and she felt freer, though the sight of her battered face in the barber's mirror had been a bit of a shock. It was twelve hours or longer since Harmon had worked her over and the bruises were really beginning to bloom. She wasn't going to make much of an impression at the employment agency, but she had decided that a day or two's work was her best option. The Dirksens would be looking for her in places where people went to lie low: cheap hotels, derelict buildings, seedy parts of town. The clan's bully boys wouldn't be looking for ordinary people doing ordinary jobs, unless they were a lot smarter than typical. She also hoped to become more familiar with life on Ostillon. A better knowledge of the world might help her locate her siblings.

The agency receptionist took in her disheveled appearance in one withering glance. She hadn't been able to find anywhere open at that early hour that sold clothes. But she clearly didn't look too awful to work. The receptionist pointed toward a row of interfaces along the wall of the shabby office. "Input your details. The system will match you with what's available today."

"I don't have any ID. I lost it."

The receptionist frowned. "Where are you from?"

"Offplanet."

"Makes sense. I couldn't place your accent. Okay. Pick out a uniform that fits, put it on, and wait outside. Someone will be along to collect the day laborers soon."

She noticed the box beside the receptionist's desk that was full of old, worn overalls.

"You get paid when you return your uniform," said the receptionist. "Dirty is okay but if it's torn or damaged the repair cost comes out of your wages."

She had thought it a little weird for the agency to provide a uniform but now the policy made sense. It was hard to avoid damaging your clothes while working manually. The agency used the uniform rule as a ploy to keep back some of the workers' wages. Still, she was there mostly for camouflage, not for money. She still had the bills Reyes had given to her.

As she rooted through the box to find overalls that wouldn't look too ridiculous on her, she wondered if Reyes had gotten in trouble for letting her go. Was Langley's mansion fitted with security cameras? She guessed not or Reyes wouldn't have been so bold. For all his brave talk, he'd acted submissively while in his mother's company.

The only overalls that didn't come up too short on her lanky legs had a tear across one knee. "I'm taking these," she said to the receptionist and showed her the tear. "But look, they're already damaged."

The receptionist said, "Sure. Okay." From her manner, it was obvious she was going to deny ever seeing the tear when Carina returned later on that day.

She put on the overalls over her dirty clothes and went outside. Over the next hour, more people went into the agency and came out again wearing a uniform. They joined her and the group grew. No one spoke much, though nods passed between workers who knew each other. She didn't talk either, not wanting to alert the others to her offworld accent. When a young girl smiled at her, however, she returned the smile. The girl reminded her of Parthenia, though she was a little older. In fact, the girl was probably her own age, Carina realized wryly. It was only that she thought of herself as older.

After another half an hour or so, as her sleepless night began to really catch up with her, a large hover transport arrived. Before it had even drawn to a stop, the workers raced to crowd around its rear entrance. The doors opened, and the people at the front of the crowd tried to climb aboard. Two men stood there, however, and they pushed the over-eager laborers back, pressing the men and women's chests with the soles of their boots.

"We need thirteen today," one of the men said. There were many more than thirteen people hoping for work. There had to be twice that number.

The men began to point and count. As they numbered off, the people they'd chosen forced themselves through the ranks to the front and the men let them aboard. When she noticed one of the men's gazes drawing near, she lifted up onto her tiptoes to make herself seem taller. "Eleven," said the man, pointing at her.

The other laborers stepped aside resentfully as she passed through the crowd and climbed into the back of the transport.

"Hey, honey," called the young woman who had smiled at her. She was smiling again, this time at one of the men. "Don't forget me."

Carina didn't rate the woman's chances. She was the smallest and weakest of all of them. Yet to her surprise, the man called, "Thirteen" and waved her aboard.

A few nasty names floated in the young woman's wake as she stepped up and into the vehicle. She put her hand behind her back and made a gesture with her fingers that Carina guessed meant something obscene on Ostillon. The seat next to hers was free, and the woman sat down.

"Phew," she remarked. "I thought I wouldn't make it. You're new, right?"

"Yeah," said Carina, and turned away to gaze out the window as the transport pulled into the traffic in the middle lane.

"Hey," said the woman, "don't worry. I'm not going to give you away." She lowered her tone. "Everyone here has a secret. Jonas over there embezzled millions from his father's company. Adrienne killed a man. Kali is hiding out from his psycho wife."

"Shuttup, Asha," said a man sitting in front of them, who Carina assumed was Kali. Ignoring him, Asha went on, "So you see, we can't turn you in because we all have something to hide ourselves."

"Okay."

Asha waited for her to say more and when Carina remained silent, she said, "What's your name?"

"Tamira. You can call me Tammy."

"Good to meet you, Tammy," said Asha. "As you're new, I'll show you the ropes. First, your uniform: don't bother trying to avoid tearing it. It doesn't matter what it looks like when you hand it back, they're gonna dock you five percent. You could turn in a brand new set of overalls and they would still dock you five. So don't worry about it. Second: we get free lunch but we only get fifteen minutes to eat it. If you're late back, they'll dock you ten percent for every minute. So if you're ten minutes late, *you* owe *them*, see?"

"Okay, I get it. Thanks."

"I haven't finished. No restroom breaks except over lunch. So try not to drink too much or you'll be in pain before we knock off."

"All right."

Asha leaned closer and said in a lowered tone, "One more thing. If you do the boys a favor, you'll get work whenever you want it."

Carina had been continuing to look out the window while Asha was speaking, but at this latest comment she turned and stared at the other woman.

"What?" Asha asked defensively. "It takes ten minutes and if you're guaranteed work from it, what do you care? I'm just saying, when your bruises go down, you won't look too bad. I bet they'd go for you. Only remember I was the one who told you, okay? I get in first."

"Yeah, thanks. But I won't be competing with you on that."

Asha shrugged. "Just trying to be helpful."

"I know. I appreciate it." Though Asha's methods weren't for her, Carina didn't think less of the woman. In that kind of life people did whatever it took to get by.

When they arrived at the job site, she was surprised to discover it was one of the complex apartment blocks, newly built. One of the supervisors told the workers they were to remove all the construction debris, dust, and dirt, ready for the decoration crews who were arriving tomorrow. She had been expecting heavier work, but she guessed that machines took care of most of the buildings' construction. The Dirksens loved their high tech.

As soon as the workers disembarked from the transport, one of the supervisors took Asha by the arm and led her away into a room. The door closed and the other supervisor addressed the remaining crew.

"There's twenty-six floors, so you have to clean two each. At six o'clock we'll check every floor and if we find any dirt or trash no one gets paid. Got it?"

Sighs and groans came from the group but no one dared to openly protest the unfair rules. Instead, the men and women began to shout out the floors they would clean. She was too slow to catch on. In a few seconds the verbal claiming was over and the only floors left were twenty-three through twenty-six. Two of them would be Asha's—when she returned from doing the other supervisor a 'favor'—and the other two would be Carina's.

Thirteen cleaning machines stood in the bare, dusty lobby. The devices were old and battered. They were also large and heavy, she discovered when she tried to move one of the two that hadn't been claimed. It was then she discovered the elevators weren't working yet.

The door to the room where Asha had gone with the supervisor opened and she emerged with the man. She walked over to Carina, who was squatting next to her machine, trying to figure out how it worked. All the other workers were leaving to begin their jobs.

"Huh," Asha said, watching the departing men and women. "I bet they left us with the broken ones."

"Have you used these before?"

"Yeah. It's always the same machines for this job, though I shouldn't complain. This is one of the best kinds of work we can get. But only if the damn machines aren't broken." She pressed a button on the remaining machine. When nothing happened, she said, "Yep. Like I thought. What about yours?"

Carina pressed the same button. Her machine started up and gave out a low hum, but then it died. "Can't we just tell the bosses our machines don't work?"

"They'd only tell us to borrow someone else's, and how likely do you think that is? No. We have to try to fix them or we're stuck." She lifted up the cowling on her machine. "But these aren't complicated. It's just a loose wire or something."

Asha fiddled with her own and Carina's cleaning machines for a while and managed to get them both working. Then together they carried the machines up to the top floors, one at a time. They were far too heavy for one person to carry alone.

After demonstrating to Carina how her machine worked, Asha went downstairs to floor twenty-three. The morning was wearing on and Carina had to clean floors twenty-five and twenty-six before the day was out. She was still sore from Harmon's beating, her hands ached from spending the night removing the bricks from the wall, and she was groggy with tiredness.

If it had only been her who would suffer the repercussions of failing to do her job, she might have lain down and gone to sleep. But if she did that twelve other people would lose their day's wages, and they were the types who couldn't afford it. She pushed her cleaning machine to the farthest apartment on the floor and started it up. They were designed to work automatically, Asha had told her.

The apartment was full of odd bits and pieces left over from the construction work, which Carina had to take all the way downstairs to a dumpster. She began to carry out the trash and build a pile next to the stairwell, thinking she could push the lot down the stairs at the end of the day.

When she returned to her cleaning machine, instead of working methodically across the floor and up the walls of the room, it was spinning in a circle. The area it had worked was spotless but the rest of the place remained dirty. She cursed and tried to turn the machine off but it was spinning too fast. Whenever she reached in to press the button, it whirled out of her reach.

She swore again, loudly. She kicked the machine and sent it

scooting over to the wall, which it rapidly climbed before continuing up and onto the ceiling where it began spinning again.

She uttered words only mercs used—and then only out of the hearing of their officers—as she jumped up to try to reach the machine's controls.

She heard laughing from the doorway. Asha was standing there, her arms folded. "I was wondering how you were getting on."

Carina ceased her efforts and rested her hands on her knees, panting. She laughed too. "Not very well."

"Don't worry. We'll get it down. I wanted to ask you something. As you're new in town, I thought maybe you don't have anywhere to stay. Would you like to sleep at my place tonight? I have a spare room."

Asha seemed nice and she was right—Carina didn't have anywhere to stay tonight. "Thanks." Although she couldn't ever tell Asha her true reason for being on Ostillon, perhaps her new acquaintance could give her some tips for finding people on that world. She could begin her search for her siblings.

FOURTEEN

Parthenia was awake before her brothers and sisters. She pushed down the smelly, hairy animal blanket they'd covered themselves with to help keep out the chill of the night and sat up. Darius had somehow worked himself fully under the remaining blanket and was lying cross ways. Oriana and Ferne were sleeping back to back, their heads resting on a thin pillow they'd made from the raggedy dress Parthenia had used to hold the food.

The barn had no windows, but pale daylight shone through cracks between the planks of the walls. On the other side of the wide space the animals were shifting about as if agitated. Parthenia wondered what was the matter with them.

Her joy at being reunited with Ferne and Oriana remained but she knew their situation was as dangerous as ever. Their Sherrerr relatives would be searching for them and the clan wouldn't give up that search for a long time—most likely as long the memory of the mage children lasted, down the generations. The children had unfortunately proven the power and value of their abilities when they blew up the Dirksens' shipyard.

As soon as the others woke, they would have to decide where to go and what to do next. Parthenia thought it might be best to find out where the capital city was and go there. It seemed to make sense that to find someone you went to the most important place in the country. What they would do when they got there, she didn't know, but she didn't have any better ideas. They might find it easier to live in a big city too, where there were jobs and lots of people to hide among.

Parthenia didn't know how they would travel to the city, or, now that she thought of it, where the capital was located. But maybe they could ask someone. More urgently, they needed to find food. Her belly was already grumbling in spite of the meal provided by Jace the previous evening. She wondered what the ranger had made of her and her little brother's disappearance. She hoped he hadn't told anyone, and particularly not the Dirksens, who she guessed were his employers.

Darius groaned and turned over, pulling the blanket off Oriana. He sat up, still under the blanket. Parthenia tugged it off of his head. He blinked and looked around, taking everything in like he was trying to figure out where he was. When he saw her he smiled. "When's breakfast?"

She was about to answer when her brother's words sparked a realization. That was why the animals were moving around so much. They were hungry. And that meant someone was on their way to feed them.

"Parthenia?" said Darius. "When's—"

"Shhh." She reached over him to shake Oriana's shoulder. "Wake up. We have to leave," she said as her sister's eyes opened. "Wake up Ferne."

Parthenia stood and helped Darius to his feet too. The only thing they had to take with them was the elixir. Where was it? She didn't know where Ferne had put the precious liquid. Ferne was sitting up and rubbing his eyes.

Just as she said, "Ferne—" the lock on the barn door rattled and a moment later the door swung open. The golden light of sunrise flooded in, silhouetting the figure who stood in the doorway. Oriana and Ferne jumped to their feet.

"What the...?" said the figure. It was a woman, though she was tall and broad. She continued more angrily, "What are you doing in my barn?" The woman stomped farther inside, swung the door closed, and dropped the latch. "Are you here to steal my horses?"

"No," Parthenia protested. "We aren't here to steal anything. We only needed somewhere to sleep. We're sorry. We haven't touched anything, honestly. We'll leave now."

"Oh no, you won't. You aren't going anywhere. You're trespassing and I'm going to call the authorities. But before I do that, I'm going to search you. I want to make sure you haven't stolen something." The woman's eyes narrowed as she scanned the children from head to toe. "Those aren't yours," she exclaimed, pointing at Parthenia's bracelets. Oriana was wearing one and Parthenia was wearing the other. "They're far too valuable for urchins like you. Hand them over."

"They belong to me," Parthenia protested. "They were a present from my father."

"Give them here. If you can prove they're yours, you can have them back."

Oriana pulled off her bracelet and placed it in the woman's outstretched hand. "Please don't call anyone. Please."

The woman frowned. "Why? Are you in trouble for something? Whatever it is you've done, you're runaways. That little boy is far too young to be away from his parents. You." She pointed at Parthenia. "Give me your bracelet." When Parthenia had done as she'd been asked, the woman slipped the bracelets inside her shirt. "And you." She was looking at Ferne. "Come here and turn out your pockets."

"No," shouted Parthenia. Ferne might have the elixir. She couldn't risk the woman taking it. They all stared at her. "Ferne. If you do have anything in your pockets, give it to me."

"Don't you dare," the woman said, striding across to Parthenia's brother. "Whatever you have, it's mine and I want it back."

Ferne reached into his pants pocket and took out a bottle. It held a small amount of elixir. Only enough for one Cast remained. As the woman moved to grab the bottle, Ferne tossed it to Parthenia. She caught it and unscrewed the lid. The woman was only one step away but Parthenia managed to swallow the last of the elixir before she snatched it.

"This is mine," the woman exclaimed, staring at the empty bottle. "You took it from the things I stored at the back of the barn. You *are* thieves."

"But it's only an old bottle," said Darius.

"How dare you," the woman blustered. She turned on the other children with narrow eyes. "What else have you taken?"

The children were watching Parthenia, however. She closed her eyes, hoping the woman would leave her alone long enough for her to Cast. She couldn't Transport all four of them but she could do something else.

"What's wrong with you?" she heard the woman ask. "Open your eyes! What are you doing?"

Parthenia struggled to concentrate and write the character she had in mind. She heard the sound of struggling.

"Mmmwharrrrr," exclaimed the woman. "Get off me!"

Parthenia was deep inside her mind, writing the strokes of the character one by one. She Cast. When she opened her eyes, the woman was on her back and Ferne and Oriana were on top of her, holding her down. Darius was sitting on her head.

Despite the seriousness of the situation, Parthenia giggled. "You can leave her alone now." When the three children stood up, the woman remained on the ground. She was limp and though her eyes were open they were glassy and unfocused.

"Did you Enthrall her?" Oriana asked.

"Yes. It was all I could think to do at the time. But I think it's going to work to our benefit. I have an idea." Parthenia walked over to the woman and looked down at her. "What's your name?"

"Marcia."

"Okay, get up, Marcia."

The woman slowly rose to her feet. Her arms hung limply and her mouth was open.

"Do you have a vehicle?" Parthenia asked.

"Yes."

"Good. I want you to take us all to the capital city."

Without a word, Marcia turned and walked out of the barn.

"Quickly," Parthenia said. "Put on your shoes." As soon as they could the four children followed the Enthralled woman.

"Don't you think we should go in her house to make some more elixir before we leave?" Ferne asked.

"No," Parthenia replied. "We don't know who else might be there. I don't want to risk it."

The strange procession marched down the path that led from the barn and across a field. Marcia was heading in the direction of the farmhouse. Parthenia hoped no one was watching from the windows. They had to be such an odd sight, anyone seeing them would be bound to come out and investigate.

"Do you know how far it is to the capital?" Oriana asked Parthenia.

"No, I don't have any idea."

"But what if your Enthrall wears off before we arrive?"

"Then I guess we'll just have to go the rest of the way by ourselves."

Ferne laughed. "Our new friend is going to be very confused when she comes out of it."

They had arrived at a shed that stood next to the farmhouse. Marcia opened both doors wide, revealing a shiny vehicle with a pointed nose. It rested directly on the ground and didn't appear to have any wheels. Parthenia wondered how it moved.

Marcia was walking into the shed. The door of the vehicle opened to her touch, and the children scrambled to catch up with her and take seats inside.

Enthrall was an unpredictable Cast. Its effect on the victim's mind varied according to their mental characteristics. Intelligent, strong-willed people could resist it to an extent, and the less intelligent who were easily persuaded could be so affected by Enthrall they lost touch with what was happening around them. Marcia seemed to be so heavily influenced there was a chance she might drive away and leave the children behind, not realizing they weren't with her.

Parthenia closed the driver's door for Marcia as she didn't seem about to. The woman started the vehicle. It rose up, causing the children to gasp. Marcia drove out and onto the small lane that ran in front of the farmhouse. She drove between the trees all the way down to a larger road and pulled out directly into it without looking for oncoming traffic. A truck blared at them and rose above and over them to avoid a collision.

It was going to be a hairy ride.

"Marcia," Parthenia said. "Don't drive dangerously. Don't drive in front of other vehicles."

"Maybe there's an automatic setting," Oriana suggested.

"Yes," said Parthenia. "Marcia. If your vehicle can travel automatically, input the capital city as the destination and stop driving."

Marcia tapped keys on a pad next to the seat. Her arms relaxed.

"Phew," said Ferne, also relaxing in his seat. "Hey," he said, "I forgot to ask. Why are we going to the capital?"

"I thought it might be somewhere we could find Carina," Parthenia replied. "I don't know what else to do."

"Will we find Carina soon?" Darius asked.

"I don't know," Parthenia replied. "I hope so."

The traffic on the highway was building up as more and more of the hover vehicles joined it from side roads. Parthenia wondered why, if the vehicles could fly, they didn't travel directly over land to their destinations, but she guessed that requiring them to follow roads like wheeled vehicles was for safety. Or maybe the Dirksens reserved the skies for their own vehicles.

She couldn't see anything resembling a city in the distance. From her seat next to Marcia, she had a good view of the vehicle's dash but nothing on it stated the distance to their destination. The capital could be hours or days away.

While they were traveling along, she prepped her brothers and sister with the story she'd made up to tell Jace. If they needed to explain themselves to strangers, they were to pretend they had gotten lost and they only needed directions to the nearest town or city, from where they would contact their parents. They were to say they were going home after visiting their relatives and that Parthenia was looking after them. She would pretend to be eighteen.

As soon as she could find out more information about the country, she would pick a distant town for them to name as their home. She told her sister and brothers they could to fill in more details to make the story sound plausible but they were not to deviate from the main parts. The children began to make up names for the relatives they had been visiting and fill in other small facts, enjoying themselves with imagining a normal family life and upbringing, until the story almost felt real.

If only it were real. Their fantasy life sounded much more pleasant than their current situation. She and Darius were still wearing the shirts Jace had lent to them. They didn't have anything else to wear. None of them had any food or water or money to buy any. As soon as Marcia was no longer Enthralled their problems would return.

Parthenia hoped they would reach the capital soon.

FIFTEEN

Asha's apartment was cramped but it contained the small, spare bedroom where she'd said Carina could sleep. What Asha hadn't mentioned was her live-in boyfriend. When they had arrived after their long day's work, he'd been lying on the sofa in the small living room. The boyfriend, who Asha introduced as Cavin, seemed to be extremely relaxed and cheerful. He was sprawled out as he played games on an interface.

"Hey, babe," he said to Asha after she'd shown Carina the spare room. "When are we gonna eat?"

"Soon, honey. Soon." Asha went into the tiny kitchen and Carina followed her. "You can take a shower while I cook," Asha said. "I'll clean up after dinner."

"Aren't you too tired to cook?" Carina asked. "How about I buy us some takeout? I saw we passed some restaurants on the way here." The little hole-in-the-wall eating joints Carina had seen were clearly off-network. Rather than taking net orders and sending out the food via drones, those kinds of places sold on the street, for cash.

Asha looked relieved. "Well, if you're offering…"

"Sure. If I give him the money maybe Cavin can go and buy us something. You two must know the best places."

"Oh." Asha peeked around Carina into the living room. "Cavin's… It's better not to do that. I'll go."

"No, in that case I'll go. You shower. I'll be back soon."

Cavin didn't acknowledge Carina as she returned through the lounge and left the apartment. She went down in the elevator to the ground floor, though the clanking of the ancient mechanism didn't inspire much trust. The streets in that area were too narrow for hover vehicles. Apartment blocks towered on both sides and skinny children played games with toys they'd made from trash.

Carina was immediately thrown back to her own childhood. She'd been a skinny kid playing with trash once too, though at the time she'd barely known life could be better. She didn't pity the kids too much. She'd been happy enough with very little except the love and care of her grandmother, for as long as the old woman had lived anyway.

Skirting the playing children, she walked down the dirty street and stopped at the first restaurant she saw. The place sold only one thing: a soup with noodles and meat. The origin of the meat wasn't specified. She bought three large containers covered with lids. The boy who was serving was so young he could easily have been one of the kids she had passed. After paying for the food, she returned to Asha's apartment.

Cavin hadn't changed position all the time she'd been gone and he was still playing on the interface. Asha came out of the shower dressed in a bathrobe. "Great, I love that soup. Thanks, Tammy. Put them down on the table. I'll get chopsticks and spoons."

Cavin finally moved, swinging his feet off the sofa and reaching for the nearest container. He peeled back the lid, took the chopsticks Asha handed him, and began to eat. Carina also dug into the steaming broth and noodles. The food was welcome after the puny, poor quality lunch they'd received at work. After the first mouthful, however, she lowered her chopsticks and stared into the bowl.

"Is something wrong?" Asha asked. "Don't you like it?"

"No," Carina replied. "Nothing's wrong. It tastes good." She resumed eating but the feeling that had made her pause persisted. The noodle soup tasted almost exactly like the one Nai Nai used to make. She wondered if she was imagining it. After her grandmother had died, Carina had never again come across the dishes the old woman had cooked. Yet the more she ate, the more certain she was that, halfway across the galactic sector from her childhood home, she was eating a dish she'd thought was a family recipe.

Asha was watching her. "Something is wrong, isn't it? Do you feel sick? We've never gotten ill from eating this before."

"It's okay. I'm fine. The food's great."

Cavin was eating at a fast rate. Anticipating the man would be back on the interface the moment he'd finished, Carina said, "I was wondering, would it be okay if I checked the news after dinner?"

"Sure," Asha replied. "Any particular reason? Not a lot goes on around here. Or at least not much that actually gets reported."

"No," said Carina. "No reason. Just want to catch up. You mean that news about the Dirksens doesn't get reported, right? I heard they only arrived a few years ago. What was it like?"

Asha made a noise of disgust. "It was awful and it's only gotten worse. The actual takeover was pretty bloodless. The Dirksens had done their research and found out exactly who held the power. After they arrived, they targeted only those people and took them out. Their families too. But the rest of us they left alone, just about. It all happened so fast, and our military was always weak. I guess no one ever thought anyone would be interested in our boring little planet. Turned out we were wrong. We hardly put up a fight. The Dirksens tried to sugar-coat it of course. They sent out propaganda telling us the planetary government was corrupt and that they were here to liberate us. They said we were backward and they would help us modernize. They gave us the hover drive technology, saying it was the first step in our "upgrade."

"But their tune soon changed. The Dirksens basically replaced everyone who had any money or influence in Ostillonian society with someone affiliated with their clan. If you weren't prepared to hand over a percentage of profits and kiss their asses they replaced you, one way or another. After news of disappearances, suicides, and accidental deaths started getting around, no one resisted any longer. Once you felt a Dirksen hand on your shoulder you gave them what they wanted, or accepted that your days were numbered."

"And what's it like now?" Carina asked, wondering how much of the mechanics of the takeover were Langley Dirksen's responsibility. The woman seemed to think her family's control of Ostillon was benevolent.

"They're slowly tearing everything apart," said Asha. "I mean, we didn't know how good we had it until the Dirksens started sticking their noses in wherever they thought they could turn a profit. You know the work we did today? Well, things didn't ever used to be that bad. There was always some kind of work if you wanted it. You didn't use to see people left behind. Now the supervisors are making ten people do the work of twenty and pocketing the extra wages. Everyone takes their cut all the way to the top and the Dirksens don't only ignore it, they positively encourage it. It's us poor saps at the bottom who lose out every time, and things are only set to get worse."

Cavin drained the dregs of broth from his container and put it down. He pushed the bowl away and reached for the interface.

"Er, could I check that?" Carina asked.

"Yeah, let Tammy use it for a minute, hon," said Asha.

Wordlessly, Cavin passed the screen over. He got up and went into the bathroom. Carina quickly set to work scanning the news for the region and the international news for the planet. There was no mention of four unidentifiable children being found. However, no reports mentioned strange, inexplicable activities or events either, she noted with relief. It looked like her mage siblings had managed to stay out of trouble so far.

While she had use of the interface, she looked up general information about Ostillon. The ritual at the Mech Battles still played on her mind. She was certain the fact that the person had created elixir was not a coincidence, but she also couldn't even guess what it meant. Mage history said their kind had lived in that galactic sector, dispersed and hidden, ever since it was first settled eons previously. The story she had learned from Nai Nai was that mages had been one of the first groups of colonizers, running from persecution on humanity's original home, a lost planet called Earth.

It made sense that something of their influence might remain in the cultures and religions of worlds they'd settled. Had Ostillon been one of those worlds? And if it had, was the fact significant? If mages had lived on the planet they appeared to have been long forgotten. No one seemed to know that elixir was being created in the ritual, so it had lost its meaning.

Cavin was getting restless. At his third cough, she returned the interface to him. "I'll take a shower now if that's okay," she said to Asha.

"Sure," Asha said. "Take your time. The hot water comes with the rent, though that's changing next month." She sighed and began to clear away the empty food containers. "Everything gets more and more expensive all the time."

Carina went into the bathroom and closed the door. She found it didn't have a lock but that didn't bother her. Both Cavin and Asha knew she was in there. She undressed. There was nowhere to put her clothes except on the basin so she piled them into it and stepped into the stall.

For the first time since Harmon's beating she could properly assess the damage. Bruises stood out on her back, upper arms, and thighs. It wasn't the first time she'd come off badly in a fight, and Stefan Sherrerr would have treated her worse, but this time she particularly hated the effects. More than ever, the injustice of what had happened angered her. The Dirksens and Sherrerrs were a menace across the sector. She wished she was in a position to fight them, but what could she realistically do? The most she could hope for would be to find her siblings and escape far from their influence, perhaps even to another sector.

As she pondered the rivalry between the clans, a memory popped into her mind. Ever since noticing the woman with the spiral hair design at Langley's party, she'd been wondering where she'd seen her before. Now she knew: it had been at the Sherrerr stronghold on Ithiya. She'd gone to see Calvaley to ask permission to visit Bryce in the men's quarters but the Sherrerr officer had been taking a holo call.

She hadn't seen the other caller's face but the hairstyle was so distinctive she was sure it was the same person. The last place she would have expected to see an acquaintance of the Sherrerrs was at a Dirksen gathering. It was no wonder it had taken her so long to make the connection. What did it mean? Was Langley's friend an informant? A Sherrerr spy? Had she interrupted a call where the woman was passing secret information to Calvaley?

As she washed soap out of her hair, she wondered if she

should do anything about her revelation. It took her less than a second to come to a decision. No. What did she care if the Dirksens had a spy in their midst? She had nothing to gain from telling them and a whole lot to lose. Yet she feared what the fact might mean for Asha and other Ostillonians. Langley Dirksen had said the planet was a hidden bolthole for her clan. If someone the Dirksens trusted was feeding the Sherrerrs classified information, Ostillon wouldn't remain a secret for very long.

She had seen first hand the devastation of a planetwide attack. Asha might think things were bad now but they were probably going to get much worse.

A creak distracted her from her thoughts. The bathroom door was opening. At first, she expected that Asha wanted to ask or tell her something but the door only opened a short distance. A male hand and arm appeared, groping toward the basin where she had put her clothes. Cavin. Cavin was trying to steal her stuff.

She jumped out of the shower and slammed the door on his arm. Cavin shrieked. She opened and slammed the door twice more, and then threw it open. He fell to his knees, still screaming. Asha ran through from the kitchen.

"What did you do to him?" she shouted.

"Not as much as I'd like to do," said Carina, grabbing her clothes.

"She broke my arm," Cavin sobbed. "I think she broke it."

"Get out of my apartment," Asha said. "After everything I did for you, you go and attack my boyfriend."

"He was trying to steal from me," said Carina. "How else do you think this happened? Why would I hit him for no reason?" She began to get dressed.

"My arm," Cavin wept. "It hurts so bad."

"So what if he was trying to steal from you?" said Asha. "You didn't have to half kill him!"

Carina pulled on her top. "Do yourself a favor, Asha. Get rid of him. He's a bum and he's using you."

"No! Don't listen to her, Asha. I love you." Cavin cursed and tenderly touched his assaulted arm.

"Get out," Asha said to Carina. "Just leave, Tammy. And don't bother turning up for work tomorrow. I'll make sure you won't be hired."

"Don't worry," Carina said. "I'm not staying here another second." She marched to the door and went out.

Too angry to wait for the elevator, she took the stairs. As she ran down the steps two at a time, she wondered where she could spend the night. The Dirksens would still be searching for her intensively. She had to find somewhere they wouldn't think to look.

Sixteen

Several hours later, Carina was dead on her feet. She hadn't slept since the night of the Mech Battle, and even then it had only been for a few hours. She'd also been beaten, she'd worked through the small hours to escape from Langley's estate, and then she'd labored all day. She was on her last legs, yet she didn't seem able to find anywhere she considered safe to sleep.

As she'd wandered around the capital's downtown, Carina had taken the opportunity to buy new clothes. After pushing her old ones down a trash chute, she'd begun her search for a safe sleeping place.

Asha's apartment had been ideal. The Dirksens would never have found her there, in one of thousands of semi-legal residences. Now her options were limited. Without ID, the more expensive places were off limits. In time, she could solve that problem, but not quickly. Yet she feared staying at the cheapest hotels and hostels where ID wasn't required. They would be the first places the Dirksens would look.

Rounding the corner of a quiet street, she saw a heavily decorated building that rose from the ground in four tiers of decreasing size. Judging by the people wandering in and out of it, the structure seemed to be a public place. She walked down the street and through the wide, doorless entrance. The interior was as brightly decorated as the exterior, only while the walls outside were covered in patterns, inside the decorations were re-enactments of stories or events.

The building seemed to be a place of worship. Several people were kneeling facing a group of deities. One person had prostrated himself, his forehead pressed against the floor as he mumbled. None of the worshipers took any notice of her.

Again, she recalled the enigmatic ritual she'd witnessed after the Mech Battles. Was this place dedicated to the same religion? On the various worlds she'd visited as a merc, several faiths usually competed for the inhabitants' devotion. But at that moment, she was too tired to investigate further. She had to sleep.

On each side of the altar holding the statues of the deities, passages led deeper into the building. She took the right-hand one. Depictions of the religion's stories continued along its walls before it opened out into a space on the other side of the statues. This room held benches, presumably for lengthier sessions of worship. Other than the benches and a low, wide, cold brazier standing on the stone floor, the place was empty. She hoped it would remain so for a few hours at least, or that anyone who came in would leave her to worship in her own way. She stretched out on a narrow bench, lay her head in the crook of her arm, and was instantly asleep.

A gentle shake of her shoulder woke her. Despite the lightness of the touch, she still barely prevented herself from punching her

awakener. Her fist stopped a whisker from the young priestess'
face, and the woman drew back in alarm.

"Sorry," Carina said, sitting up. "I'm so sorry. You startled
me." She didn't know how long she'd slept but she remained
groggy with tiredness.

"I apologize for waking you," said the priestess. She wore a
long cloak and a cowl so her features and figure were obscure, but
she was so slight and her voice was so high and soft she seemed
very young. "We have a morning ceremony. You're welcome to
remain here but we need to use this bench."

"No, it's okay. I'll leave."

"You really don't have to leave," said the priestess. "Perhaps
you would like something to eat after the ceremony?"

Now that she was fully awake, Carina gave some thought to
the young woman's suggestion. Perhaps it wouldn't hurt to stick
around in the place of worship for a while. She might be able to
discover something about the ritual at the Mech Battles. "Thank
you. I'll stay."

The priestess nodded. "You may stand in the corner over
there." She left through a small door at the back of the room.

Carina stood up and stretched. Then she winced as her
bruises reminded her of their existence. Music began to float
through the open doorway—twangs of stringed instruments and
the regular beat of a drum. She went over to the corner and
waited.

Figures wearing the same hoods and floor-length robes as the
priestess entered the chamber in single file, each carrying a scroll
of plaspaper. She spotted the young priestess, the shortest in the
ranks. The twelve disciples took seats, one at each end of the
benches. They began to chant in a foreign language, repeating
what sounded like six or seven words over and over again. Then
one of the priests stood and stepped solemnly to the brazier. He

pressed a switch and flames sprang up. At the same time the whine of a fan came from above. When the fire was burning strongly, he unfurled his sheet of plaspaper and dropped it into the flames.

She glimpsed some writing on the sheet, then it was gone to ashes that were drawn upward to the fan. The priest returned to his bench. When he had sat down, the other devotee sitting on his bench did the same thing, though she thought the word he uttered was different from the first's. She was a little disappointed. She'd been hoping the disciples might make elixir on the brazier, but perhaps they didn't follow the religious practice she'd witnessed in the Mech Battle stadium.

The ceremony continued. Each disciple disposed of their sheet in the brazier's flames. As she was thinking wryly that it might be less effort to put the scrolls down a trash chute, she saw the writing on the paper clearly for the first time. She stood bolt upright. Then the sheet was gone and the fan above hungrily vacuumed up its ashes.

She'd seen a character. She hadn't been able to make out which one, but the sweeping strokes were so familiar she was sure she hadn't been mistaken.

Only one sheet remained unburned. It belonged to the young priestess. As the child approached the brazier, Carina craned to see what was written on it but the priestess was carrying the scroll close to her chest. She unfurled the sheet. The flames burned high as she held it out. The priestess spoke her word and dropped the paper into the fire.

Her heart sank. There was no character on the paper. It only displayed a random pattern of dots and numbers. She slumped against the wall. Had she imagined the character on the other scroll? Perhaps it was only because she'd just woken up and was still tired that she thought she'd seen something significant.

Someone had turned off the brazier and the priests and priestesses were filing out of the chamber. The young priestess was at the end of the line. Before she left the chamber, she gestured to Carina to wait.

She returned to a bench and sat down. After a few moments, the priestess reappeared carrying some food wrapped in a napkin.

"It isn't much," she said, "but you're very welcome to share with us."

"Thanks," Carina said. Thinking she might as well inquire about the religion anyway, she added, "Do you have a moment? I wanted to ask you something."

"What would you like to know?"

"I was at the Mech Battles the other night and I saw the ceremony at the end. Is that something your sect performs?"

"The Libation? Yes. We do that, though I've never had the privilege myself. It's a great honor and it will be many years before I am worthy, if I ever am."

"I was wondering what it meant."

"The Libation means many things. It gives thanks for the protection of the people, for one. You see, many years ago two great superpowers on Ostillon were at war. It was to put an end to the war that the Mech Battles were invented. Legend says that originally it was only two fighters representing each side, who fought with weapons. The mechs came later. A second reason for the Libation is to absolve the fighters' guilt if they killed their opponent. The Libation absorbs the sins of the competitors and washes them away when it is poured onto the soil."

"I see," said Carina. "But is there any significance to the ingredients used to create it? I thought I saw the priestess drop wood and soil into it." She didn't go into any more detail. She didn't want to give away how familiar she was with the creation of elixir.

"Oh yes, the ingredients are very significant. They... I can show you if you'd like me to when you finish eating."

Carina had been munching on the moist wafers the priestess had given her. She popped the last one into her mouth and said, "All finished."

Though the young girl's features were almost entirely obscured by her cowl, Carina thought she saw her smile. The priestess rose, and Carina followed her through a passage into the front of the building.

Daylight from the doorway now illuminated the room, washing out the colors of the friezes. The priestess led her to a section of the wall that displayed a pastoral scene. As she drew nearer, she realized the scene portrayed the five Elements. A stream ran through grass, representing Water. Lightning was striking a tree, and the first flickers of flame were outlining its branches. So there was both Wood and Fire. It was a natural land-scape, so Earth was all around. Buried to its hilt in one spot next to the stream was a dagger or a sword, obviously made of Metal.

Beneath the scene was writing in a script she didn't recognize. "What does this say?" she asked, pointing.

"The language is very old," the priestess replied, "but it explains what sins belong to each material. Water represents lust. Wood is stubbornness. Metal is impatience..."

Carina was looking at the wall, but she was facing the entrance. As the priestess spoke, someone poked their head in briefly, withdrawing the second they saw her.

Not waiting to hear the rest of the priestess' explanation, Carina sped out of the building. The person who had looked in was running away. She set off in pursuit.

How Reyes had discovered where she was, she didn't know, but she was going to find out.

SEVENTEEN

Parthenia realized she hadn't heard any of the other children speak for a while. She checked over her shoulder. Darius was lying with his head on Ferne's lap and Ferne had his head on Oriana's shoulder. Oriana was slumped against the door. All three were deeply asleep. Parthenia sighed. She was tired too but she had to remain awake. Marcia could return to her normal self at any minute.

The woman had stared blankly ahead all the hours they'd been traveling, only slowly blinking every so often and shifting a little in her seat. Parthenia could hardly believe how long the Enthrall Cast had lasted. Yet despite their long journey they still didn't seem to be drawing near to the capital city.

The countryside was much greener than any place Parthenia had seen on Ithiya. They'd passed through farmland and alongside wide, lush estuaries before they'd reached the forest that currently lined the road. The place looked similar to the woods she and Darius had wandered through for hours and she wondered if it was in fact the same place, though she hadn't seen the ranger's tower.

Jace had seemed a nice man but she dreaded seeing him again. Not because he was so large and foreboding, but because she'd disappeared right before his eyes. She hoped he hadn't told anyone. She resolved to absolutely avoid Casting in front of anyone else again. Then she remembered that was exactly what she'd done around Marcia. Once more, she sighed.

She had allowed herself to be Enthralled more than once when the twins and Darius were learning the Cast. She recalled that coming out of it was like being in a dream and you slowly realized that you weren't in a dream at all—that everything around you was real. It wasn't like waking up from sleep. It was a strange sensation and quite unsettling.

Watching the farmer's profile, she wondered when she would wake up. It had to be soon, and then what would happen? She hoped Marcia didn't grab the vehicle's controls in her shock and surprise and cause them to crash. As they were traveling on automatic, she didn't think that was likely but she wished she could be sure.

When Marcia did come around, they would have to deal with her reaction and get away from her somehow. If only they would reach the city outskirts, then she could command Marcia to stop the vehicle and let them out. But the capital was nowhere to be seen, and if they left the vehicle while they were in a forested area, they would be in the same position she had been in with Darius when they arrived.

As she was about to turn away and refocus her attention on the road, Marcia closed her hanging jaw and smacked her lips.

Oh no! "Oriana," Parthenia hissed toward the back of the vehicle. "Ferne!" But the twins didn't wake.

Marcia's limp hands twitched.

Parthenia reached over her seat to prod her siblings to wakefulness. She didn't want to hasten Marcia's return to reality by speaking loudly. Parthenia could just reach Darius' leg. She poked him. He brushed at his leg but didn't properly wake up. She nudged her brother again.

"What?" he said sleepily.

"Wake up Ferne and Oriana. Quickly! Marcia's coming around."

The farmer began to blink rapidly. Her eyes regained their focus. Darius had sat up and he was shaking Ferne. Marcia lifted her hands onto her lap. A frown creased her forehead.

Parthenia had perhaps a few seconds remaining while the Enthrall Cast had some power. "Marcia," she snapped.

The woman's head turned toward her. Marcia's eyes grew wide.

"Stop the vehicle," Parthenia said sternly.

"Wh-what...? Why? What am I...?"

"Do as I say," Parthenia said. "Immediately."

Marcia shook her head in confusion but her hands took the controls. "How did I get here? I don't remember..." The hover vehicle rapidly slowed and sank toward the ground.

"Get ready to bail," Parthenia said to her siblings.

"Hold on," Marcia exclaimed. "You're the children who were in my barn. I remember now. You're a bunch of thieves." Her voice rose in volume as she spoke.

The vehicle was on the side of the busy highway. Ignoring Marcia's words, Parthenia went to open her door. It was locked.

"We can't get out," Oriana said.

"Open the doors, Marcia," Parthenia commanded.

"No way," the woman replied. "What am I doing here? How did you all come here with me? What did you do to me?"

"I said, open the doors," Parthenia repeated, hoping against hope that some tiny dreg of the Enthrall Cast might remain.

"I will not," Marcia said. "I'm taking you all to the authorities. I don't know what you did to me, but you're all criminals and I'm not letting you get away with it. Wait. I know what's happening! You want to steal my vehicle, don't you? And you want to kidnap me too." She moved her hands to the controls again.

Parthenia desperately tried to think of a way to stop her from turning them in. The only solution that occurred was almost ridiculous but she couldn't think of anything else. "Marcia, I'm telling you, if you don't let us out of this vehicle right now, I'll control you again. I can make you do whatever I want. How else do you think you came to be here? Open the doors now or I'll do it!" She tried to look angry and threatening though inside she was quaking with fear.

Marcia seemed about to refuse. Her lips twisted in anger. But then she relented. She gave the voice command and the locks popped. The children scrambled out.

"Quick, into the forest," Parthenia shouted, grabbing Darius' hand. She wanted to get everyone out of sight of the road and away from Marcia before the woman changed her mind. Holding onto her youngest brother, Parthenia slithered down the embankment at the road's edge and under a wire fence.

"She's comming someone," shouted Oriana as she tumbled down beside Parthenia. "I saw her."

"Run," yelled Parthenia. Gripping Darius' hand, she set off through the low plants and in amongst the trees. Then she slowed and turned, worried they might become separated if they didn't take care. Oriana wasn't far behind but Ferne was veering away. She called her brother's name. "This way," she shouted. "We have to stick together."

As soon as she saw her brother change direction, Parthenia plunged once more into the undergrowth. The plants weren't thorny like the ones in the first forest she and Darius had encountered on Ostillon, she noticed with relief.

Parthenia pushed deeper and deeper through the densely packed trees. She didn't have any idea where she was taking everyone but it was the best she could do for the moment. They had to avoid capture and if that meant getting lost again, that was how it had to be. Regularly checking that Oriana and Ferne were keeping up, Parthenia ran on, panting, for a short while.

"Ow," Darius exclaimed.

She had accidentally dragged him into a tree. "Sorry!" She slowed and stopped. "Are you okay?"

Darius rubbed his nose. "Yes, I'm all right."

They'd put considerable distance between themselves and the road. She thought it would be safe to stop for a moment and catch their breath. Ferne bent over, his hands on his knees. Oriana leaned against a tree. For several minutes, no one spoke. Then, after their breathing began to return to normal, Ferne said, "What's that? Can you hear it?"

Parthenia had to listen hard before she heard the noise too. It was a soft thumping sound. She'd mistaken it for her heartbeat at first but then she realized it was coming from somewhere not far from where they stood. The children stared at each other. What could be causing it? Darius opened his mouth to speak but Parthenia raised a finger, motioning him to silence. She beckoned Oriana and Ferne to come closer. She cupped a hand to her mouth to whisper to them but a second noise interrupted her. This time it was unmistakable—it was the sound of voices, and they were rapidly getting louder.

Oriana crouched down and Ferne and Parthenia quickly followed her lead. Parthenia pulled Darius down with her. Luckily, the undergrowth was tall enough to hide them. The children sat on their haunches beneath the leafy fronds, staring at each other through the plant stalks.

Parthenia still hadn't figured out what the soft thumping sound was. Like the voices, it was growing louder.

No one dared to speak. They could only hope the people wouldn't see them or come so close they tripped over them. Parthenia strained to hear what they were saying.

"So that's four for me and only three for you," a man said. "Shall we call it a day?"

"No, absolutely not," said a woman. "That isn't fair. If I go back with fewer kills than you, they'll never shut up about it. No. Let's stay out a while. I'm sure I can bag another."

"If you like," the man said, "though I don't fancy your chances."

"I know. We haven't seen much game at all today."

"That's true, but that isn't what I meant."

"Huh? What did you mean?"

"Isn't it obvious? I'm a much better shot than you."

"What? What are you talking about? You just got lucky."

Parthenia was looking in the direction of the approaching voices. The light was dim under the plants, but eventually she spotted movement. She gasped. Legs were coming toward them, but they weren't human legs. They belonged to the kind of animals she'd seen in Marcia's barn. Ferne and Oriana's eyes were round as they saw the legs too. The animals' steps were what was making the thumping sound. Even Darius noticed and pointed. Parthenia nodded at him and put a finger to her lips.

The most amazing thing about the approaching legs wasn't what they were, but what was missing from the scene. Along with the thuds of the walking animals, the voices were growing louder. But no people were visible. What could it mean? Were the people on the animals, sitting on their backs? Parthenia had never seen such a thing, not even on vids.

Her heart was racing. Two of those huge animals she'd seen in the barn were almost upon them but she didn't dare try to move out of their way. The slightest shift would bring her into contact with plant stalks—the plants would move and the people would know there was something in the undergrowth.

Another painful realization hit: the people on the animals were hunting. That was what they'd been talking about when they mentioned "kills." If she or one of her siblings changed position, the hunters might mistake them for game and shoot at them. She cringed and tensed. She was right in the path of one of the animals. It was going to step on her. She braced herself.

But the long legs shifted slightly to one side, narrowly avoiding her, as if the beast knew she was there. With much rustling of leaves, the two animals passed by, leaving everyone unscathed. Parthenia let out a long, silent exhale and watched the eight legs retreat out of sight.

When she could no longer hear the animals or the people, she cautiously poked her head out of the foliage. The forest looked the same as when they'd first hidden. Aside from the plant life and insects buzzing in shafts of afternoon sunlight through the trees, it was empty. Parthenia stood and helped Darius to his feet.

"Can we talk now?" he asked.

Ferne and Oriana also stood up.

"Yes," Parthenia replied. "But only quietly."

"Where should we go?" Ferne asked.

"I'm not sure," said Parthenia. "We definitely can't go back to the road. If anyone's looking for us we'll be very easy to spot there. I guess we'll just have to walk until we finally reach the city, or maybe a town."

"Which way is it, though?" Oriana asked. "What direction were we headed in when we left the vehicle?"

"Uhhh..." Parthenia didn't know. She'd entirely lost her sense of direction when they were running through the trees. Oriana and Ferne also looked confused, however, so she said, "I'm pretty sure it's this way." She took Darius' hand again and walked confidently ahead. She didn't want her siblings to know how lost they were. It would only make them worry. Perhaps she'd guessed correctly, she reasoned. Or maybe they would hit upon a village or town eventually.

Trying to be brave for the sake of her sister and brothers, Parthenia led the little party through the forest. She pushed her memory of her previous desperate walk with Darius to the back of her mind.

EIGHTEEN

Carina caught up with Reyes at the end of the street. She launched herself at him and grabbed him around his thighs. They both hit the ground. Before Reyes could get up, she climbed onto his back and pinned him down. Passersby drew back in alarm and hastened away.

Reyes struggled to squirm out from under her for several moments before saying, "Okay, okay. I give up. Get off of me."

"Don't try to run," she said, releasing her pressure on his shoulders, "or I'll catch you again and I won't be so gentle next time." She moved off his back and stood up.

As he also rose to his feet, Reyes said, "I didn't think you were gentle this time."

"Then don't risk it."

"You really were a soldier, weren't you? Like Mother said. I didn't think a girl could hold me down."

She snorted derisively. "Plenty of female soldiers could beat your ass in a fight without trying. If I were you I wouldn't go around saying they couldn't."

Reyes rubbed his shoulder. "I don't know why you were

chasing me anyway. I haven't hurt you. I let you escape, remember?"

"As soon as you saw me looking at you back there, you set off running. If you didn't have anything to hide, why run away? You weren't in that place by accident. You knew I was there and you came to check on me. How did you know that?" Pedestrians were still staring at the two as they passed by. "Wait. Let's get off this street."

She took Reyes' skinny upper arm and guided him along the sidewalk before pushing him down the first alley they arrived at. She walked along the narrow lane with him until they reached a spot between two towering apartment blocks that was empty of people. After halting, she pushed Reyes against a wall—not roughly but hard enough to reinforce that she was in charge.

"How did you know where to find me?" she reiterated.

"Honestly, it was just a coincidence. I often go to that temple. When I saw you there, I knew you would think I was spying on you, so I ran."

"No. You're lying."

"I'm not. Really."

She was tempted to force the truth out of the kid with the threat of—or actual—violence, but she'd experienced plenty of that kind of persuasion herself. She wanted to avoid dispensing it to others if she could. She tried a different tactic. "Okay. So if you go to that place all the time, what's the main picture on the left wall? What does it show?" She had been looking at the frieze only minutes before. Her question wasn't difficult for someone familiar with the building's interior.

Reyes looked panicked. "It, er, shows... It's a scene of... of—"

"Right," she said. "So we've established that you lied when you said it was a coincidence you were at that place. You don't always go there. Yet you knew where I was. But how?" She was directing the question at herself as much as at Reyes. Carina was fairly confident she hadn't been followed, and she had no identity or footprint in Ostillon's systems.

Reyes protested, "Like I said—"

"Oh, stop wasting my time," she snapped. She regarded the young man. He seemed about the same age as Parthenia. "Look. You're still young enough to not involve yourself with criminals and thugs, even if they are your family. You don't have to go along with everything they do just because you're related. You don't seem like a bad kid. Why don't you get out while you can? Go someplace else and start a new life. A clean life where you aren't hurting anyone. Only first tell me how you knew where I was."

Her words seemed to penetrate Reyes' conscience. He lost his guarded expression and looked down as if ashamed to meet her gaze. "It isn't as easy as you think, even if I did want to leave. But I can't anyway. It would break Mother's heart. I know she doesn't seem like a good person to you, but she isn't as bad as the others and she loves me. I'm all she has."

"Then take her with you."

"Huh. She'd never listen to me. Besides, she loves being a Dirksen. It's her whole life."

She gasped. While she'd been talking to Reyes, in the back of her mind she'd continued to try to figure out how he'd found her. The answer had just come. "I'm carrying a tracer, aren't I? Where is it? How did your mother get it into me?"

"Nnnno. That isn't true."

She grabbed Reyes' bony shoulders and pushed him into the wall. "Yes it is! There's no other way you could have found me. Have you been following me all this time?"

"I, er..." Reyes slumped and hung his head. He nodded. "I haven't been following you the whole time, but you are carrying a tracer. More than one, in fact. I'm sorry."

She swore. "Where are they?" She tried to remember everything that had happened at Langley's mansion. Had they injected tracers into her while she was asleep? No. She would have woken up. She was sleeping on a hair trigger these days. Had they drugged her? She was sure she would have noticed.

"They were in the food you ate at breakfast the morning after we went to see the Mech Battles," said Reyes. "The type mother used passes through the stomach and latches onto the inside of the small intestine. You ate several but you wouldn't have noticed anything."

Feeling nauseated, she pressed a hand to her stomach. She had to get the tracers out immediately. "So that's why neither of you came down to breakfast that morning. You couldn't eat the food."

Reyes nodded again. He looked up at her, a defeated expression in his eyes. "Would you be willing to come with me somewhere?"

"Where?" Carina asked. "And is this to do with getting these tracers out of me?"

"No. I honestly don't know how to do that. But you'll be safe with me. I just want to talk."

She wasn't sure if she could trust the young Dirksen. On the other hand, if he really was wavering in his allegiance to his mother's clan he could be very useful. She was willing to take a chance. "Okay."

Reyes continued down the alley and she walked with him.

The young man said, "Mother isn't as bad as you think, you know."

"You mentioned that already." She wanted to tell Reyes what his family's thugs had done to her brother. That might open Reyes' eyes about exactly what he was involved in. But sje couldn't say anything about Darius' experiences at the hands of the Dirksens without revealing more to Reyes than was safe. She hadn't yet admitted to anyone that she was the merc who had rescued Darius and she wasn't about to, despite the evidence of the vid. It didn't matter how different from the rest of the Dirksens Reyes thought he and his mother were. Yet she wanted to find out whatever she could about the clan. Perhaps she might learn something that would help her locate her siblings.

Reyes seemed to be looking for something as they walked along the alley. When they reached the end, they turned into another narrow lane and continued along it. The district was seedy. The residents were too poor even for clothes driers. Rows of wet garments hung across apartment balconies and the street didn't look like it had seen an autocleaner in a long time.

She was having second thoughts about going with Reyes. She needed to take out the tracers and she didn't know for sure what Reyes would tell her. He might not know anything useful.

Finally, after turning down several more alleyways and entering deeper and deeper into the poverty-stricken neighborhood, Reyes seemed to find what he was looking for. He stopped at a door that didn't seem any different from the others except that the wall next to it bore a pattern of scratches. The door had no security panel. Reyes tapped at it instead. When it opened a burly man not unlike Harmon stood there, his expression angry and sullen. But then he recognized Reyes and stepped backward, ducking his head.

"Wait a minute. If you think I'm going to follow you into some clandestine hideaway guarded by your mother's henchmen, you're mistaken."

"And if I wanted to recapture you, I could have done it at the temple," said Reyes. "I'm not forcing you to go in. You're free to leave now if you want."

She hesitated then said, "I do want to. I worked too hard to escape from your clan to risk this."

"Okay. Maybe we can go someplace else."

"No. I changed my mind. I've wasted too much time already. Goodbye, Reyes, and good luck living with thugs. I hope you don't turn into one of them." She began to walk away.

"Hold on," Reyes said, running after her. "What are you going to do about the tracers?"

She replied, still walking quickly, "Don't worry. I'll figure something out."

"Wait. I was going to say that maybe I can help you."

"Really? How?" She wasn't sure she believed him. After all, he'd already said he couldn't help her, or at least not with the tracers. When Reyes didn't reply immediately, she continued, "Forget about it. And stop following me or I'll force you to stop."

The young man halted. As she walked away from him, he called out, "I still don't know your name."

NINETEEN

Carina had to find somewhere private to try to extract all the tracers. She wasn't looking forward to the task. When she'd Transported the Sherrerr tracers out of her brothers and sisters while they were escaping on the shuttle, she'd only been working on one per child and she'd known exactly where the devices were. Now, she didn't know how many Dirksen tracers were clinging to her guts, or their precise location. She would be using guesswork with her own body, and a delicate area of her body too. A damaged muscle would heal naturally in time, but she hated to think what she might do if she hurt her intestines.

Where to go? She continued deeper into the maze of streets. It was a warren of cheap apartment blocks served by small eateries and convenience stores. After stopping and checking behind her several times, she was finally convinced that neither Reyes nor anyone else was following her. Not that it mattered as long as she carried the Dirksen tracers.

Langley had tricked her into swallowing them in case she attempted to escape, of course. The Dirksen matriarch had been right on that score. Reyes hadn't mentioned what had happened at the estate since her escape. Did his mother know that he'd let her go? He also hadn't explained why he'd been checking up on her.

Or had she been set up? Had Langley Dirksen deliberately made it easy for her to get out of the mansion? Reyes had even been carrying cash to hand to her. It was all too convenient.

So many questions. And she had walked away from the only person who might answer them. Perhaps she'd done the wrong thing. Her friend, Bryce, had told her once that she was too distrustful. He'd said that not everyone was out to exploit mages for their own ends; that some people genuinely wanted to help.

He'd been right. The soldiers aboard the Sherrerr flagship had deliberately missed with their shots, allowing her and her family to escape. Perhaps Reyes really was a good guy, despite his family affiliations. Ah well. Now she would never know.

Then, as her hand touched the bills in her pocket, she realized she hadn't quite shut the door on Reyes Dirksen just yet.

She finally spotted what she was looking for: a small sign in a window high up in an apartment block. After counting the stories down to the ground, she walked through the security-free entrance. Only one elevator served the building and it was broken. She began to climb the stairs, counting each floor as she went up.

When she reached the story where the sign had been displayed, she tried to figure out which apartment it belonged to but she couldn't tell which it was. She couldn't remember in which direction the street lay and the hallway was windowless.

She went from door to door, pressing the panels until someone finally answered. It was a child, perhaps only seven or eight years old. She wondered if Ostillon was entirely staffed by children and if that explained why they were always hanging around. Didn't the planetary government provide schools? The little girl looked up at her expectantly.

"I want to speak to the person renting out a place on this floor."

The little girl only continued to gaze at her.

"I said, I—"

"That would be me," said a portly middle-aged man, waddling hurriedly toward the doorway. "Go back to your room," he said to the girl.

She moved away, but slowly, casting backward glances at Carina as she dragged her feet down the hall.

"So you'd like to rent my apartment?" the man asked eagerly.

"I'd like to *see* the apartment," said Carina. She didn't want the landlord to know she was desperate for a place. She only had a limited amount of money and no means of getting any more right now. She asked, "But if I like it, do you take cash?"

"My dear," the man replied. "I only take cash."

It turned out the apartment for rent was directly next door. The landlord keyed a code into the panel and the lock clicked open. The place was almost exactly as Carina had expected it to be —awful. It hadn't been cleaned in a long while. The windows were so grimy they were almost opaque and the bathroom and tiny kitchen were covered in stains.

"The place cleans up beautifully," the man said. "I would do it myself only I have a bad back. And with my grandchild to look after, I simply don't have the time. I was going to—"

"How much for a week?" she interrupted.

When the man named the figure, she didn't know if it was expensive or cheap according to the local rates, but she guessed he was probably trying to rip her off. He would be able to tell from her accent that she wasn't an Ostillonian.

"Are you joking?" she spluttered. "You think you'll get away with charging that much for a place like this?"

"Oh, wait," said the man. "What am I thinking? That's the rent for my other apartment that has twice as many rooms." He dropped his figure by a third.

She said, "That's still far too much."

The man shaved off a small percentage of the proposed rent. She was tired of haggling and she needed to remove the tracers as soon as possible. "All right, I'll take it—"

"Excellent."

"If you include an interface."

"An interface? You don't have one?"

"Mine was stolen and I haven't ordered another yet. I need something to bridge the gap."

The man frowned disbelievingly but said, "Well, that's easy enough. You can have one of my old ones, though I'll want it back at the end of your tenancy."

"Agreed," said Carina.

"And you pay me your week's rent up front. Now."

She reached into her pocket to pull out the cash. When her hand touched the bills Reyes had given her she stopped and took out the money she'd earned for her day's labor instead. It wasn't enough. She added some notes from Reyes' money to the pile and handed it to her landlord.

He counted the bills carefully and slipped them into the money belt he wore. "What's your name?" he asked.

"Tamira."

"Tamira what?"

"I'll tell you if I stay longer than a week."

"Ha," the man said. "If you say so. I'll send my granddaughter over with the interface later. Water and power aren't included in your rent, by the way." He told her the door code and left.

Adding the point about the utilities after the deal was struck was a typical trick, but she dismissed it. She hoped she wouldn't be in the place for longer than a few days. She couldn't contact her siblings through Casting, but she hoped she could find them through more conventional means, perhaps utilizing the planetary network.

She had an urgent task to complete first. She was about to take a sip of elixir and set to work when her door chimed. When she went to open it she found the little girl standing there wearing a solemn expression and holding an interface.

"Thanks," she said as the girl handed the device over.

She didn't reply but only skipped slowly back to her grandfather's apartment and went inside.

Carina carried the interface into the bedroom and put it down. Searching for information that might lead to the whereabouts of her sisters and brothers would have to wait just a little while.

She sat down on the bare, dirty floor and gently rubbed her stomach. She wasn't sure exactly where her small intestines were. Transporting objects you couldn't see was tricky. Transporting objects out of your body when you only had a rough idea of their location was plain stupid. But what choice did she have? Until she was free of the tiny electronic bugs, the Dirksens could swoop in at any moment and pick her up.

As soon as she'd removed the tracers, she would have to take them somewhere else and dump them or destroy them. When the Dirksens came for her they would go to the devices' last known location, and she didn't want that to be her newly rented apartment.

She took a sip of elixir, placed a hand on her stomach, and closed her eyes.

TWENTY

A wind was rising, setting the trees into motion. The noises of the forest increased, rustling, creaking, and murmuring. The insects had retreated since the temperature dropped and the breeze arose. Parthenia hoped rain wasn't on its way. She and Darius were still wearing nothing except the shirts Jace had given them and Oriana and Ferne weren't much better clothed.

At least they were heading toward the capital city, or so she hoped. She'd spotted shuttlecraft traveling overhead and because they always went in a particular direction she'd concluded they were on their way to or from a spaceport. She'd taken her pick of the two possible directions in which the spaceport might lie and for the last half an hour or so they'd been walking toward—or away from—the place. Her chances of being correct were only fifty-fifty, but they were the best odds they were going to get.

Ferne was carrying Darius. Not because her youngest brother was tired, but just for fun. Parthenia was grateful to Ferne for entertaining the little boy and taking his mind off the thirst, hunger, and fatigue they all felt. Ferne was pretending to be one of the animals from Marcia's barn and Darius was pretending to be a hunter. He was holding an imaginary weapon and firing behind while telling Ferne to go faster.

"What are you shooting at now, Darius?" Oriana asked. Previously the boy's targets had been various monsters of his imagination. This time, however, he replied, "Father's guards are chasing us. But it's okay. I'm killing all of them."

Oriana caught Parthenia's eye, her eyebrows raised. Parthenia returned the look. Poor Darius. It would take them all a long time to get over their terrifying escape from Father's family. She was still struggling with the role she'd played in his death. She didn't think she would ever come to terms with it.

"You get 'em, Darius," said Ferne.

Her little brother screwed up one eye to take aim and fired his finger at the invisible guards.

A loud thunk resounded, and a thick cylinder of wing-tipped metal appeared in the tree trunk next to Ferne's head.

The children froze.

Someone was firing at them.

"Run," Parthenia shouted. The children sped away through the trees. She wanted to tell Ferne to give Darius to her. Her little brother was heavy for a twelve-year-old to carry. But she didn't dare stop long enough to make the switch.

Another loud thunk sounded. "Hurry," she called. She hoped they wouldn't get split up, but putting distance between themselves and the hunters was the priority.

Why were they being shot at? Did the hunters really want to kill children? A third wooden thunk resounded and Oriana squealed. The bolt had nearly hit her.

Now, above the sound of the wind, Parthenia could hear the thump of the feet of the animals the hunters rode, getting closer. How the large beasts maneuvered between the trees, Parthenia didn't understand, but they managed it. The thought gave her an idea.

Over to one side was a dense grouping of trees. Ordinarily she would have avoided such a place, but in this case it was ideal. "Over there," she panted to her siblings. They changed direction and ran for the trees.

A fourth bolt whistled past her ear. She bit back the shout of fear that rose to her lips. The trees were giving the children some cover. She didn't want to give the hunters a clear indication of their whereabouts.

Oriana was the fastest runner of them all. She'd reached the thick trunks of the dense clump of trees. In a moment, she'd slipped between them and disappeared. Parthenia reached them next. She hopped behind a tree and watched. Ferne was lagging far behind, struggling with Darius' weight, but finally he ran up with his little brother clinging to his back.

Just as he reached her, Ferne cried out and fell forward. Darius tumbled off of him. One of the hunter's bolts was sticking out from the back of Ferne's thigh.

"Ferne," she screamed. She couldn't help herself. Her brother raised his head, his face twisted with pain.

A burst of sound and movement a short distance away distracted Parthenia from her brother. The hunters on their animals were speeding closer. Then the animals slowed, making a strange, high-pitched sound. One of the hunters cursed. "It's kids," he said. "What are they doing here?"

Parthenia helped Ferne to his feet. "Run, Darius," she said. "Run into the trees. Find Oriana."

The woman exclaimed, "You shot one of them!"

"No, I didn't," the man protested. "That was you."

"Can you walk?" Parthenia asked Ferne.

He was white and shaking but he nodded. She wrapped his

arm over her shoulder and half-helping, half-carrying her brother, she took him out of sight of the hunters. As soon as they'd made it a short way through the narrow spaces between the trunks, she lowered her brother to the ground. Blood was running down his leg and he looked ready to pass out. If the hunters followed them and caught up with them, there wasn't anything she could do about it. She only hoped Oriana and Darius might get away.

But while she sat with her injured brother on the forest floor, no sounds of pursuit followed them. Parthenia guessed the hunters might get into trouble for accidentally shooting children, even if they were trespassing.

"Ferne," Parthenia said. "I'm so sorry. That must hurt really badly. I'm going to do whatever I can to help."

Her brother only nodded, his lips tightly compressed.

But what could she do? If she had elixir, she could Transport the bolt out of Ferne's leg and then Cast Heal on the wound. But she had no elixir nor a way of making any. The children were alone and friendless.

For the thousandth time, she wondered what had happened to Carina. If only she were there she would know what to do. Parthenia felt she'd made one mistake after another.

"Ferne," Oriana exclaimed as she came through the trees, holding onto Darius' hand. She fell to her knees at her brother's side and burst into tears. "Ferne, don't die. Please don't die. We're nearly there. We can make you better."

"What?" Parthenia asked. "We're nearly where?"

"We're at the city," Darius said. "Oriana and I found it. Come and look, Parthenia. We can take Ferne to a splicer and make him better. Come on, I'll show you." He grabbed her hand and tried to pull her to her feet.

Leaving Ferne with Oriana, she got up and went with Darius. Not more than a minute away, the trees faded out entirely. She found herself looking at a wire fence. Beyond the fence stood a landing bay, and beyond that were the low buildings of a spaceport. Farther away the city stood, its buildings rising higher in the distance.

They'd made it to their destination, but Darius wasn't right in all he'd said. They would never get Ferne to a splicer from their current location. She would have to fix her brother's leg somehow before they could go on.

Twenty-One

As Carina sat at the edge of the bedroom in her rented apartment, she recalled removing the Sherrerr tracers from her siblings when they were escaping on the shuttle. That had been so much easier. For one thing, she'd seen the tracer that the Dirksens had cut out of Darius, so she knew the size and appearance of the devices. And she'd known almost precisely where to find them in her siblings' bodies.

By contrast, removing the Dirksen tracers from her intestines was going to be like hunting in the dark with a double-edged knife. One false step and she could cause herself some serious harm.

She swallowed. The truth was, she was almost certainly going to inflict some damage. She doubted the best mage in the galaxy could Cast with the accuracy required to lift out the tiny tracers without affecting the surrounding tissue, even without operating blindfolded. No, there was no point in kidding herself—this was going to hurt.

She took out the bottle of elixir she'd carried with her all the way from Langley's mansion. She'd hoarded the liquid, saving it for emergencies just like this. She unscrewed the cap. Then she paused.

She couldn't figure out why the Dirksens hadn't picked her up yet. Should she have given Reyes a chance to explain? No. That would have been too risky. The information he held might have been useful yet she felt she'd made the best choice in the circumstances. It was time to get as far away from the Dirksens and the Sherrerrs as she could—after she found her brothers and sisters.

She realized she was going over her decision as a way of putting off something she dreaded to do. She refocused and mentally reached out, feeling for the tracers. Now she knew they were there, it wasn't too hard to sense the devices in the depths of her gut. Their material was different from the rest of her flesh, but she couldn't tell how many there were. The tracers were all bunched together.

It wouldn't be a good idea to try to Transport all of them out of her at once. She was fearful of accidentally pinching out a large piece of her intestine at the same time. Although she could Cast Heal and fix the injury, she might not be able to do that if she was in too much pain or had passed out.

She breathed in and out, deeply and slowly, and centered her mind on the tiny devices embedded in her intestines. She wrote the Transport character and sent out the Cast. She winced as she mentally gripped a tracer and lifted it out and away, placing it on the floor beside her. She opened an eye to look at the thing. It was a tiny metal bead—a red-stained, silver fleck on the grimy floor.

One.

She couldn't feel any ill effects yet. No pain or even discomfort. She took another sip of elixir. It was time to remove number two.

———

She wasn't sure if she'd removed seven or eight tracers. She'd lost count, and the devices were too small to see clearly in their little bloody pile beside her. She was in pain and she was feeling faint, though she wasn't sure if the faintness was due to the repeated Casting or the damage she'd caused. The more tracers she'd removed, the harder it had become to locate the devices. She thought she could sense one final tracer but she wasn't sure. Her foggy mind and her aching stomach were strong distractions.

She took another sip of elixir and pressed on. She had to get all the tracers out. The Dirksens only needed one in order to find her. She forced her tired mind to concentrate and reached inside herself. Was there something still there? It was so hard to tell. The site where the tracers had burrowed was damaged and bleeding. She would have to Cast Heal soon.

But only when she'd removed the final tracer from her system. She only had enough elixir to Cast twice more. She had to save Heal until last. She strained her senses and mentally probed her gut. She felt something—some kind of anomaly. Was it a tracer? Perhaps her damaged tissue was confusing her. No matter. She would Transport a small piece out and then immediately Heal herself.

As she Cast Transport, a sharp pain pierced her insides. She gasped and opened her eyes. Something was wrong. She'd gone too far. Pain radiated from her gut. She had to Cast Heal. She swallowed the last of her elixir and closed her eyes. She tried to center herself and write the character, but she was in too much pain. She was slipping away. Everything went black.

Twenty-Two

Carina awoke to a familiar sensation. She could feel the faint vibration of a starship's engine. For a moment, groggy with pain and too much Casting, she thought she was back aboard the Dirksen ship. She opened her eyes, expecting to see the shaven-headed officer watching her, waiting for her to slip up during his subtle interrogation. Instead, she saw a young man's profile. Reyes was sitting at a starship's flight controls. A low ceiling was above her and she was pressed against a wall. She was lying in the reclined seat of a small shuttlecraft.

She sat bolt upright. Pain from her stomach lanced through her and she cried out.

Reyes turned and looked down. "Stay still." He placed a hand on her shoulder, gently restraining her. "I'm taking you to a doctor."

She didn't have the strength to resist. She was so tired and she'd definitely done something to her gut. If she had some elixir left she could fix herself but she remembered she'd drunk the last of it. As she gave up struggling, Reyes lifted his hand.

"I'm glad you've come around," he said. "I was worried about you. We'll be at the hospital in another minute."

"You tracked me through those tracers."

"Of course."

"Damn."

"It was lucky for you I did. I don't know what's wrong with you but you were out cold when I found you."

"Huh. An old guy let you in, right?"

"A little girl, actually. She said her pops was sleeping."

Carina guessed the old man hadn't taken long to spend her week's rent money on his favorite addiction. There wasn't a lot else to look forward to in districts like that, she knew too well. "You carried me out all by yourself?"

"Hey, I'm stronger than I look. ... And you came around a little and helped. Maybe you don't remember. I only had to get you to the roof where I'd landed my star racer."

"Why did you come for me? I thought you were going to leave me alone."

"You did? I never said that."

"It was kind of implied, I thought. After the whole kidnapping thing." Her wooziness wasn't dissipating. If anything, it was getting worse. She wasn't sure if she was going to pass out again or throw up. The latter alternative won. Her vomit was brown and granular. "Sorry."

Reyes glanced down at her production, now slowly spreading over the shiny floor of the tiny shuttlecraft. "Don't worry about it. I'm sure glad I decided to come and get you though."

"How come you turned up just then? Did you know I was sick?"

"Yeah. The tracers don't only signal their position. They transmit the subject's health status along with a few other things."

"Pretty clever. You Dirksens love your high tech."

"Don't call me a Dirksen, please. Just call me Reyes. I don't like to think of myself as one of them anymore. I decided I'm going to divorce myself from my clan, just as soon as I exploit the benefits of being a member one more time." He gave a wry smile. Returning his attention to the controls, he said, "We're here. There should be medics to meet us. I comm'd ahead."

The shuttlecraft rapidly lost altitude, increasing her nausea. The engine cut out and half of the roof of the vehicle lifted. It was raining outside. She was instantly soaked. Two medics were suddenly checking her over. The next moment, she was being lifted out and onto a gurney. The medics raced with her across the rooftop, through open double doors, and into an elevator.

Reyes stepped in as the elevator doors closed. He stood over her, resting his hand on the gurney rail. One of the medics was cutting open her clothes.

"I only just bought these," she protested. Everyone was over-reacting. She'd been injured plenty of times while working as a merc. If she only had a mouthful of elixir she could fix her problems herself.

A medic was running a scanner across her stomach. The woman showed the other medic the results.

"Did you eat something sharp?" the female medic asked.

"No, someone fed me something noxious." She glared at Reyes, who looked away.

The medics didn't say anything else. Did they know Reyes was a Dirksen? Would the hospital check Ostillon's databases for her genetic profile? What would the staff do when they couldn't find her on the planetary system?

She couldn't stay here to be treated. It was too risky. But as she tried to sit up she gasped with pain.

"Lie down," admonished the female medic, pushing her shoulders to the gurney. "Where do you think you're going?"

"Away from here," Carina exclaimed, struggling with her.

"Please stay still," said Reyes. "I'm really only trying to help you. No one here is going to hurt you or even ask you who you are. You don't have to worry."

In her current state of health, she didn't have much choice but to give in. She wouldn't be able to fight off three people and escape. She wasn't sure she could even stay upright.

As the elevator reached its floor and the doors opened, she passed out again.

———

When she came around for the second time the pain in her stomach was gone. She was in a hospital bed and Reyes was sitting beside her reading an interface, not yet aware she was awake.

Though she felt a lot better, her wooziness hadn't entirely gone away. She guessed it was an after-effect of the drugs she'd been given while her insides were being fixed. Relief washed through her. While she'd tried to pretend to herself that the damage she'd inflicted while removing the tracers was no big deal, deep down she'd actually been quite scared. She hoped she wouldn't ever have to attempt such a thing again.

Now she was better and the tracers were gone she could begin searching for her siblings right away. They'd been on their own for days. She hated to think what might have happened to them.

She pushed back her covers and sat up half way but the movement made her head spin. She slumped down.

"Whoa," said Reyes. "Take it easy." He pulled the covers over her.

She noticed she was wearing a hospital gown. "Where are my clothes?" She wouldn't have gotten far dressed as she was. What had she been thinking?

"The medics cut your clothes off you, remember?" said Reyes. "Your money is in the drawer next to your bed. I can get you some more clothes. I'll order them for you now. What do you want?" He took up his interface again.

"Wait. What are you doing?"

"Huh? I'm buying you some clothes. Didn't you hear? Don't worry. The anesthetic will wear off soon."

"I mean, what are you doing here, now, with me?"

"What do you think I'm doing? I'm looking after you. The surgeon said your operation went well. Said you're as good as new now."

"Thanks, but..."

"But what?"

"I don't get it. What's all this about?"

Reyes said, "I told you already. I'm leaving my mother's clan. What you were saying was right. They *are* a bunch of thugs. I never really saw it before because I was brought up in the middle of it. I believed Mother when she explained that we Dirksens were helping to develop and modernize other societies to their benefit. It just took me a while to realize it was all garbage. Excuses.

"It's hard when it's your close family who's doing evil things. That was what I wanted to talk to you about before, only you didn't give me a chance. Then I saw what you'd done to yourself trying to remove the tracers. That made up my mind. I'm never going back home. I still love my mother but I can't accept what she does and I don't want to be a part of it.

"I haven't told her about my decision yet," Reyes went on. "I'll let her figure it out for herself. Until she does, I can make use of my status. But only to do good things. Like helping you. No one here will ask who you are or what happened to you. There won't be any record of your treatment on the hospital records.

And…" he smiled slyly, lifting his interface, "I can order whatever I want until my account is closed."

"Yeah," Carina said, "and your mother will be able to find out exactly what you ordered and where it was delivered."

Reyes' face fell. "I didn't think of that."

"If you do plan on doing a disappearing act, you'll need to be a lot more careful. It isn't easy to stay hidden. Not easy at all."

"I guess that's true."

The young man looked troubled and she felt a little sorry for him. It was a bold, brave, and perhaps foolish step he was taking. She didn't think he was mature or experienced enough to understand all the implications. Yet he was doing the right thing. Overall, she was glad her previous goading seemed to have tipped him into a decision he'd been brooding about for a while.

"What do you plan to do?" she asked, wondering if he had a plan at all.

"I'm not sure."

He didn't.

"Maybe I can get a job," Reyes continued. "I have my star racer. I can sleep in that."

"You don't think your mother might have put a tracer on it?"

"I don't think so but you're right, it's a possibility. I should have it scanned. It was my present for my sixteenth birthday. I don't think it's registered. No Dirksen registers anything."

"Of course not," she said. "Why would they? That might force them to operate within the law, which would be ridiculous."

Reyes' wry smile returned. "I like your sense of humor. How are you feeling now?"

In truth, she was still feeling the effects of the anesthetic, but she felt much better than she had before. "I'm okay. I think I'll be able to leave soon."

"Don't do that," said Reyes. "Rest a while longer. The surgeon said you should wait until tomorrow to go home."

"That isn't going to work for me. I have some things I have to do urgently."

"Please, stay here for a couple more hours. Allow some time for the drugs to wear off. Maybe I can help you do whatever it is that's so urgent."

"Well..." She considered. Could she trust him? Reyes had saved her when she was in a dangerous position. Bryce had always said she too distrustful. She wondered what had happened to her friend. She hoped he'd made it back to his family.

She looked into Reyes' eyes. He gazed back openly, unblinking.

"Maybe you can help me."

Twenty-Three

"I can't do it," Oriana sobbed. "I just can't do it."

"It's okay," Parthenia replied, taking her sister's hands in her own. Oriana's palms were red and raw from trying to start a fire. "I'll think of something else."

"The wood's too wet," Oriana said. "In the barn it was bone dry, and even then it took me ages to make it smolder. Here, outside, it's too damp. I'm sure that's the problem."

"I guess you're right," Parthenia replied. "It was a miracle you started a fire at all the first time you tried. I wouldn't have known how to do it."

"I saw it in a vid," said Oriana. "Ferne showed me." She burst into sobs again.

Ferne was lying to one side under a tree. He was on his front, the bolt the hunters had shot him with still sticking out of the back of his thigh. He was awake but in so much pain he'd hardly spoken over the last few hours.

"Just pull it out," he said between clenched teeth. "I can't stand having that thing stuck in me. Please, pull it out. We can tie something around my leg and then we can go into the city."

Parthenia had been trying to avoid that solution to their problem. As it was, Ferne's wound currently only bled when he moved. She was worried that if they pulled the bolt out they might not be able to stop the bleeding and her brother might bleed to death. She didn't want to tell him that, though. If only they had some elixir. Just a couple of mouthfuls was all it would take. But they couldn't start a fire.

Oriana was holding her poor, sore hands under her armpits. Parthenia put an arm around her sister's shoulders. Her own hands were hurting too from trying to help.

Darius was where he'd been for hours, sitting at the wire fence watching shuttles take off and land at the spaceport.

Parthenia was trying to be strong but she felt like crying. No matter how hard she tried she couldn't figure a way out of their situation. If she could make it into the city, it might be easier for her to make some elixir. The process was so simple and the ingredients so mundane, it shouldn't be too hard. But she didn't want to leave Ferne, even if Oriana stayed with him. What if the hunters came looking for them? She didn't know what might happen while she was gone.

She'd been parted from the twins once already. She didn't want to leave them on their own again. The responsibility weighed on her heavily. At some point during the trials of that day, she had given up hope of Carina finding and helping them. For whatever reason, her older sister clearly wasn't going to turn up. They were on their own. Yet Parthenia had learned she wasn't up to the task that had befallen her. She'd made so many bad decisions.

Dusk had fallen and was turning to night. The lights from the spaceport meant they weren't in darkness, but Parthenia remembered with a shudder the sounds of night creatures in the forest where she and Darius had first been lost. Also, though no one had complained, she knew everyone was extremely thirsty and hungry.

Perhaps it was time for her to face the truth about what she had to do. As she made her decision, Darius turned away from the fence, stood up, and walked over to her. He wrapped his arms around her neck and hugged her. Her little brother didn't say a word. She knew he had sensed her mood and was trying to offer some comfort.

"It's no good," Parthenia announced. "I'm going to have to leave you and find someone I can ask for help."

"No," Ferne muttered. "I keep telling you. Pull the damned thing out. I'll be fine. I would do it myself if I could reach it."

"We can't," Oriana said. "Parthenia's right. It wouldn't be safe. We aren't splicers. We don't know what we're doing. It isn't like Casting. You could die."

"Dying would be better than going back to living how we were," Ferne said.

He'd spoken the thought that was on all their minds. If anyone discovered who they were or what they could do, the best they could look forward to was a life of captivity. But while their lives with Father and Mother had been luxurious, they couldn't expect the same treatment at the hands of the Dirksens. Parthenia wondered what the clan might do to her if they figured out she was responsible for many of their business deals going awry.

But what else could she do? Feeling like a failure, she said, "I'm the oldest and I'm making this decision. We can't stay here trying to make fire forever. At least this way we have a chance. It doesn't automatically follow that whoever we ask for help is going to do something bad to us. Maybe they'll be kind and not ask any questions. When Darius and I were lost we found someone who helped us."

"I agree with Parthenia," Oriana said. "You can't stay as you are, Ferne. You need help. If we have to take a risk to find someone to help you that's what we have to do."

Ferne closed his eyes in pain and turned his head away.

"Okay," Parthenia said. "Let's go over our story one more time. We don't know the name of any places here, so we'll make one up. We'll say we're from Riverfield. There has to be somewhere called Riverfield. Then the rest of the story is the same as we said before."

All the children except Ferne rehearsed their cover story. Parthenia wasn't sure it sounded authentic but it was the best she could come up with. It would have to do. When they'd repeated all the details a few times, she said, "Right. I want you all to stay here. I'm going to try to find someone."

"Where will you go?" Darius asked.

"I'm going into the spaceport. It's the closest place that has people in it. Now, none of you must move from this spot while I'm gone. Especially you, Darius. No matter what happens, you mustn't leave Oriana. Do you understand?"

"I want to go with you," said Darius.

"No, you can't." If something bad happened she didn't want Darius with her.

"What if you don't come back?" Oriana asked, her eyes glistening in the darkness.

Parthenia didn't know what to reply. As she struggled to think, a shuttle passed overhead, momentarily lighting up her sister and brothers with its beams. She ran to hug and kiss them, just in case. "I will come back."

―――――

The spaceport was full of passengers. Parthenia had walked around the perimeter fence until it met the road that led to the facility. She went through the transparent doors as they parted and entered the busy hall. After the quiet of the forest the noise of announcements and crowds of chattering people were almost painful. Everyone seemed to be in a hurry. Who should she approach? She didn't want to speak to anyone in authority in case they asked her awkward questions.

She decided to target people who were on their way out of the spaceport because they wouldn't be in a hurry to catch their flight. Yet after glancing at her odd clothes—she had never felt so aware she was still wearing Jace's shirt up until that moment—everyone she went up to ignored her and went on their way.

"Please..." she said, trying to catch the attention of a mother with two children. "Please, can you help me?"

But the mother only pretended not to hear her and hurried her children along. Parthenia tried to approach another passenger but the result was the same. She'd never felt so alone and helpless as she stood by herself in the shifting crowds. What a change it was from the last time she'd been in a spaceport, with Father and Mother. Father had been so haughty and arrogant, arguing with the official about having to walk through the public departures hall.

She had to make someone stop and listen to her request. Ferne and the others were counting on her. A young couple were walking slowly over to the exit, arm in arm. They seemed to have kind faces.

"Excuse me," she said, planting herself in the couple's path so they couldn't avoid her. "My brother's had an accident. I need some help."

The couple had been entirely focused on each other. At her interruption, they looked surprised and then embarrassed. "I'm very sorry," said the woman, side-stepping her.

She grabbed her arm. "How can you be so uncaring? My brother's seriously hurt. Why won't you help?"

"Hey," the man shouted. "Let go of her." He tore her hand away. "Come on, honey," he said to the woman. "She probably wants money for drugs."

"No, I don't," she shouted, at her wit's end. If she didn't get some help soon, Ferne might die. She was worried her siblings might give up on her and try to pull the bolt out of his leg. "You have to help me! Someone has to help."

A guard she hadn't noticed before began to march toward her. She tensed. She didn't want that kind of attention. After a moment's indecision, she turned and ran... directly into another guard who had been approaching her from behind.

"Got you," the guard said as she grabbed her arm and twisted it behind her back.

Parthenia cried out at the sudden pain. She struggled but the guard only twisted her arm more tightly. She gasped. "Let me go! I haven't done anything."

"I don't believe that for a minute," said the guard. "But we'll soon find out. Come on. Let's go." By this time the other guard had also reached her. The two of them manhandled her across the spaceport hall. Suddenly, all the passengers to whom she'd been invisible only a moment before stopped and stared.

"I'm only here because I need help for my brother," she protested. "He's been hurt. He was shot in the forest. I had to leave him there with my other brother and sister."

"Shot? In the forest?" the male guard asked.

"Save your lies," said the female guard. "They won't do you any good."

"Why would I lie about something like that? I'm not asking for money. I'm asking for help. Please. You have to believe me."

The male guard was grave. "If your brother really is lying

injured in the forest, there isn't anything we can do. That's Dirksen land. Whatever goes on in there is up to them."

"No! You have to help him. If you can't help him, let me go! Let me go back to him." She twisted and fought, trying to bite the guards' hands, trying anything to make them release her, but she couldn't break free.

The two guards hauled her, struggling and kicking, into a security room. She was beside herself with fear and rage. The guards pushed her into a corner, left the room, and locked the door.

Twenty-Four

As Reyes checked the Dirksens' comm records, Carina was having grave misgivings. Why had she told him she was looking for her brothers and sisters? If she hadn't been groggy from the anesthetic at the hospital she doubted she would have taken the risk. On the other hand, without his help she might never be able to locate Parthenia and the others. What chance did she really have of locating four children in an entire continent, or perhaps a whole planet?

Reyes had arranged new clothes for her after she insisted on leaving the hospital. They still hadn't quite left, however. They were sitting in Reyes' star racer on the roof of the building and he'd been going through the recorded comms for ages. She had passed some time looking out over the city while the sun came up and she'd passed some more examining Reyes' vehicle. It was tiny, holding only two people, yet he'd assured her it was interplanetary.

"Maybe this was a bad idea," she said as she finally lost patience waiting for him. "If there was any mention of my siblings on those files I'm sure you would have found it by now."

"Not necessarily," Reyes replied. "These are personal files and they aren't searchable. I have to go through them individually."

"Personal files? You mean that Dirksens have access to other clan members' personal comms?"

"Of course not."

"Then how come you can read them?"

"I figured out a way into the intra-clan comm system a few months ago. It was what I read there that partly fueled my decision to leave. Some of my family are depraved. It's sickening. Mother is about the best of all of them. Ah, wait. What's this?" His fingers swiped down the screen. "Huh. That's odd, and interesting."

"What?" She looked over his shoulder.

"It's an audio file that was deleted only a few minutes after it was made."

"That could be anything. And it's gone now anyway."

"Not from my records, it hasn't. Let's see..." He continued to work at the interface for a few moments. "Got it. I'll play it back."

"But you said it was deleted."

"When I discovered that deleting conversations and messages was somewhat of a habit in my clan I set up a system to automatically copy all comms. It's the deleted files that are the juiciest. I only have room to store the information for a few weeks before I have to clear it out but this comm was only made yesterday evening. Let's hear it."

The first voice they heard was a young woman's. It was tremulous. "Father?"

"Hello, Kiva. Where are you? Is everything all right?"

"No, it isn't. I think I... I..."

"What's wrong? Are you still out hunting? We wondered what had happened to you. Come home now. It's late."

"Father, I think I might have accidentally shot a child. I don't know what to do. Should I call for a medic?"

"A child? Don't be ridiculous. How could you have done that? You must be mistaken."

"I don't think I am. It was twilight and I couldn't see very well, only their moving shapes. There were four of them. They were running away. I shot at them, thinking they were game. Oh, Father. I hit one of them. I know I did. Pol saw it too. One of them fell down."

Carina's heart froze.

"I'm telling you you're mistaken," the man said sternly. "What would children have been doing in our hunting grounds? No Dirksen child has been shot. I would have heard about it."

"I don't think they were Dirksen children," the woman said. "I think—"

"Then it doesn't matter, does it? Come home immediately, Kiva, and never mention this again."

The comm ended. Carina's hand was over her mouth as she stared at the interface.

Reyes said, "I'm sorry. That might be them, right? It makes sense. If they're from offplanet, they wouldn't know it's dangerous to enter woods unless they know who owns them. I seriously doubt any Ostillonian child would have been wandering through a Dirksen hunting forest."

She struggled to reply. She could see visions of Darius lying dead on a forest floor. "Do you know where the comm originated?"

"Yes," Reyes replied. "I have the exact coordinates. It's a hunting lodge on the outskirts of the forest by the spaceport. Strap in and I'll take you there."

Reyes' star racer, as he called it, was a high-class spacecraft. She could barely feel or hear the engine as Reyes started it, and the ship's motion was as smooth as silk as they flew up and away from the hospital roof. She guessed the star racer's drive included the hover technology the Dirksens had brought to the planet.

As soon as they were high above the city Reyes accelerated. The force pushed her back into her seat.

"How long will it take to get there?" she asked.

"Not long. Ten or fifteen minutes," he replied, checking the controls.

"This place is close by then?"

"No. It's on the other side of the city. But up here we can fly direct and the star racer is fast."

She was twisting her hands in her lap, trying to ignore the image in her mind of Darius dying. "So your relatives go hunting?"

"It's a popular sport. They have forests all over the planet and hold competitions using ancient weaponry." He glanced at her. "Sorry."

"Do you go to them... These competitions?"

Reyes shook his head. "Not my kind of thing. Plus there's the fact that Mother's always there trying to partner me up with some girl or another."

"What, other Dirksens? Do you marry your cousins?"

"Only distant ones. Don't you?"

"No. I don't think so anyway." In fact, she had no idea how mages met and married. Nai Nai had never told her and during the brief time she'd spent with Ma the subject had never come up. She didn't know how her parents had gotten to know each other.

"That's another reason I want to leave the clan," Reyes said. "Mother's obsessed with making a good match for me, as she puts it. Like I shouldn't have any say in the matter."

"You're a bit young to be getting married."

"That's another objection of mine."

"Do we have far to go now?" Perhaps they wouldn't find anything at the hunting lodge. Perhaps the woman, Kiva, had been mistaken. Or if she hadn't, perhaps the children weren't Carina's siblings.

"Nearly there."

They continued the rest of the short journey in silence, Carina telling herself it probably wasn't one of her siblings who had been shot. Even if that had happened to any of them they would have Cast Heal.

The star racer slipped smoothly and quickly out of the sky. Its nose was tipped downward and the screen displayed a green expanse with a small clearing that was growing rapidly larger. At the center of the clearing a wooden building stood. The bare ground surrounding the lodge was empty.

"Wait," she said. "Is there any point in landing here? If that woman did shoot a child in the forest, she probably didn't do it right here. This is just where she was when she comm'd. And she won't be here now. She would have gone home like her father told her to."

"You're right," Reyes replied. "No one will be here at this time of day but it's the only clear space for kilometers around. If your sisters and brothers are nearby, they might have headed here."

He brought the star racer down on the lot outside the hunting lodge and opened the hatch. The air that flooded in was fresh, cool, and scented with tree oils. Carina climbed out and scanned the surrounding trees but the space below their canopies was dark and silent.

"Hey," she yelled. "Is anyone there? Are you hurt? We can help you."

No reply came.

She didn't want to give away the names of her siblings. She'd been hoping that if they heard her they would recognize her voice, but her brothers and sisters might not reply to someone yelling *Hey*. She cupped her hands around her mouth. "Parthenia," she called. "Parthenia! Can you hear me?"

Her voice echoed through the trees but received no answer. Reyes strode to the edge of the clearing. "Parthenia," he yelled. "Parthenia!"

They waited in silence as the sun crept over the tree tops and lit up the roof of the hunting lodge. They called again, but it soon became clear that if her siblings were in the forest they weren't within earshot.

"I don't know what to do," she said, her voice thick. She could tough out almost any situation, but the idea of one of her siblings lying injured somewhere was crippling her.

"I'm not sure either," Reyes said. "We can fly across the forest to look for them but the canopy makes it hard to see anything. Oh, wait. Maybe there is a way."

Twenty-Five

"Yes," Reyes exclaimed. "I do have a scanner." He was at the controls of his star racer. "I wasn't sure. I've never needed to use one."

"Can it tell humans from other living things?" asked Carina. "This place must be full of animals."

"Hmm... No, it can't. Good point."

"And it would take us forever to scan this place anyway. It must cover hundreds of square kilometers."

"It does." Reyes paused. "I'm sorry. I want to help. I feel responsible."

"Well, you didn't shoot anyone. Or did you?"

"No! I've never even fired a weapon. I hate the idea of hunting, and Mother always insisted that I work in the business side of the family, not the military. But these people are still my clan, and I don't think you would be split up from your siblings if we hadn't captured you."

"I can't deny that," Carina replied. "But I'm not giving up yet. I'm going to continue looking until I find them." She climbed out of the star racer into the lot once more. Her gaze searched the trees that brooded over the place. *If I were lost in a forest, where would I go?*

Reyes joined her. "Have you had an idea?"

"Just wondering how I might try to find my way out of here if I were on foot."

"It would be hard if you didn't know the place well. As soon as you're in the trees you can't see very far ahead, and all there is to follow are bridle paths and animal tracks."

"What about streams?" Carina asked. "They might have followed a stream, thinking it could lead them to a river and people."

"I don't recall any streams. Wait a minute and I'll check."

She wondered how Reyes remembered being in the forest when he'd said he didn't like hunting.

He returned from the star racer. "No. No streams. The land's pretty dry around here."

As they stood and thought a shuttle passed overhead. She looked up. "Where's that going?"

"How would I know?"

"You seem to know a lot of things. What I mean is, is it heading to the spaceport?"

"No. It's heading away from it."

"So shuttles fly over the forest when they take off from the spaceport?"

"Yes. Some do. Why?"

"Because if you were lost in a forest, a shuttle might be the only sign of civilization you could see. Come on. I have an idea."

———

"But that's about the only place I can't fly," Reyes protested.

They were nearing the spaceport and Carina had announced

her idea of scanning along the forest edge. It was a long shot but it was somewhere to begin their search. She would head in the same direction as a shuttle was flying if she were lost. "Why not? I thought the Dirksens could do anything." She needed him to do as she wanted. It would take hours to search the area on foot.

"Because it's incredibly dangerous," said Reyes. "I'd be flying right across shuttle flight paths."

"I think as long as you keep low it shouldn't be a problem. The shuttles must have to clear the trees by a wide margin as a safety precaution. If you fly just above the canopy, nothing will even come close to colliding with us."

"But then I might hit a tree instead."

"Really? I didn't think you were that bad a pilot."

"I'm not a..." he exclaimed. "Huh. Very clever. Okay. I'll try. But don't blame me if the military arrives to escort us away."

"I'll take that chance."

He turned the star racer and headed in the opposite direction to the flight of the shuttle they'd seen minutes earlier. She was hoping her siblings had traveled toward the spaceport and not away from it. The departing shuttles were flying in different directions, which would mean her sisters and brothers could be anywhere if they'd followed one.

In truth, she didn't hold out much hope for her idea but it was the best one she had. If her siblings weren't near the spaceport, they would just have to search every square meter of the forest. And she would ask Reyes to continue searching the news and comms for any sign of them. They would have to turn up somewhere. She only hoped that when they did it wasn't because they'd revealed their abilities to the world.

They were approaching the spaceport, and at the same time a shuttle was approaching them, rising at a steep angle. She turned on the star racer's scanner, which registered heat from living bodies. She could already see the moving forms of animals beneath them, otherwise invisible beneath the canopy, but she couldn't see anything that appeared even vaguely human.

Reyes tutted.

"What's wrong?"

In answer, he spoke a voice command: "On speaker."

"Star racer pilot," said a voice, "your craft is not registered. Who are you? Please reverse your heading immediately."

"Spaceport Traffic Control?" Carina asked.

"Yeah," said Reyes. "Speaker off." He slipped his headset off his head and let it rest on his shoulders. "They're gonna get real mad at me real soon. What can you see?" He glanced at the scanner display.

"Lots of animals. No people."

"We're nearly at the spaceport. I'll start at the northern end and fly south."

The star racer turned again as another shuttle passed overhead, closer this time. She was certain that if the shuttle's pilot had a warning klaxon, he would have blasted it.

They reached the northern boundary of the forest, which was a highway that also ran along the edge of the spaceport. She peered even more keenly at the scanner. "Go as slow as you can. We're so near the ground I can barely register what I'm seeing before we're a long way past it."

What she could see were the shadowy shapes of trees dotted with the moving green forms of warm objects. Some were only sparks on the image: birds. Others were long, four-legged animals with even longer tails. Other figures were more human-shaped but they were moving rapidly through the trees in a non-human manner.

They were about halfway down the line of the fence when she saw them: three green shapes quite close together. They didn't look very much like people but they also didn't look like anything else she'd seen. "Wait. I might have something. Can you circle back?"

"Are you sure it's worth it?" Reyes asked. "I don't think Traffic Control is going to tolerate me here much longer."

"Just circle back," she snapped.

"Okay, okay."

She felt the star racer turn. When they arrived at the spot where she'd seen the strange forms on the scanner, Reyes hovered above it. Two of the forms had changed position. They were moving, heading away from the third figure, which she now recognized as a person lying down.

"Land here," she commanded.

"I can't. There isn't room."

"There has to be. This thing is tiny."

"There's no space. The trees are growing right up to the fence."

She cursed. She was sure the forms she could see were people. If they were her siblings, she didn't know why there were only three of them. But the story of one of them being shot tied in with the person lying on the ground, and if the two figures running away were her other siblings, it would make sense for them to leave at the approach of an unknown spacecraft.

"Open the back hatch," she told Reyes.

"What? While we're in flight? You're crazy."

"Open the hatch and I'll jump into the canopy."

"No. You'll kill yourself. Let me find somewhere to land then we'll walk back to this spot. There's probably a clearing nearby."

"Just do what I say. Don't worry. I've done this loads of times before." She had never done it before but she didn't want to waste time. They might never find their way to the spot, or find the two children who were running.

"If you're sure," Reyes said. He gave the command and the hatch opened. "Make sure you jump well away from the ship. The exhaust is hot."

Now she could see the tree canopy below, she wasn't so sure about her plan anymore. So, before she had more time to think about it, she took three fast steps over to the open hatch and leapt out.

A heartbeat later, she hit leaves and branches, breaking them and falling through until she collided with a thick branch, which knocked the wind out of her. She wrapped her arms and legs around the branch but the force of her fall carried her around it to the other side. She found herself clinging on upside down and struggling to breathe. Her ribs seared with pain every breath she took. She'd broken at least one rib and probably more as far as she could tell.

But she was alive. She wriggled along the branch toward the trunk, each movement agony. By the time she reached her goal she could breath again. She tried to inhaled deeply but stopped and gasped at the feeling of knives piercing her lungs.

She tried again. "Parthenia," she yelled. "Oriana! Don't run. It's me."

She climbed onto the tree trunk and half-scrambled, half-fell down the tree, stopping only once to call out to her siblings again. She hit the forest floor, covered in bleeding gashes and her chest a mess of pain. "Parthenia," she repeated, though she couldn't muster much volume.

The forest was silent. Had she been wrong? Were the figures she'd seen not her siblings after all? Her eyes filled with tears. Then she heard the noise of something running—something human, and perhaps more than one of them.

A little boy burst from the trees. *Darius!*

"Carina," he shouted joyfully. "I knew you'd come. I knew it." He barreled into her, causing her to cry out in pain.

Oriana was close behind him but she wasn't so happy to see her. She looked distraught. "Do you have some elixir?" she blurted. "Please, give it to me. Ferne is dying."

Twenty-Six

Ferne was lying on his back beneath a tree near the fence. He was deathly pale and the forest floor all around him was stained reddish-brown. His eyes were closed.

"I didn't want to do it," Oriana protested, almost hysterical. "I didn't want to do it, but when Parthenia didn't come back he made me. He said it was the only way he could come with us. He said either pull it out or leave him here."

Carina guessed her sister was referring to whatever it was Ferne had been shot with.

"So I did it," Oriana went on. "It was hard, and I really hurt him. Then when I finally got it out, blood started pouring out of his leg. I couldn't stop it."

Carina turned her unconscious brother over. The wound was on the back of his thigh and still seeping blood. She pushed the heel of her hand deep into it. Still, Ferne didn't stir. She guessed he didn't have long to live. If she had elixir, she might save him, but she'd drunk all of hers when she removed the tracers. They had to make some more, fast. But how?

"You couldn't make elixir?" she asked. "What are you missing? What do you need?"

"We only need fire," Darius replied. His recent joy at being reunited with her had entirely dissipated.

"Did you look for firestones?"

"What are they?" asked Oriana.

"You don't know?" Ma clearly hadn't told them. Or rather Stephan Sherrerr had made sure she didn't. "Never mind. Oriana, come here and do what I'm doing. Press down as hard as you can. I have to look for a firestone." She removed her hand as soon as her sister was ready to take her place.

She set off on her search. It wasn't likely there would be firestones or any other kinds of stone lying on the surface of the forest floor, but it was the only way she might save Ferne. Darius was following her.

"Go back to Oriana and Ferne. Wait with them."

"I want to stay with you. Please, Carina."

"No, I'm sorry. You'll only slow me down."

He turned and sloped back the way he'd come. She returned her attention to the forest floor. It was littered with dry leaves that overlay dark brown mold. The leaf mold had to be centuries old. It was moist and spongy.

She was concentrating so intensely as she searched she didn't notice Reyes until he called. She looked up to see him some distance away. "Did you find them?" he shouted.

She sprinted toward him, yelling, "Do you have anything that can start a fire?"

"A fire? No, of course not. Why do you want to start a fire? Did you find your brothers and sisters?"

She reached him. "I found them. But I have to make a fire. Don't you have anything at all? Please, think. Is there something on your star racer? Where did you land it?"

"Sorry, I would help you if I could but I don't have anything like that."

She grabbed the front of his jacket with both hands. "Where's the star racer?"

When Reyes turned to point, she set off immediately, not waiting to hear what he had to say. There had to be something inside the spacecraft she could use to make a spark and light some tinder. Perhaps she could short a circuit.

As she neared the star racer, she found her problem had been solved. The forest was burning. The heat from the landing spacecraft had ignited the dry leaf litter. It wasn't a big fire yet but it grew fiercer as she approached it. The flames were being blown toward her. She could see the rear of the vehicle through them.

She grabbed a fallen branch and ran over to a patch of burning forest floor. The end of the dry tree limb soon kindled. On her way back to the children, carrying the torch over her head, she passed Reyes as he caught up to her. "I'd get your spacecraft out of here fast if I were you."

She would have to get the children out of the forest quickly too. Just as soon as she Healed Ferne.

———

As the color began to return to Ferne's face, Carina put her head down and listened at her brother's chest. His heart was beating strongly. For a moment, she couldn't move. Tears of relief welled up and spilled from her eyes onto him. She'd Healed him just in time.

"Is he going to be all right?" Oriana asked anxiously.

She couldn't speak. She nodded. Oriana threw herself over both of them. Carina gasped as the agony of her broken ribs tore through her.

Hearing her sister's reaction, Oriana quickly moved off. "Are you hurt? I'm so sorry."

Carina grimaced. She took a sip of the hot elixir and set about Healing herself. As soon as she'd finished, the acrid scent of smoke filled her nostrils. The forest fire was getting closer, but Ferne remained unconscious. She would have to carry him.

"We have to go," she said to Oriana and Darius. She grabbed Ferne under his armpits and put him over her shoulder before rising slowly to her feet. But she was forgetting someone. "Where's Parthenia?" Oriana had said something about their sister not coming back.

"She went to get help," said Darius. "But that was last night."

A shadow settled over her as she wondered what had happened to her oldest sister. "Don't worry. We'll look for her. But we have to get out of the forest first. A fire is heading this way." Smoke was already making the sky hazy and wreathing between the trees. She was sure the air had grown warmer too.

Carrying Ferne, who was as limp as a rag doll, she led Oriana and Darius into the trees. She didn't get far before she realized she was walking toward the fire, not away from it. The ash in the air was growing thick and she could hear the roar of the flames. The conflagration had spread quickly. She doubled back toward the fence, thinking they could walk along it to reach the highway that lay to the north. As they walked, however, a tree a short distance in front of them began to smolder.

She cursed and turned. They would have to go the other way. But the smoke in the place they'd only just left was growing thick.

Darius' hand slipped into hers and gripped it tightly. He looked up, his eyes wide and scared. Oriana coughed and pulled her shirt up and over her mouth and nose.

It was no good. The only way to avoid the fire was to climb

over the fence. Carina looked up at the top of it, which was twice her own height. She might make it there carrying Ferne, but she didn't know how she would climb over and hold onto her brother at the same time. She might easily drop him and a fall from that height could kill him.

"We're going to have to climb our way out of this," she said. "But you two are great climbers, right?"

"Yes," Darius said. "I'm a good climber."

"You go first. Oriana, you climb under Darius. And both of you be careful when you're climbing down."

"But what about all the shuttles on the other side?" Oriana asked. "Won't it be dangerous out on the landing ground? Won't we get arrested?"

Neither of Oriana's points had escaped her attention but she couldn't do anything about them right now. They would have to face those problems after they'd avoided becoming forest barbecue.

Darius hadn't waited to be told twice. He was already halfway up the fence.

"We'll figure that out later," she replied. "You go up now. I don't want Darius to be on his own."

Oriana began climbing. The air was beginning to choke Carina and she was coated in sweat. She adjusted Ferne so he was sitting firmly pushed up against her neck. Grabbing the links of the fence, she started to climb.

It wasn't easy but she thought she could do it, though she still hadn't figured out how she would climb over the top. Darius was already over and heading down the other side. Oriana was nearly there too.

When Carina reached the top she paused. Her toes were pushed into gaps in the wires and one hand gripped the fence while the other held onto Ferne's side to prevent him from slipping off. She needed two hands free to climb over, which would mean letting go of Ferne. She continued to hesitate, not knowing what to do.

Then Reyes arrived.

His star racer was lowering out of the sky, a safe distance from Darius and Oriana but at the edge of the spaceport's landing ground. He was really going to annoy Air Traffic Control. He landed and the hatch opened.

Oriana was looking scared. She didn't know who Reyes was.

"It's okay," Carina called down. "He's a friend."

"Wait there," Reyes shouted, running toward her. "I'll help." He worked his way up the links of wire. "Can you pass him to me?"

"Yes, but please be careful. Don't let go of him."

"Of course I won't."

With great care, she transferred Ferne over to Reyes, who balanced the boy's limp form on his shoulder. As Reyes began to descend the fence, Carina climbed over, catching a glimpse of tree tops on fire. She sped down the wires to catch up to Reyes and shadow him, ready to catch Ferne if he started to fall. They reached the ground together just as a tree bordering the fence burst into flames. Military vehicles were speeding toward them across the shuttle landing field.

"Quick, everyone into the star racer," Reyes shouted.

"We can't all fit in that," Oriana said.

"We're going to have to," said Carina. Reyes was already at his vehicle, still carrying Ferne. She took Darius' hand. "Come on."

They piled into the tiny space. Reyes had lain Ferne on the passenger seat and taken the pilot's seat.

"I'm closing the hatch," he said. "Breathe in."

Carina, Oriana, and Darius squeezed into whatever spare

space they could find. The hatch of the star racer closed against Carina's back, pushing her down. The spacecraft lifted and everyone was crushed together further by the acceleration force as Reyes flew away from the spaceport.

Three out of four of her mage siblings were safe—for now. But what had happened to Parthenia?

Twenty-Seven

Parthenia had spent the night in the security room. The guards hadn't even given her a cot to sleep on and so she'd been forced to curl up on the cold floor, napping fitfully over the long hours she'd been left alone. Aside from a couple of restroom visits, she hadn't been allowed out and no one would tell her what was going to happen to her or listen when she tried to tell them her brother needed help.

She couldn't stop thinking about Ferne, Oriana, and Darius, alone in the forest overnight. She'd told them she would be back but she'd failed to keep her promise. They needed her but she didn't know how to return to them. She was out of her mind with worry, to the extent that she barely considered how much danger she was in herself.

The female guard had brought her breakfast then left her alone, once again refusing to hear her pleas. Parthenia guessed something would happen to her soon. The guards had taken her into custody late the previous evening. Their boss had probably gone home by then but now it was morning he or she would be back at work and ready to deal with the stray girl who had been annoying the passengers.

Parthenia was mentally rehearsing her cover story when the door to the small room opened and the female guard came inside. Someone else entered behind her—an older man wearing a civilian suit, not a uniform. His hair was white with age, which was odd. Having your genes spliced so your hair never changed color no matter how old you grew was a standard treatment. Even the servants at Parthenia's family estate on Ithiya had undergone the procedure.

The older man also wore a small, neat mustache—another anomaly. Parthenia knew few men who hadn't arranged for the permanent removal of their facial hair not long after puberty, for convenience's sake.

The man sat down and put a finger to his mouth as he regarded her. "Would you mind telling me your name?"

"Penny. Penny Sharp."

"And where are you from, Penny?"

"I'm from Riverfield." Her next words fell out of her mouth in a rush. "I was traveling with my family but we got lost. My brother's hurt and he needs help. I've told your guard many times but she won't listen to me."

The man turned to the guard. "Check her again. I want to be sure."

The guard was carrying an ID scanner. She leaned over Parthenia. "Open up."

She had been subjected to the same test twice before during the previous evening. She opened her lips. The result would be the same, and it meant she was in trouble.

The guard put a probe into Parthenia's mouth and wiped it along the inside of her cheek. The machine bleeped. The guard turned the display screen toward the man.

"Well, Penny Sharp," he said, "according to this you don't exist. Now, ordinarily I wouldn't be very surprised to come across an unregistered vagrant hanging around the spaceport. But you aren't a regular member of the invisible fringe, are you? There's no such place as Riverfield on all of Ostillon, and the fact that you lied about your origins tells me you have something to hide. What is it? Are you working with smugglers?"

"Am I working with smugglers?" Parthenia asked, her worries temporarily forgotten in her amazement at the man's question. "If I were a member of a smuggling gang, do you think I would go around drawing attention to myself by dressing like this and asking people for help?"

Even the guard looked embarrassed by her superior's question.

The older man colored and coughed before muttering, "You could have been acting as a diversion. Anyway, what you were doing is irrelevant. As an unregistered individual we have a duty to hand you over to the appropriate authorities. It's clear that you aren't Ostillonian, therefore I'm going to send you to the Illegal Migrant Holding Facility." He stood up. "Someone will be along to collect you soon." He went out.

The female guard tutted. "If you'd been more polite and asked nicely, he might have let you go." She also left, and the lock click closed.

Parthenia's head sunk onto her arms. Why had she been rude to the spaceport official? Now she would never get back to Ferne and the others.

———

The Illegal Migrant Holding Facility was full to the brim. She was put in a cell with at least ten other girls and women. They all stared at her when she arrived. And after the cell door was locked and the guard walked away, no one spoke to her.

"Excuse me," she said to the person nearest to her—a girl about her own age who had bouncy blonde curls, "what happens here? Do we ever get to leave?"

"There's a few ways out," the girl replied, looking Parthenia up and down. "Proving your identity, bribing the warden, or sleeping with the guards. Those are the main ones anyway."

At Parthenia's shocked expression the girl laughed. "I was kidding for the last one."

"Yeah," another woman chipped in. "You have to sleep with the guards just to eat."

"That's why Laury's so fat," said a third.

The golden-haired girl turned and glared at the speaker.

Parthenia asked, "And what happens if you don't do any of those things?"

"It's off to the asteroid mines with you," Laury replied.

"What? Forced labor? Can they do that?" Parthenia realized what a fool she sounded as the words left her mouth. Her own clan had done the same, if not worse.

"If you don't exist," said Laury, "they can do what they like."

Parthenia's low mood sunk even further. How could she help her brothers and sister if she was stuck on a mine somewhere? She might never see them again. What would become of them all by themselves? And what would happen to Ferne if he didn't get medical help?

She eased through the crowded cell, stepping over women who were sitting or lying on the floor, until she reached the little window. It looked out onto a square yard where a few of the inmates were wandering aimlessly. Shuttles from the spaceport were crossing the small patch of sky. Parthenia felt like crying but she didn't want to show her emotion in front of all these strange women.

She rested her elbows on the ledge of the high window. Ever since escaping from the Sherrerrs, everything had gone from bad to worse and Parthenia had no idea how to turn things around. Fate seemed to be pushing her down a road that ended in nothing but loneliness and despair and there wasn't anything she could do about it.

Was she going to live out the rest of her life slaving away on an asteroid, never seeing her family again or finding out what had happened to them? The only saving grace in her situation was that things couldn't get any worse.

As she aimlessly watched the sad figures of inmates meandering around the exercise yard, the murmur of voices in the cell behind her grew louder. She heard snatches of comments like, "Here he is again," and, "I wonder who he's looking for."

Mildly curious about what the women were talking about, she turned around. A young man was moving down the corridor that linked the cells, accompanied by a guard. He looked so different from the last time she'd seen him, she almost didn't recognize him. When she did, she nearly froze. She had just enough presence of mind to turn away.

Her back facing the visitor, her heart raced as she stared sightlessly out of the window, hoping beyond hope he would pass by without noticing her.

But her brother wasn't so unobservant as to not recognize his sister, even from behind.

"Parthenia," Castiel said. "How nice to see you again."

Twenty-Eight

"Where are you taking us?" Carina asked Reyes, her neck painfully scrunched up. Before he could answer, she also said, "Darius, could you scoot under Ferne's seat? I can see some room there."

Her little brother did as she'd asked him, shuffling along on his bottom to the space under the reclined passenger seat, where he fitted comfortably.

"That's better," Oriana breathed, moving into the place Darius had occupied, which allowed Carina to change position and straighten up.

"Back to the hospital, of course," Reyes replied. "Your brother needs a medic."

"No," Carina said. "He's fine."

Reyes gave her a quizzical look over his shoulder but at that moment, Ferne stirred and his eyes opened. The first thing he saw was her. Before she had a chance to warn him, Ferne blurted her name and tried to sit up.

"I feel terrible," he said as he gave up his attempt and lay back down. "What happened?" He reached for his leg. "Did you—"

"Ferne," Oriana hissed. "Shuttup."

He finally noticed Reyes. His lips clamped closed and he gave Carina an apologetic look.

Reyes said, "Were you the one who was shot? Are you hurt?"

"I..." Ferne began.

"He wasn't shot," said Oriana. "Or, he was nearly shot. He was just exhausted because we'd been walking through the forest for so long."

It was a terrible excuse to explain Ferne's unconsciousness, but Carina didn't blame her sister. She couldn't think of a credible explanation herself. And Oriana had thought it through: if Reyes found out that Ferne had been shot he would want to know why he didn't have an injury, and that would require a whole lot more explaining.

"Okay," Reyes said. "I understand there are things you don't want me to know, *Carina* and family. But don't forget I helped save your lives back there. You don't have to treat me like an enemy."

"Reyes," said Carina, "you're right. I'm sorry. Thank you for helping me find my sister and brothers. I couldn't have done it without you." Then she said, "Ferne, if you're feeling better, can you raise your seat? We can hardly move in here."

After some more shuffling around the star racer was still cramped but more comfortable. They couldn't stay in it forever, though. More to the point, they had to find Parthenia. "Reyes, can you turn back to the spaceport? I think my other sister might be there. She left to go and get help but she didn't come back."

"Return to the spaceport?" Reyes asked, incredulous. "I was lucky I wasn't arrested. If this spacecraft was registered Mother would be pulling a lot of strings for me right now."

"I thought Dirksens could do whatever they wanted," Carina said.

"He's a Dirksen?" Oriana exclaimed, her voice laced with disgust. She tried to ease away from Reyes' seat but there was no room.

"He says he's leaving his clan," said Carina.

"I am leaving them," Reyes said. "I would have thought what I just did would prove that to you."

"I do appreciate it. But we can manage by ourselves from here. So if you wouldn't mind landing and letting us out?"

"You said you think your other sister might be at the spaceport? Let me see what I can find out."

"You can check official comms as well as your clan's?"

"Official comms are easier." Reyes set the star racer to automatic flight and began to search again on his interface. This time, he found the information within a few minutes. "A young woman was detained at the spaceport on suspicion of smuggling. She was transferred to the Illegal Migrant Holding Facility around an hour ago."

"That has to be her," Carina said. "Can we get her out? You can use your influence, can't you?"

"Not so keen to get rid of me any longer?" Reyes asked sarcastically. "I don't know. Maybe. Mother's comms have been building up for hours. She's going crazy but I don't think she suspects what I plan to do yet. She probably thinks I'm rebelling a little but I'll come home soon. So if we turn up at the facility I'll still be a Dirksen to be feared, rather than one to be reported. I guess it's worth a try."

"Thank you," said Carina.

"I hope you'll accept I'm on your side if I manage to do this," Reyes said as he input a new destination to the star racer's navigation.

She sighed but didn't say anything. The problem was, she and her siblings didn't belong to a side. She only wanted to gather them together so she could protect them and decide what they were going to do next. She didn't know what vision Reyes had of his involvement with them once they'd found Parthenia, but she had no intention of having anything else to do with him. He already knew her name and was probably wondering about Ferne's mysterious unconsciousness and how that fitted in with the comm that stated a child had been shot. It was far too much dangerous information.

They landed outside a dark, one-story building. Black, unmarked hover vehicles were parked outside, and the whole place exuded a depressive air. Carina hoped that if Parthenia had been taken here, they could get her out as soon as possible.

A guard was leaning nonchalantly against the wall in the lobby when they went inside, but he quickly stood to attention when he spotted them. She wasn't sure if it was because he recognized Reyes or because they were strangers.

Reyes walked up to a woman in uniform who was sitting behind a transparent screen. She glared at him. "Yes?"

"I'm Reyes Dirksen."

The woman's expression softened a little but not much. "Can I help you, sir?"

"I'm looking for a young girl. She was brought in this morning from the spaceport."

"Do you have a name?"

Reyes looked over his shoulder at Carina, but she didn't know what to tell him. She doubted Parthenia would have told anyone her real name, especially her surname, but she didn't know what name she would have given.

"Penny Sharp," Oriana called out.

The woman checked her list. She looked up, frowning. "We did have a Penny Sharp here this morning but she was taken away."

"What?" Carina said, stepping forward. "Where did she go? Who took her?"

"Well, I'm surprised you don't know. She was checked out by a Dirksen."

Twenty-Nine

Ferne, Oriana, and Darius waited outside Reyes' star racer while he combed through the Dirksens' personal comms once more, this time trying to discover which of his relatives had removed Parthenia from the Illegal Migrant Holding Center. Carina sat next to him, watching over his shoulder in case he missed something.

The back hatch of Reyes' vehicle was up, allowing in the noises of the busy street. Hover vehicles hissed passed, and every so often a large, unmarked, multi-passenger van stopped to unload or pick up detainees at the center. Carina would glance at these scruffy, unkempt individuals just to check that, by some miracle, her sister hadn't been returned. She was clinging to the hope that whatever Dirksen had taken Parthenia hadn't known about the girl's powers, and that she'd been removed for some other reason.

But Parthenia didn't appear, and though Reyes searched for hours he couldn't find anything that alluded to Carina's sister.

"It's odd," he said. "We do use people from the center for various things, but there's nothing in the official record about someone being picked up today and no mention of it in any personal comms."

"What do you think that means?" Carina asked. "Could the receptionist have been lying?"

Reyes shook his head. "She wouldn't dare, even if she had a reason to lie, which she didn't as far as I know. It's very strange."

Outside the star racer, Darius suddenly burst into tears. He wailed, his face pressed into his hands. Carina jumped out and went to him. "What's wrong?" she asked, putting an arm around his shoulders.

"I'm hungry," he sobbed.

"Oh, I'm so sorry," said Carina. Her concern about Parthenia had made her forget that her other siblings had spent the night and probably the previous day in the forest without anything to eat. And Ferne had spent a lot of that time severely injured.

She stuck her head inside Reyes' vehicle. "I have to buy some food. Do you know where I can go? Is there somewhere nearby?"

Looking up from his interface screen, Reyes replied, "I can do better than that. You're all going to need somewhere to sleep as well as food and clothes and everything else. If you squeeze inside once more, I can take you somewhere."

"Er..."

"What's wrong?"

"I don't know if that's a good idea. Maybe it's better that we part ways now. You need to continue with breaking away from your family." She didn't want Reyes to know where she and her siblings were staying and she didn't want him to get to know them well. She might be able to hide her abilities from him but she wasn't confident her sister or brothers could.

"You're never going to get your other sister back without my help," Reyes said, his expression grave. "I can assure you. The fact that I can't find any mention of her probably means the security surrounding her is very high level. You'll never breach it alone. I can't force you to stick with me for a while longer, but you would be stupid if you didn't."

She hated it but what he was saying was true. She called to Darius and the others to climb inside Reyes' tiny vehicle.

———

The apartment he showed them wasn't much better than the one Carina had rented from the old man, but it was sparsely furnished. There were two bedrooms.

"Great," said Ferne. "One for boys and one for girls."

"I'll sleep on the sofa, thanks," said Reyes.

Carina stared at him. "You're planning on staying here too?"

"Why not? It makes sense, doesn't it? That way I can help you more easily. And I don't have anywhere else to go."

"Uh, okay."

Reyes had paid their landlord from his own money, so Carina felt it would be ungrateful and churlish to refuse him, yet she remained deeply uncomfortable about the Dirksen man's proximity to her siblings.

Ferne had declared which room belonged to the boys, and he and Darius were already bouncing on the bed, Darius' ravenous hunger of less than an hour ago apparently entirely forgotten.

"Come and eat," Carina called to the boys. She opened the bag of takeout food Reyes had bought on their way over and began to take off the lids. "Ferne, check in the kitchen for bowls and cutlery," she said to her brother as he pulled out a chair at the rickety table.

Darius didn't wait on niceties. He reached for piece of meat poking out from a dish. "Wash your hands," she admonished.

"Yes," Oriana said. "Come on, Darius."

As Carina was laying the table, she could hear Oriana speaking in a hushed tone to Darius in the bathroom.

"I know," the little boy exclaimed.

Carina winced internally. Her sister had undoubtedly been reminding their brother not to allude to anything to do with Casting while Reyes was around.

There were only four seats at the table, so Reyes took his food to the sofa to eat. Carina sat down and waited while her brothers and sister filled their bowls. For the first time since she'd found them in the forest, she could stop what she was doing and simply appreciate the fact that most of her family were reunited. She resolved to do her damnedest to prevent them from being separated again.

When everyone was eating, she also spooned some food into her bowl. The cereal was white grains and the main dish was meat in a sauce. She ate a mouthful, but as she was chewing, she stopped and put down her spoon.

"Don't you like it?" Ferne asked, his mouth full. "I think it's great." Before he swallowed he piled another spoonful of grains and sauce into his mouth.

She had stopped because she had the same sense of deja vu she'd experienced at Asha's apartment. The flavor of the food was familiar. The last time she'd eaten it, however, she'd been living with Nai Nai. Like the noodle soup, the dish they were eating had been another of her grandmother's specialties.

"It is good," she said. She continued to eat. If Reyes hadn't been present, she could have told Ferne and the others about her discovery, but she hesitated to mention anything personal around a Dirksen, no matter how strongly he professed that he no longer wanted to be a part of his clan.

After everyone had eaten, she insisted that the three children go and lie down. Though they were excited to be reunited with her and anxious to find Parthenia, they could hardly have slept the previous night. Also, though she didn't know what had happened after she'd Transported them from the Sherrerr shuttle, she doubted it was anything good. They would need time to recoup their energy.

As she'd predicted, Oriana, Ferne, and Darius quickly fell asleep. She closed the blinds in the bedrooms and went out into the lounge, where Reyes was searching for information on Parthenia once more.

She sat down beside him. "Still nothing?"

The young man's long, fine hair hung over his face as he leaned forward. "Nope." He sighed, leaned back against the sofa, and brushed his hair out of his eyes. "There isn't a single reference I can see. I'm sorry. I'll continue to look after I've had a rest."

"Thanks. I do appreciate what you're doing for my family."

"Consider it my way of trying to put things right. When I think of all the things my clan have done over the years.... And I'm probably not even aware of half of it. It was only a couple of years ago I began to realize what Mother and other Dirksens were doing was wrong. Up until then I accepted that was how life was. I thought we deserved everything we had and that if people didn't have anything it was because they'd hadn't worked hard enough. The sheer evilness of what we were doing went over my head."

"Well, it's good you realized it finally. It's a shame the rest of your family haven't arrived at the same insight."

"Yeah." Reyes frowned. "You know, I've been putting something off that I really ought to do."

"What's that?"

"I should read Mother's comms. I won't reply. I want to make use of my status as long as I can to help you, so I'm not going to declare anything to her. But I have to face up to what I'm doing."

He leaned forward again and lifted his screen. Even from her position she could see he had tens if not hundreds of messages waiting from his mother. Reyes began to open and scan them, spending no more than a few seconds on each. She could imagine what they said—variations on *Where are you?* and *When are you coming home?*

But then Reyes opened a message that seemed to occupy a lot of his attention. He read it top to bottom, then his fingers flicked as he quickly opened the next message, and then the next. He let the interface fall to his lap.

"Is everything okay?" she asked, wondering what Langley Dirksen had said to her son that could be so devastating.

Reyes turned to her. "My mother has her—your sister. I'd swear it."

Thirty

The estate Castiel had brought Parthenia to reminded her of her home on Ithiya, only it was far larger. The house was at least three times as big and the grounds stretched so far she couldn't see the boundaries.

Castiel had wanted to walk in the grounds while they waited for someone. He hadn't said who. Nahla trailed behind Parthenia and their brother. The little girl hadn't spoken a word since Parthenia had arrived. A man called Harmon walked even farther behind the group. He was large, with broad shoulders and a thick, muscly neck.

Parthenia guessed he was there to prevent her from running away. Yet in fact his presence wasn't required. She wouldn't have dared to run from Castiel—not after he'd demonstrated that he could now Cast.

He'd used Nahla as a subject for his demonstration. In a room inside the mansion, he had sipped elixir he must have made himself, and he'd Cast Transport on their sister. Parthenia had thought he would do something simple like move her from one side of the room to the other, but instead he'd lifted her up to the ceiling.

Poor Nahla had hung there, plainly terrified but uncomplaining. It had been Parthenia who had begged Castiel to put their sister down, and safely, knowing he could release Nahla and let her fall. In the end, he had lowered the little girl rather than dropped her—until she was a meter above the floor, when he did allow her to drop.

He had smiled with satisfaction at the cry of pain she gave when she hit the floor.

Later, as they walked across the lawn, he said, "I know how sentimental I must sound, but I'm glad to see you again, Parthenia."

"Really?" she replied. "I can't say I feel the same."

"Oh, now that's unkind. Did you hear that, Nahla? Parthenia doesn't like us. She isn't happy to be reunited with her own flesh and blood."

"I don't know why you say *us* like that. I am pleased to see Nahla, or maybe *relieved* is a better word. Relieved that you haven't seriously hurt her, yet. Though that demonstration in the house just now tells me you're perfectly capable of it. Probably looking forward to it, in fact."

His expression darkened. "If anything bad happens to Nahla, it will be entirely justified, I'm sure."

She made a noise of disgust. "You sound just like Father."

"I certainly hope so. He was a great man, and he was in the prime of his life when he was cut down by our evil bitch of a mother—with *your* help." He turned to face her, malevolence simmering in his eyes. His voice was soft, which made his words all the more terrifying. "And believe me, I haven't forgotten it."

"Huh. Full of bravado after the fact, aren't you? I don't recall you doing anything to help him at the time."

He drew himself up and clenched his fists. Between his teeth he said, "That was because I wasn't sure if I could Cast at the time. Now I know I can, I won't allow anyone to do anything I don't want them to." His rage abated and he walked on. "Besides, I wanted to get away from our clan. We never received the respect we deserved from them. After everything we did—turning around their failing businesses, increasing their power and influence—we were still treated little better than slaves. They should have been bowing down to us, asking for our help and giving us rich rewards instead of locking us away and only bringing us out whenever they needed their performing monkeys."

Parthenia inwardly smiled at his words. Once more he was using "us" incorrectly. He had personally done nothing whatsoever to help the Sherrerrs and he'd enjoyed favor and numerous privileges that hadn't been allowed to his mage siblings. Also, it had been their father who had treated the mages like slaves—the very man Castiel had just been praising. From what she could understand, the other Sherrerrs were either disinterested or uncaring about how Stefan Sherrerr used his children, providing the clan could benefit from her and the others' abilities.

However, she was careful to show no sign of her wry amusement. She had already angered him once and gotten away with it but she might not be so lucky again. It was a lesson she'd learned well at the hands of their father.

"*There* you are," said a voice.

She turned to see a middle-aged woman standing in the mansion at a set of open double doors. She was richly dressed. Smiling warmly, the woman stepped out of the doorway and walked toward them over the neatly clipped grass.

"I wondered where you'd gone," the woman said as she drew nearer. "Castiel, please introduce me to our guest."

"Naturally." Smiling sardonically, he said, "I'd like you to meet my sister, Parthenia. Parthenia, this is our host, Langley Dirksen."

"I'm very pleased to meet you, Parthenia."

She didn't reply. While she knew she would never get away with being rude to Castiel, she was willing to test the boundaries with this new person who was clearly colluding with him.

As she saw her reaction, Langley Dirksen grimaced. "My, that look is familiar," she remarked to Castiel. "I can see the resemblance to her sister."

"Yes, she does look a bit like Carina, doesn't she? Though Carina isn't a Sherrerr like the rest of us. Parthenia and I only share a mother with her. We had different fathers."

Parthenia wondered what else Castiel had told the Dirksen woman. She had a feeling it was probably everything, including all he knew about Casting. He might even have exaggerated his explanation of mage powers. He had always been prone to boasting. She was also curious about what her brother was doing on a Dirksen estate and, more importantly, what he intended to do with her. It was unlikely to be anything pleasant.

"So is this the one your father used to take to business meetings?" Langley asked.

"Parthenia did do some of that, yes, though I also performed several key roles."

Parthenia could hardly believe his last remark, which was utterly false. Before she could say anything, however, he flashed her a warning look.

"And it was Carina who extracted your youngest brother from our custody."

"That's right. Though we didn't know anything about her at the time."

"Hmmm...." Langley glanced at Parthenia. "Would you mind

taking a stroll with me?" she asked Castiel. "Your sisters can wait here with Harmon."

"By all means," Castiel said. The pair walked off across the lawn, away from the huge house.

Turning to her large guard, Parthenia said, "Can we go inside? I want to sit down."

Harmon considered for a moment before giving a short nod. She went through the double doors into a lounge. Nahla traipsed along behind her. While both the girls sat on sumptuous sofas, Harmon stood with his back to the doorway, blocking most of the light.

As they waited for Castiel and Langley to return, Parthenia wondered what the Dirksen woman's words had meant. She seemed to know Carina somehow and she didn't particularly like her. Parthenia was certain the feeling had been mutual. On the one hand, she was relieved to hear her sister was alive and well, but on the other she was dismayed to discover Carina had been captured by the Dirksens. She wondered how it had happened. Her sister was so smart and resourceful she would never have fallen into Dirksen hands easily.

Where was Carina now? Was she somewhere in the mansion? Or had she managed to escape? Langley Dirksen's words hadn't made it clear. Parthenia resolved to find out and help her sister if she could. If Carina was being held captive that explained why she hadn't come to find her mage siblings. She hadn't been able to Cast Locate using one of her bracelets.

My bracelets! She gasped. The farmer called Marcia had taken them when she'd found Parthenia and the others in the barn, and they'd forgotten to take them back before they'd fled into the forest. Now Oriana had no way of finding where she was, and she had none of her siblings' belongings to use to Locate them either. They might never find each other again.

Her throat tightened and her eyes filled with tears as she was reminded of poor wounded Ferne, and Oriana and Darius, who might still be waiting for her in the forest, though they'd probably realized by now she wasn't coming back. What would they do without her?

Harmon stepped aside to allow Castiel to enter the lounge from the garden. Parthenia rubbed her eyes to rid them of tears but Castiel noticed the gesture.

"Are you upset, dear sister?" he asked. "Don't worry. You don't have anything to fear. Our lives are going to be so much better than the exploitation we suffered at the hands of the Sherrerrs. Langley has made it clear how highly she values our skills, and she appreciates that we will truly commit to the Dirksen cause."

"I think you mean *your* life with the Dirksens," Parthenia retorted. "You don't have any right to tell me what I can and can't do."

"I may not have the right, but I have the means," Castiel said. He took out his bottle of elixir. "As long as I have this and you don't, I can do what I like."

"As long as you have that and I don't, I'm useless to you. So that's an empty threat." Parthenia didn't go on, guessing she was skirting the limits of what he would tolerate from her.

"You'll soon find out whether my threats are empty. What do you have that belongs to Carina? Hand it over. I'm going to find that bitch and bring her here."

"I don't have anything."

"Don't lie. She must have given you something before she Transported you off the shuttle. She knew you would need something to Locate her. Of course, she didn't give anything to Nahla and me because she never wanted to see us again."

He was close to the truth of what had actually happened, but she kept her lips sealed. It was clear from what he said that Carina was free, which was some consolation. Even if Parthenia had one of her sister's belongings, she would never willingly hand it over. She would never betray Carina.

"Hmpf." Castiel dropped into a seat and folded his arms over his chest. "It doesn't matter. She'll find out where you are eventually and she'll try to rescue you. We can grab her then, and we'll get the rest of them."

With a sinking heart, she realized he was correct. No matter how hard she tried to avoid helping him capture their older sister, she couldn't prevent herself from being bait.

THIRTY-ONE

Carina was uncomfortable with the idea of leaving Oriana, Ferne, and Darius alone while she went to rescue Parthenia but she didn't have any choice. It was far too risky to take them with her. Reyes, however, would be coming along. Although she knew her sister was probably somewhere in Langley Dirksen's mansion, she didn't know exactly where. The place had to have a hundred rooms. She needed Reyes to find out her sister's exact location and guide her there.

Langley's comms to her son hadn't explicitly stated that she was holding Parthenia captive. The implication of the woman's words was clear, however. She'd said things like: *Come home soon, darling. I have exciting news. It doesn't matter that the Sherrerr girl left us. Someone else is here who possesses the same abilities.* Carina could only conclude that, somehow, the Dirksen matriarch had discovered Parthenia's abilities—perhaps the young girl had been observed Casting—and Langley had wasted no time in removing her sister from the Illegal Migrant Holding Center and taking her to the Dirksen estate.

Reyes had never mentioned Carina's 'abilities,' though he had to know his mother's reasons for holding her captive. And when he'd picked them up from the burning forest he'd been curious about Ferne's unconscious state, knowing that one of the children had supposedly been shot. Yet Reyes hadn't followed up with any questions about their powers. She guessed he didn't want to broach a sensitive subject. It followed that he hadn't mentioned anything when showing her his mother's comms. He let her draw the same conclusion from them as he had.

"Are you sure you can get Parthenia?" Darius asked as she prepared to leave.

"I'm going to try my hardest, but I can't promise anything. If I can't bring her back tonight I won't stop trying until I can."

"But you won't let them catch you, will you?"

"Of course not."

"Because I'll be really sad if I don't see you again."

"I'd be sad about that too." She squatted down to look her youngest brother in his eyes. "You must do whatever Oriana and Ferne tell you, no questions asked, okay?"

"Okay." Darius looked down. "I just wish we could all be together again."

"We will be, hopefully after tonight." She kissed and hugged him and Oriana and Ferne, then turned to Reyes. "I'm all set. Are you ready?"

"I don't have anything to prepare. I'm waiting on you."

She had prepared. While she'd kept Reyes distracted in the living room, Ferne and Oriana had made more elixir in the kitchen. She was bringing a full bottle with her. She was very reluctant to use it within Reyes' sight, but if she needed to Cast while he was around in order to get Parthenia out, so be it.

They left the apartment and went to his star racer. The plan was that he would land in his mother's estate grounds, far from the house. She would exit the vehicle, then Reyes would continue on to the mansion, returning home as if he hadn't been missing for two days. After he'd endured his mother's predicted ire, he would discover where Parthenia was being held. Next, he would meet Carina at one of the rear entrances to the home after everyone had retired for the night.

According to Reyes, the final part of the plan entailed her, Parthenia, and himself then leaving his home together. But for her, this was the part where her own plan deviated. As soon as she was in sight of her sister, she would Transport them both out of the house and far away. Though she appreciated what Reyes had done to help them, she didn't think she would ever feel safe with him around. Nai Nai's lesson remained ingrained in her mind, despite her friend Bryce demonstrating that not everyone was out to use mages for their own ends.

The minute she reunited Parthenia with her mage siblings, Reyes Dirksen would be on his own.

———

The metropolis was bright with artificial light, outshining the starlight. Reyes had input his mother's estate as the destination and his star racer made its own way while he leaned back in his seat, resting the ankle of one leg on the knee of the other. He seemed unusually pensive.

"I guess it's got to be hard for you to go home tonight," said Carina.

"Yeah." Reyes picked at his nails. "I'm not looking forward to pretending I'm back for good, or that I don't have a problem with what my family does." He bit off a hangnail. "Or lying to Mother, if I'm honest. You know, she isn't really a—"

"Bad person. Yeah. I know."

"You sound like you don't."

"Reyes, I know she's your mom and it's hard for you to see her behavior objectively, but just think about what her and the rest of your clan have done. You know a lot more about that than me, but I know Langley Dirksen kept me captive and she tricked me into eating tracers that nearly killed me to remove. Are those the actions of a good person?"

"But if you'd only agreed to what she was proposing she wouldn't have done either of those things," Reyes said. "She really wanted to work with you, not against you. And she couldn't afford to let you go. What if you'd gone back to work for the Sherrerrs? It would have been stupid of her to allow that to happen. The Sherrerrs are evil. If they take control of the entire sector, everyone will suffer for it."

She sat up in her seat. She could hardly believe what she was hearing. Did the kid really have no idea of the suffering of people on Ostillon, like Asha? "First of all," she said, "I thought you didn't want to be a Dirksen any longer. Why are you defending them? And secondly, I've seen what Sherrerrs *and* Dirksens do to the people they control and they're equally bad. People on both sides try to justify their evil acts by saying they're necessary to achieve peace and prosperity. But that's all their arguments are: attempts at justification. I don't know who's worse—the people who don't care they're cruel or the people who behave cruelly and pretend to themselves they have some kind of higher purpose."

Reyes didn't answer.

She went on, "Your mother might think she would treat me well if I agreed to do what she said, but it wouldn't last. As soon as I said no to something she wanted she would try to force me to obey her. She would stop seeing me as a human being. I would become an impediment to her plans and all her fine words would fly out the window, as I soon found out after a day at your place."

"I really don't think—"

"You really have no idea what you're talking about," she snapped. She was tempted to tell him about all that had happened to Ma. That might convince him of the truth of what she was saying. But the last thing she wanted to do was give Reyes Dirksen any more information about herself or mages, especially considering that she hopefully wouldn't see him again after tonight. Instead, she said, "If you start out a relationship in a bad way, like by coercing someone or lying to them, things won't ever change, they'll only get worse. You can't do something bad and tell yourself that in the future you'll behave better. It isn't going to happen. What you did at the start sets the pattern. So please, don't try to assure me that the woman who kidnapped me and whose guard beat me up has my best interests at heart. It's insulting."

A corner of his lips lifted. "Well, that told me, I guess."

They'd left the city and were flying over dark countryside. She could make out faint lights in the distance, which she assumed were shining from the windows of the Dirksen mansion.

"Just another couple of minutes," said Reyes. "I'm going to set down just inside the estate walls. You'll have an hour's walk to the house. Is that okay?"

"If that's the safest way to do it, that's absolutely fine."

"It'll be a while before Mother goes to bed, so we have plenty of time. Only make sure to watch out for guards. They patrol the grounds sometimes, but not much. Dirksens don't expect to be attacked on a home planet, so the guards are only checking for vagrants and burglars."

"I am a kind of burglar, only I'll be stealing my own family's treasure."

Thirty-Two

The Dirksen mansion was silent as Carina approached it after her long walk. The dark windows were blank eyes. She wondered which window it was she'd looked out of during her captivity. A shudder ran through her as she recalled her time there. Her experience had been nothing like what Ma had endured for years, but she was in no doubt that, had she stayed, her life would have been similar eventually.

She was armed with nothing except elixir. She hoped it would be all she needed to slip inside the place and Transport herself and Parthenia out. Once her sister was free and her mage siblings were reunited, she could begin to think about how she would get everyone offplanet. She hadn't forgotten about the Sherrerr spy at Langley's party and what her presence probably meant.

Several pairs of double doors ran along the first floor at the rear of the mansion. She was pleased to see that, as arranged, Reyes had left one of them slightly ajar. Her heart was thumping as she opened the door wider. She peeked through into a quiet, dark room. It seemed empty. She slipped inside.

Reyes was waiting. He stepped out of the shadow of a corner

and beckoned her. She tiptoed across the room, avoiding the large chaise longue that stood in her way.

"She's in the suite you slept in," Reyes whispered as soon as she was close enough to hear him.

So Langley was trying out her soft coercion on Parthenia too. It was better than throwing her in the cellar immediately. She hoped the Dirksen matriarch hadn't already fed her sister their tiny tracers.

She followed Reyes out of the lounge into the downstairs corridor. "You should wait here," she said to him quietly. "I can remember where the suite is." As soon as she laid eyes on Parthenia, she would Transport them both out of the place. She wanted Reyes out of the way so he wouldn't witness her Casting. Also, Reyes would probably be more of a hindrance than a help if she had to deal with Harmon.

Reyes shook his head. "I want to help."

It wasn't the time or place to argue about it. She went in front of him and walked softly down the corridor to the stairs. Her hand on her bottle of elixir, she began to climb the steps, placing each foot gently on the treads. Reyes was directly behind her. She listened intently, hoping to hear the sleep-breathing of Harmon or another guard. Surprising an unconscious guard was the best break she could hope for. She heard nothing.

As she approached the top of the stairs, she unscrewed the lid on the elixir bottle. She didn't want to Cast in front of Reyes but she also knew that if Harmon was on guard duty she would never defeat him without some extra help. She sipped and swallowed a mouthful of elixir as her head rose above the level of the second floor.

Harmon was standing, silent and bulky, in front of the suite door. Unlike the man who had been guarding her the night she escaped, he hadn't brought along a chair to nap the night away.

She turned to Reyes and gestured to him with a flat hand. *Wait.* She closed her eyes and Cast her first—but hopefully not her last—Transport of the evening. She sent out the Cast and opened her eyes. To her great satisfaction, Harmon flew upward. His head struck the ceiling with a crack, but before he fell down the Cast also caught him and dropped him quietly to the floor. He landed with barely a bump and lay sprawled out and motionless.

Harmon was out cold, but she didn't know for how long. The man's skull was probably extremely thick. She ran lightly along the hall to the suite door, leaving Reyes to do whatever he wanted. She tried the door but it was locked, of course. With plenty of elixir on her, that wasn't a problem. In a few moments, the Unlock Cast had done its work. A quick glance at Harmon told her he remained dead to the world. She went inside the room. Her plan had nearly succeeded. Her heart lifted.

The lounge of the suite was exactly as she remembered. It was empty, so Parthenia had to be in the bedroom, asleep. No problem. She could Transport her sister without waking her up. Swallowing another mouthful of elixir, she opened the bedroom door.

She was surprised to see the bed was empty. Had Reyes misunderstood and directed her to the wrong suite? A muffled whimper drew her attention.

She swung around and nearly froze in shock. In a white nightgown in a far corner of the bedroom, Parthenia stood. She was gagged. Even more of a surprise was the person standing by her side: Castiel. Carina reacted instinctively. Castiel's presence didn't matter. Now she could see Parthenia she could Transport her. She closed her eyes. With a great effort of concentration, she Cast.

Almost immediately, a shockwave hit her, knocking her from her feet. The wave was so intense, so reeking of evil, she was momentarily dazed. She was on the floor. Parthenia was staring at her, eyes wide and panicky above her gag. Then she figured out what had happened. As she'd Cast Transport, someone else had Cast Repulse, throwing the force of her Cast back at her.

Parthenia wouldn't have sent the defensive Cast, which meant only one thing.

Castiel was smiling triumphantly. "You have no idea of the satisfaction that gave me, Carina. I have finally demonstrated my natural superiority over you. All our brothers and sisters thought you were so wonderful and powerful and wise, just because you'd learned true Casting, not the watered-down version Mother taught. But I knew *I* was the one who truly deserved their respect and awe, not you. Now my gift has finally arrived and my chance has come to receive my due, from you and all the others. The things I'll do, Carina, the victories I'll achieve with me leading all of you."

She was barely listening to Castiel as she went over her options. Of all the obstacles she'd imagined she might face in rescuing her sister, this one had never entered her mind. She couldn't Transport Parthenia while their brother was here to stop her. Though the power of his Repulse had surprised her, she thought she could probably defeat him at Casting. However, she was entirely unprepared. She would need time to think up a strategy and tactics.

A sound came from the other room. She saw with relief that Reyes had come into the suite. Maybe he could pin Castiel down or otherwise distract him and she could retrieve Parthenia. She rose to her feet. "Reyes, quick, come here. Grab that boy."

"Oh, no," Reyes said, advancing. "It isn't him I'll be grabbing." He lunged at her. She stepped aside just in time, and his momentum carried him past her. What was he doing?

Then she saw it all. Right from the beginning, the entire escapade had been an elaborate trap set by Langley and her son.

They'd allowed her to escape and since then they'd been stringing her along, hoping to find out more about Casting and her connections with other mages.

Reyes lunged for a second time. She kicked out at him, catching him in his stomach. That stopped him, momentarily. He bent over, coughing.

She had to act fast. Harmon would be returning to consciousness any minute and Castiel could Cast at her. She would be entering into a battle she could not win. If she remained here, both she and Parthenia would be trapped. She only had one choice, though it broke her heart to do it. She tipped the elixir bottle into her mouth and swallowed. "I'm sorry," she said to Parthenia. "But don't give up hope. I'm coming back."

With that, she Cast Transport and was gone.

THIRTY-THREE

Carina appeared in the street outside the temple. Luckily, it was the middle of the night so no one was around. She hoped the twins had done exactly as she'd asked and Transported themselves and Darius to the same place not long after she and Reyes had left.

The Dirksen kid had betrayed her after all. Just when she'd begun to trust him. For a while, she'd believed he might be different from the rest of his clan. But he'd only been pretending so that he could be around her and learn about Casting. He and his mother had probably wanted to see if she knew other mages—maybe they were hoping she was in contact with Darius. The Dirksens had known about his existence for a long time. She was glad she'd taken the precaution of telling her siblings to leave the apartment. Reyes had probably arranged for his people to go there and kidnap her sister and brothers as soon as she was gone.

And Castiel.... Her brother's reappearance had been even more of a surprise. His Casting ability was a serious concern, especially the nature of his Casts. The Repulse she had experienced had felt *wrong*. And the fact that his ability had shown itself so late in his development was odd too. What it meant, she didn't know. Not for the first time she rued the fact that she'd been so young when Nai Nai died and that Ma had been so sick and with so little time to live while she had known her. As a result, her knowledge of mage lore was sparse.

She walked through the quiet courtyard in front of the temple and passed across the doorless threshold. The temple had been the only place she could think of to send her siblings where they would be safe, and then it would only be for a little while. Dirksen thugs would search everywhere Reyes could think of that she might go. She would have to take her siblings somewhere else soon.

The ancient frieze on the wall of the temple's antechamber seemed to greet her. What had the priestess been telling her about the painting when Reyes had stuck his head in the door? It had been something about how each Element in the scene represented a sin. She couldn't remember which material represented which sin, but the priestess' explanation had seemed very strange. It was nothing like her understanding of what they meant, based on the knowledge Nai Nai had passed down.

Yet in the morning ritual, she had seen a priest burn a character. The other acolytes may have been burning characters too. She hadn't been paying attention. However, the final scroll to be burned had displayed only dots and figures. The religion of the temple seemed to be tied up with magehood but she didn't understand how.

She also didn't have time to figure it out. Quickly, she went down a passage to one side of the central statues of deities and emerged in the larger, rear room where she'd spent a night sleeping on a bench. The room was empty. Where were Oriana and Ferne and Darius?

Her stomach clenched. Had her siblings Transported here or

not? Were they still in the apartment or, more likely, in the custody of the Dirksen clan by now? As she stood hesitating about what to do, the young priestess who had helped her the last time she was here came out of the door at the rear of the chamber.

"I believe you're looking for some children?" she asked.

"Yes, I am."

"They're waiting for you in here. Please come through." The hooded figure returned through the door.

She hesitated again. Was this another trap? Had the Dirksens arrived here before her?

Darius popped out. "Carina!" He called behind him, "She's here, everyone!" before running over to her and grabbing her hand. Then he stopped. "Where's Parthenia?"

"I'm sorry, Darius. I couldn't get her."

The little boy's features fell.

She continued, "But I'm going to go back." Just as soon as she'd figured out how to free her sister.

His face brightened. "You'll get her. I know you will. Come on. Everyone's waiting for you."

He pulled her through the doorway into a small, dingy room lit by nothing but an old lamp and a small fire burning in a grate. The priestess was nowhere to be seen. Oriana and Ferne were here, however, sitting down facing her as she came through the door. Someone else was here too. A man sat opposite the twins, his back toward her. Her hand gripped Darius' tighter. Who had infiltrated her family this time?

The man stood up and turned. At first she didn't recognize him. Then she took a closer look and nearly fell over. It was Bryce.

"Carina." He strode over and enveloped her in a hug.

Through her surprise, she hugged him back, but then she pulled away. "What are you doing here? I thought you'd gone back to Ithiya."

"Why would you think that?"

"You have to run your family's business."

He frowned. "Yeah, I remember that's what you thought I was going to do the last time we were separated. You were wrong then—what made you think you'd be right this time around? Carina, don't you get it? I want to be with *you*."

Ferne put his hand over his mouth and snickered. Oriana elbowed him in the side. Bryce glanced at the twins over his shoulder then returned his gaze to Carina, mildly embarrassed but not really caring. Before she could think of a suitable reply to his declaration, he went on, "Wait. Where's Parthenia? The kids said you'd gone to rescue her from the Dirksens."

"I couldn't," she replied, entirely forgetting her surprise at Bryce's appearance as she recalled the scared eyes of her sister. "Everything's worse than I thought. Castiel has her."

"Castiel?" exclaimed Ferne and Oriana in unison.

She told them Castiel had skillfully inserted himself into Langley Dirksen's household. "He must have decided to ally himself with the Dirksens. Then he set about trying to find us so we can be his acolytes. I have to try again to get Parthenia out, and soon. They might move her somewhere else and I don't trust Castiel not to do something awful to her."

She knew that if her oldest brother was anything like his father, there were no depths he wouldn't sink to, though she didn't want to go into details in front of the children.

"Why is Castiel helping the Dirksens?" Oriana asked. "He's a Sherrerr. It doesn't make any sense."

"He probably has some deluded idea about lording it over them. Idiot. As if any of the Dirksens are going to allow some kid to boss them around. He'll receive a wake-up call soon enough. But I plan on us being long gone before that happens. I just need to get Parthenia first."

"Well I'm here to help you," Bryce said.

She studied her friend. Though they'd only been apart for a short time, he seemed to have changed. His beard was thicker and he'd filled out a little. That was why she hadn't recognized him immediately. "I don't understand. How did you find us? Is it just a coincidence you were here when the children arrived?"

"No coincidence. When you Transported me to the planet—alone...." He glared at her. "I appeared in this city. I nearly frightened the life out of a tramp. He ran off shouting something about ghosts. You ran out of elixir, didn't you? That was why you sent me here by myself."

"Yeah, I'd used it all up. I only had enough left for one person."

"So whoever was boarding the shuttle—you decided you were going to face them alone? Don't do that to me in the future, okay? I would have stayed with you if I'd known the situation but you didn't give me a choice."

"Okay." Having Bryce with her when she'd been captured by the Dirksens would have complicated matters tenfold, but her friend did have a point.

"When I realized you hadn't Transported yourself too," he continued, "I thought I would try to find you and your brothers and sisters. From then onward I've been wandering the city, visiting places where people might go to lie low. A couple of days ago I came here. It was the only place where someone who fitted your description had been seen. The priestess said you'd been interested in the pictures out in the front, so I guessed you might return. Since then I've been back two or three times a day, hoping you would show."

"Bryce was just leaving when we Transported to the courtyard," Oriana said. "We made him jump."

"You certainly did," he said.

She smiled. She was relieved that Bryce was okay, though she was also somewhat alarmed by his feelings for her.

The priestess returned to the chamber. "Will you be spending the night here?" she asked. "We have a small room for the homeless, though it only holds two beds. However, you're all welcome to stay."

"Yes, we are," Darius said. "I'm tired."

"No," said Carina. "Thank you, but we're leaving now."

"Why?" Oriana asked.

"Yes, why can't we stay?" asked Ferne. "I'm tired too."

"It isn't safe for us. Other people might guess we're here. People who want to hurt us. We'll have to find somewhere else to sleep tonight." She paused. "But..." She didn't know when she would return to the temple, if ever. She might never have the chance to find out what link the religion had with magehood. "Before we go," she said, "could you tell me more about your religion? Or do you have anything I could read about it?"

Thirty-Four

After finding a hotel to stay at, Carina opened the room's interface to find the religion's database while the children settled down to sleep. The holy book of the religion was too old and fragile to be handled, but each page had been copied onto a database that was free to anyone to read. The priestess had given her the name of the site before they left. Bryce sat down beside her as she studied the pages.

The pictures of the holy book were in the same style as the friezes that decorated the temple, only much better quality and in greater detail. She hadn't seen much art in her life, but the images in the religious text looked well-painted to her. Though the figures were tiny, their facial expressions were naturalistic and nuanced, and the landscapes and buildings represented looked realistic, though they were unfamiliar and archaic.

"I wonder why they put all this stuff in a book?" Bryce asked. "Why not create it on an interface? A file wouldn't suffer the same wear and tear."

"I guess they thought a book would last longer."

"They thought a book would last longer? From what I can tell, the thing's falling apart."

"Yes, but the priestess said the book was thousands of years old. Do you know of any files that old? I don't."

"True enough. What does it say?"

The text was legible but the language was indecipherable. "Oh, look. There's a translation." She opened the relevant page.

In the beginning, the People came, arrived from the stars that gave them birth. They traveled in celestial vessels filled with every food they might desire in an unending supply, provided to give them nourishment throughout their long voyage.

First to set foot on the Given Planet was Lomeq. She brought with her two sons: Sear and Sorn. Sear and Sorn brought with them their wives, Lani and Pirlu. Sear and Lani brought with them five children...

"Do we have to read this?" Bryce asked. "It's just a long list of names."

"You don't have to read anything. Go to bed if you like. But you're right. I don't think I'm going to learn much here."

"What are you looking for anyway? I didn't know you were interested in religion."

"I'm not." Carina explained what had prompted her to investigate the religious beliefs on Ostillon.

"You think it might have something to do with mages? I would have thought you would know all about them, considering you are one."

In the time she and Bryce had spent on the shuttle after escaping from the Sherrerrs, Carina hadn't told him much about her past. She'd been careful to keep the conversation about him or other, neutral, topics. But she guessed he had proven his loyalty and trustworthiness enough for her to tell him about mage lore.

"I only know what my grandmother told me," she explained,

"and she died when I was young so I don't remember everything very well. Mage history, how to Cast, everything in fact, all we know about being a mage is passed on orally. Nothing is ever written down, and we don't have family photographs or anything else that might link us to other mages. It's the only way we can remain safe."

"So you don't know any other mages apart from your family?"

"That's right. I didn't even know them until I happened to rescue Darius from the Dirksens. And then I didn't find out he was my brother until Stefan Sherrerr found me and reunited me with Ma."

"Wow, that must have been a lonely life."

"Yeah." She paused, thinking that Bryce was one of the few people she'd met who had some idea of what she'd been through. "Anyway, if there is something in this religion that has to do with mages, I want to find out more if I can."

"Okay. What else does it say?" He swiped to the next page.

The initial chapter of the holy book went into a lot of detail about the first settlers on the planet. It also explained that the world was a paradise provided for the colonists by their deities. The information was quite interesting, but it wasn't until the second chapter Carina saw anything that seemed significant.

In the second year, the People tilled the fields, grew crops, and harvested them. The People hunted in the woods and brought home meat. They birthed more children and their numbers swelled. All was good and the People lived in peace and prosperity.

But then they discovered their new world was blighted. An alien race had arrived before them and stolen their rightful home. These others were not People. They had disguised themselves to resemble People so they could walk among them and befriend them.

Yet these others tricked the People, doing things that People could not. The aliens could disappear in the wink of an eye and reappear in another place altogether. They could move objects without touching them. They could bend the People to do their bidding.

The alien race was evil and the People knew they would never be safe until the aliens were expelled from the world.

Her hand went to her mouth.

Bryce said what was on her mind. "The aliens sound like mages."

————

By the time Carina finished reading the holy book, it was so late it was nearly morning. She closed the interface and went to bed. She had time to sleep for a couple of hours before the children woke up. Then she had to make a plan on how to rescue Parthenia.

Bryce was squeezed into a narrow space between Darius and the wall on one of the two beds, with Ferne sleeping at the other edge of the bed, on the verge of falling off. Darius was lying on his back between them, arms outstretched, looking like a sea creature she had seen once on a forgotten planet. The animal had been flat and its five limbs splayed out.

With only Oriana to share a bed with, she had more room than poor Bryce or Ferne, yet though she was exhausted, she didn't fall asleep right away. The stories from the ancient book replayed in her mind, though she saw them from the perspective of the mages.

What had happened during the time in which the book was set had become clear to her when she'd read between the lines. Thousands of years ago, mages had settled on Ostillon. The planet might have been one of the first they'd fled to after leaving Earth. Then, some time later, another group of settlers had arrived. The new colonists might have already been following a religion that told them the planet was their rightful home, or the religion might have sprung up as divine justification for the persecution of mages.

It was plain that the newcomers had felt threatened by the mages' powers. Her ancestors might have become lax about hiding what they could do since leaving Earth possibly many generations before. Whatever the reason, the new settlers hadn't wanted to share their world with these people who had strange abilities. They deemed the practices of mages immoral and probably made them illegal. The Elements that were so important to mages became representative of sins, and the Characters had to be destroyed—perhaps a metaphor for what the colonists wanted to do to the mages.

The ritual at the end of the Mech Battles performance suddenly made sense. The priestess had said that pouring the elixir into the sand was to cleanse the participants of their sins. At some point, the newcomers had justified pouring away stocks of elixir by saying they were purifying the mages of evil.

The only reminder that mages had once lived on Ostillon were their inaccurate representation in stories in a holy book and a few traditional dishes in the local cuisine.

Though in her time the planet was a nowhere place at the edge of the galactic sector, at one point in its history it must have been one of the first to have been settled from Earth. Her heart skipped a beat. Did that mean Earth was comparatively nearby?

"Can't sleep?" Bryce whispered from across the room.

She lifted herself onto her elbow. "No. You neither?"

"Uh uh. I know it's asking a lot, but I need more than a hands-breadth of space to relax in."

She chuckled. "Sorry about Darius. Push him out of the way if you like. I don't think he'll wake up."

"It's okay. I just realized... I never told you how happy I was to find you again."

"Bryce, I'm happy you found me too." She really meant it. For the first time in her life, she thought she'd met a non-mage she could completely trust.

THIRTY-FIVE

Parthenia had cried herself to sleep, and the following morning when Harmon woke her and told her she had to go down to breakfast, she refused. The large man bristled but seemed to think twice about his response. He said nothing and left the suite. Another guard arrived to take his place. Harmon had been watching her all night, presumably to catch Carina if she repeated her rescue attempt.

A few minutes later, Langley Dirksen arrived and sent the replacement guard out. She was dressed in loose fitting, light pajamas covered by a robe made of a similarly fine, expensive material. She was only lightly made up. Perhaps it was due to the dim light through the window blinds or the woman's age and luxurious clothes, but Parthenia was briefly reminded of her mother. Another bout of sobbing threatened and it was as much as she could do to control herself.

Langley seemed to sense her vulnerable state. The woman's expression was soft with sympathy as she stood in the bedroom doorway. "Do you mind if I come in?"

Determined not to open her mouth lest she begin to cry, Parthenia didn't reply.

Langley came in anyway. She sat next to her on the side of her bed. "My dear, you look exhausted. I imagine that you hardly slept. There's no need for you to come down to breakfast if you don't feel like it. I can ask one of the maids to bring something up to you. How does that sound?"

Finally, Parthenia trusted herself to speak. "I'm not hungry."

"Is that so? I'm surprised. Your sister had quite the appetite."

At the mention of Carina's name, Parthenia's lower lip turned out and she had to swallow. She'd seen Carina for only a moment —less than a minute—for the first time since she'd arrived on Ostillon. After waiting and hoping for so long her sister would find and help her and her siblings, Carina had finally appeared, but then she'd left again. She'd left her in the hands of Castiel and the Dirksens. She was trying hard not to feel abandoned but she wasn't succeeding.

Langley reached out and placed a hand on top of hers. She snatched her hand away and thrust it under the coverlet.

"Parthenia... May I call you that? I understand how you feel and I know I would feel the same in your circumstances. You've had a very difficult time recently. Your brother has told me all about it. You must have been terrified to find yourself alone on a strange planet with no one to turn to. I can't imagine what you must have been forced to do to survive. You must be very brave and resourceful. I doubt I could have done the same. I have so much admiration for you."

Langley was gazing in her eyes, a soft, compassionate expression on her face. She continued, "You see, you and I are quite alike, aren't we? We were both raised within the comfort and privilege of a powerful clan. We wanted for nothing, and—if your parents were as indulgent as mine—we could have whatever we asked for. To live a life like that and then suddenly find yourself in an entirely different environment where you had absolutely nothing and were in fear for your life, what a challenge that must have been, and yet you met it." Tilting her head, Langley paused, allowing her words to linger.

She was right, Parthenia realized. She'd had a terrible time when she had walked with Darius through the forest. She'd had to seek help from the ranger, and do so many other things including going for help when Ferne had been shot. All the time she'd worried that she was making bad decisions, but actually she'd done as well as could have been expected. Perhaps she'd been too hard on herself. But what did any of that matter? She wanted to make sure that Carina had helped Ferne and her siblings. "I want to leave," she blurted.

"But why?" Langley asked. "Don't you like it here? This is a beautiful room in a beautiful house. We have wonderful grounds for you to wander in. You can have whatever you want. You only need to ask for it. Isn't this the life you're used to?"

"I want to be with my family. It doesn't matter that this is the kind of life I used to lead. Maybe I wasn't happy then. Have you considered that?" Despite her words, Parthenia recognized the truth of what Langley was saying. Her time on Ostillon since Carina had Transported her down here had been awful. A small part of her did yearn for the indulgent life she was accustomed to, even though she'd known that Mother was unhappy and no one except Father had much freedom. At least she'd never suffered a moment's physical discomfort. At least she'd been safe.

"Your brother has told me about your lives on Ithiya, and, to be honest, it doesn't sound that bad. None of us can have everything we want. That would be selfish and unreasonable. We must accept that sometimes sacrifices and compromises are necessary.

That's the correct, mature attitude to have in life. Don't you agree?"

Parthenia *did* agree, but she didn't want to say so. Agreeing with Langley Dirksen felt wrong. Of course it was wrong. The woman was holding her against her will. Parthenia was muddled. "You shouldn't listen to Castiel. He's a bad person. He scared and hurt Nahla and last night he gagged me and forced me to stay beside him when Carina came to rescue me."

"Ah, your sister," said Langley. "Another troubled young lady. She also didn't understand the advantages of using her powers for good. But you were talking about Castiel, weren't you? I agree, his behavior is excessive at times. I shall speak to him about it. Of course, he had to prevent your sister from taking you from us and returning you to hardship and a difficult life, but he must learn to be more kind and reasonable. Perhaps you can help me to persuade him."

Once more, she was at a loss. Castiel certainly did need to learn to behave better, but she didn't feel she was the person who should teach him. That wasn't her responsibility. Or was it? She was his older sister after all. And Mother had loved Castiel the same as she'd loved all her children. Perhaps she'd seen good in him that wasn't apparent to anyone else. Maybe Mother would have liked her to show Castiel some compassion.

"I... Er..."

Langley smiled. She pressed her hand where it lay beneath the covers. The woman's touch felt warm and comforting. She suddenly missed her mother very, very much.

"Don't worry, dear," said Langley. "You're still upset from everything you've been through since you arrived. It's entirely understandable that you need to recover and think things through before making any decisions. Take all the time you want. You're at a very important crossroads in your life. One way lies a wonderful life doing good and helping people while enjoying the best every world has to offer, the other way lies uncertainty, never knowing where your next meal will come from, and fear of discovery preventing you from helping others." Langley stood up and tightened the ties on her robe. "Would you like something to eat? Breakfast is still warm."

She looked down. This time, guilt bothered her while she refused to reply. For a powerful member of a powerful clan, Langley Dirksen didn't seem as bad as she would have imagined.

Langley left, and she gave vent to her feelings again, burying her face in her pillow. Even when she'd been trapped in the security room at the spaceport or in the cell at the holding center, she had never felt so alone. At those times, she'd been focused on returning to her siblings and desperately worried about them. Now she guessed Carina was with them. That had to be how her older sister had discovered where she was. It meant that Darius, Oriana, Ferne, and Carina were all together and Parthenia was the one who was apart from them.

Carina had come for her just as she'd said she would. Her sister had kept true to her word, and yet... The awful feeling that had pervaded her the previous night returned. Carina had left her. She'd left, even though she knew she was trapped and Castiel was holding her hostage.

Why had Carina gone away? She could do anything. She was an amazing fighter and she could Cast expertly, while Castiel was new to the skill. He should have been easy for Carina to defeat. Yet after only a brief try, she had abandoned her to the Dirksens. She'd said she would come back but would she? And when?

THIRTY-SIX

Carina, Bryce, and the children crowded around a table at a diner. It was a small, cheap, grubby place, but she had still checked the establishment took cash before they sat down. Bryce had money from some casual labor he'd picked up to survive while searching for them. The man behind the counter nodded in reply without removing his gaze from an erotic holo playing on a lower counter, barely out of view. She asked him to turn down the volume a little so the children wouldn't hear.

Oriana, Ferne, and Darius squabbled over who would be first to order from the interface at the table until she made them stop. She told them she would order the worst-tasting breakfast on the menu if they didn't behave.

She rolled her eyes at Bryce, reflecting that, for children who had been brought up by a cruel monster, they sometimes showed little sign of it. She guessed that Ma must have shielded them from Stefan's nastiness much of the time.

Bryce was wearing an amused expression.

"What?" Carina asked. "Is something funny?"

"You're pretty young to be a mom."

"Huh. I didn't get a lot of choice about it."

"Well, you're doing a great job, especially considering it was thrust upon you."

She glanced at the twins and Darius, who had begun to argue again—this time about what the others were ordering—though more quietly. They seemed distracted enough to not be listening.

"Honestly, though it's hard," she said, "I couldn't be happier. I didn't have anyone I could be open with about being a mage until I met this little gang. It's isolating to be always keeping back a part of yourself from everyone you know. For a long while, I thought I was used to it. But then when I met Darius and I discovered there was perhaps an entire family of mages I could meet, I was so excited.... I realized I'd been sad, deep down, for a long time." She drew breath, a feeling of panic rising in her. Although she knew its cause—her words to Bryce were probably the most frank she'd ever been about her feelings to anyone, ever—that didn't dampen her visceral reaction.

"Anyway," she went on, quickly steering away from dwelling on her emotions, "now I only need to get Parthenia back. Then we can all be together. I just haven't figured out how yet."

Perhaps sensing her discomfort, he also focused on the new topic. "What happened when you went to the Dirksen estate?"

She filled him in, finishing with, "Part of the problem is that in any plan I think up, Castiel is an unknown. If we end up Casting directly at each other, it's hard to be sure I can defeat him. I got some sense of his power last night and at the time I thought I would probably be stronger than him if it were put to the test, but I wouldn't like to bet on it."

"What if you had the others helping you?"

She shook her head emphatically. "I'm not taking them with me. It's too risky."

An ancient servitor trundled up to the table, its shelves bearing breakfast dishes. She lifted the plates out and slid them across to the children, who had already forgotten what they ordered. Three dishes were passed back due to their being apparently unfit for human consumption. Bryce picked up some kind of toasted vegetable, nibbled on it, and announced it was the most delicious thing he'd ever tasted.

"Wait," Ferne said, "I remember I ordered that."

"It's mine now," Bryce retorted. "You said you didn't want it."

"But I changed my mind."

"Oh, okay. Here you go then." Bryce pushed the plate back.

She grinned. "How come you're so good at this?"

"I'm the eldest of a similar brood."

"Well, don't do any more of that. I'm hungry, and from the look of it there aren't going to be any leftovers."

As everyone ate, she tried to think up a plan for extracting Parthenia from the Dirksen estate. If it had only been non-mages she was facing, she didn't think she would have had too many problems. Casting gave her an edge in most situations. But going up against another mage brought up the possibility of an entirely different set of scenarios. Castiel's time spent witnessing Ma's lessons on Casting with his siblings probably meant he knew just about everything she could do. He would be able to think up defenses and counterattacks to defeat her.

Darius was fidgeting vigorously in his seat.

"Is something wrong?" she asked.

"I need to go to the bathroom."

She slid across the bench and stood up to let him out. As she sat down again, Darius said, "I know how we can get Parthenia back."

"Really?" Carina said, wondering if her little brother could read her thoughts. "How?"

"We fly in on Reyes' star racer and grab her. Then we fly away again."

"That's a good idea, Darius, but we can't borrow Reyes' star racer. He isn't our friend anymore."

"Oh, good," Darius said. "I never liked him. I didn't like the feeling he gave me."

"You didn't? Why didn't you tell me?"

"I don't know. You didn't ask."

"Uh.... Next time you get that feeling about someone, Darius, let me know, okay?"

"Okay." The little boy skipped off to the restroom at the back of the diner.

"What was that about?" Bryce asked.

"Darius is a special kind of mage, I think. Ma suspected it too. He picks up on people's emotions very strongly."

"So he knew there was something off about the Dirksen guy?"

"Yeah, I think he did. I wish I'd thought to ask him."

"Shame he didn't tell you."

"It probably wouldn't have made a lot of difference. I would have gone to get Parthenia anyway, thinking I could easily Transport us both out of there, no matter what trap the Dirksen woman had laid for me. I didn't know Castiel was waiting."

"I was wondering," Bryce said, "if Castiel can Cast, why didn't he just put you in a locked room the minute he saw you?"

"Because I had elixir with me and I would have Cast my way out again. He needed to get the elixir off me first. Besides, I think he's playing a longer game. He wants all of us, not only me and Parthenia. Then he can play at being the head of a mage family, just like his dad. Maybe he's hoping I'll bring everyone along next time."

Darius returned and she moved again to let him back into his seat.

"Did you figure out how we're going to get Parthenia?" he asked.

"Not yet."

"I wish we had a star racer. Then it would be easy."

She didn't think that rescuing their sister was going to be easy at all, star racer or not. But Darius' suggestion had given her an idea. Maybe she'd been focusing too heavily on Castiel's mage power and not enough on what he couldn't do. Her brother had no military experience, and Langley and the other Dirksens wouldn't suspect she might try to extract her sister with brute force. An armed attack would take them by surprise. But how could she buy weapons?

"What's wrong?" Darius asked.

"I thought I had an idea but I realized it won't work. It would cost a lot of money that we don't have."

"We could work for it," said Bryce. "Or maybe I could ask my parents for some."

"Both of those would take too long. We have to get Parthenia out soon. If we wait weeks or months they might move her somewhere else, even offplanet. My plan would require a lot of cash and we would need it fast, like in the next few days."

Her eyes widened and she sat up straight.

"You thought of an idea," Darius exclaimed. He clapped his hands. "Yay! We're going to get Parthenia."

THIRTY-SEVEN

The Mech Battle company secretary didn't take Carina seriously. The woman looked her up and down before saying, "Sorry, we're all booked up for the next few months. Come back later."

"I'm an ex-merc," Carina said. "I've used mechs before."

"Sorry, that wouldn't make us any less booked up even if I believed you."

"Please. Give me a chance. I would put on a really good show."

"Look, I'm trying to do you a favor. Find another way to earn a fast buck, okay? Because if you go in that pit, you aren't coming out alive."

As she spoke a door behind her slid open and a heavily muscled, very hairy man walked out into the lobby.

"Mech fighting is for people like this great lunk," the secretary said. "It isn't for young women."

The man grinned at being called a 'lunk.' "Another idiot kid who wants to fight?" he asked the secretary, not making eye contact with Carina.

"Yeah," she replied. "You finished for the day?"

"Yep. Off to get this scar taken out." He showed the woman a broad, angry, fresh scar running from his shoulder down his back. "I like to leave them a while to impress the girls, but this one's a pain in the ass. Restricts movement in my arm."

"Call that a scar?" Carina asked. "That's nothing. Take a look at these." She turned and lifted her top over her back. During her time as a merc she'd gotten into plenty of scrapes where the cheap armor provided by the company hadn't been adequate protection. Shipboard medical facilities didn't cover scar removal and Carina never wanted to go to splicers planetside. She guessed that mage abilities were in her genetic code and she didn't want anyone getting their hands on hers if she could help it.

From the silence behind her, she guessed that the secretary and the lunk were suitably impressed. She lowered her top and turned to face them. "What do you say?" she asked.

The woman glanced at the Mech Battle fighter, whose eyebrows were raised. She pointed toward an old cargo mech standing in the corner of the room. "If you can operate that, I'll put your name down. Don't get your hopes up too much though. The boss has the final say."

Carina went over to the ancient machine. It was even older than the outdated models she'd worked with during her time on her company's ship, *Duchess*. Stepping backward and upward into the mech's center, she sought out the feet and hand controls. The front shield lowered automatically, also giving her access to the eye-tracking controls. She was locked in and ready to go.

She walked the mech forward. Its response time was slow, each leg moving as much as a quarter second after she activated it. She hoped the models they used for fighting weren't similarly sluggish.

Odd mechanical parts were piled in the middle of the floor.

She was supposed to demonstrate she could pick them up and manipulate them, but she needed to do something much showier and more memorable if she were to be picked to fight.

She walked the mech past the pile and approached the secretary's desk, the hiss, clunk, hiss, clunk of the mech's legs loud in her ears. The secretary looked alarmed. "No, no, no," she exclaimed. "Go back there. Move those things around."

Carina continued on her original track. The secretary jumped up and backed against the wall. But it wasn't her she wanted.

The lunk was standing behind the desk, his hands on his hips, smiling broadly. Carina guessed he must be impressed. She was about to impress him further. She reached forward with the mech's pincers. At the last second, the man realized what she was about to do and he tried to jump out of the way. He was too late.

She grabbed him around his biceps. She held him firmly enough that he wouldn't slip but delicately enough not to hurt him. When she had a good grip on his biceps, she used the mech's second set of pincers to grab his thighs.

"Whoaaaaa," the lunk exclaimed, chuckling. "Take it easy, girl."

She lifted him up, then turned him horizontal so he was parallel with the ceiling.

"Oh my stars," the secretary wailed. "Put him down!"

Carina spun the man around once. As he was roaring with laughter, she spun him around a second time. Then she lowered him to his previous position. As soon as she'd released him, he doubled over, slapping the desk and laughing too hard to speak. Carina walked the mech back to the wall and climbed out of it.

The secretary had been crouching while all this had been going on. She stood and straightened her clothes. "Well, that was quite the demonstration," she said as she returned to her desk. "You didn't need to go quite that far. I would have put your name down anyway." She opened her interface. "What is it?"

"Tamira... Lan."

"Can I see your ID?"

"Oh. I don't have any."

"Ah," said the secretary. "That could be a problem."

"Give her a chance," said the lunk. "You know half the IDs you see in here are fake. The boss will love her."

"Hmm... Okay, Tamira—"

"Call me Tammy."

"Tammy. The owner will be here at five, a couple of hours before the show starts. If you come back then, perhaps he'll give you a shot."

"Tonight?" Carina asked.

"No. Definitely not tonight. But he might find you something within the next few days."

Her disappointment must have shown.

"It's the best I can do," said the secretary. "Take it or leave it."

Without a large sum of money, her plan to attack the Dirksen estate military-style would never work. She needed a hover vessel, weapons, and ammunition at the very least. Ideally, she would like smoke grenades and other accessories that would make the rescue attempt easier. Winning a Mech Battle was the only way she knew that she could obtain the necessary funds quickly.

She hoped a few days wouldn't make too much of a difference to Parthenia, and that Langley wouldn't move her sister someplace else. Then it occurred to her that the waiting time would allow her and Bryce to earn more money, which they could then bet on her winning her fight.

Of course, there was the small detail of her winning to consider. That wasn't guaranteed at all. She'd never actually fought in any mech, let alone the monsters used for the Mech

Battles. But what the secretary offered was better than any alternative she knew. "I'll take it. I'll be back later."

Bryce was waiting for her outside. "They turned you down, right?"

"What? Of course not. They were practically begging me to fight, and tonight. I had to put them off for a few days. We need to earn some money and make some arrangements."

They walked down the long road through the lot that led into the city. The last time she had walked this road she hadn't thought she would ever be back, and least of all that she would be fighting in a Mech Battle.

"They turned you down at first, though," Bryce said, "didn't they?"

"Yeah. I had to show off a bit to persuade them."

"I thought so. Where to next?"

"Wait a minute." She took out a flask of elixir, sipped a little, and then Sent to Oriana. After checking the children were okay in their hotel room, she said, "We have to see about those arrangements."

THIRTY-EIGHT

Langley Dirksen had given Parthenia an exquisite dress to wear to the soiree. Somehow the woman had known exactly the most flattering colors, style, and fitting. Though Parthenia felt embarrassed to admit it as she gazed at herself in a mirror, she had never looked so beautiful. Mixed in with her embarrassment was a large portion of guilt.

She shouldn't have agreed to meet Langley Dirksen's relations, friends, and business associates at the informal party. She felt sure that Carina wouldn't have agreed to it in her position. Yet Parthenia had feared what might happen if she said no. When Langley had asked her, she had noticed the woman's expression turn rigid as she waited for an answer, then relax when she had reluctantly said yes.

She'd only acquiesced because she was worried what Castiel might do to her if she didn't, or—even worse—what he might do to Nahla. Her brother had already caught on that she was frightened he would hurt her little sister and, like his father before him, he wouldn't be slow to exploit the fact. Castiel had been watching from the corner of the room when Langley

Dirksen had made her request and he'd smiled when Parthenia nodded.

A familiar feeling of suffocation was sinking over her. Though it was only her second day in the mansion, she was beginning to feel very much at home. So many things contributed to the sensation: luxurious surroundings, servants, expensive, perfectly cooked meals and polite, well-mannered behavior expected at all times. Most influential of all to her, however, was Castiel's presence. Like a brooding malevolence, he seemed to be around her wherever she went, watching and judging, ready to pounce when she stepped out of line. Just like their father.

She hated how she was so used to the environment that it felt comfortable. She didn't know how she could ever break out of it. She didn't dare to try. Perhaps she didn't want to try. If she failed in her attempt she might lose all hope.

Don't give up hope, Carina had said. But she hadn't said when she would be back, or how she would help her escape. A constant guard meant that Carina couldn't Transport in and Transport out with her. And the Dirksen estate was probably heavily defended. What chance did Carina stand against the might of the Dirksens? She was only one person and their siblings were too young to be of much help.

On the other hand, Carina had managed to escape from the Sherrerrs, Parthenia had to admit. If her sister could do that, maybe she could defeat the Dirksens too. She would try not to give up hope.

In the meantime, she would go along with whatever Langley Dirksen wanted. It would keep Castiel happy and hopefully prevent him from hurting Nahla as a coercion tactic. It shouldn't be too hard. All her life, Parthenia had been wearing pretty dresses and smiling nicely to keep everyone happy. Another short period of the same wouldn't hurt.

———

When she arrived at the party downstairs, Langley Dirksen's guests all turned to look at her. They seemed apprehensive, almost afraid of what she might do or say. She could feel herself blush in response to all the attention. She hovered in the doorway, tempted to turn around and go back to her suite.

"Come in, dear," Langley called from across the room. She was sitting with a group of women who all wore fantastical hairstyles. Langley rose and swept across the room to take her arm. "You look *stunning*," she whispered in her ear as she guided her through the groups of partygoers, who were returning to their conversations now she had made her entrance.

She experienced the same guilty thrill she'd felt when she'd looked at herself in the mirror in her bedroom. Her feelings were in turmoil. Her younger mage sisters and brothers were struggling to survive, even if Carina had found them as she hoped. Yet here she was, wearing beautiful clothes and going to parties. It wasn't what she'd chosen, yet she hadn't refused to participate either.

She caught sight of a pair of dark eyes through the crowd and inwardly flinched. Castiel was here, watching her. He was wearing a suit and looking much older than his years. He gave her a wink and turned away to speak to someone in his group. It was as though he knew exactly how she felt and the knowledge of her discomfort and inner conflict pleased him. She wondered if Castiel was like Darius: able to pick up on the emotions of those around him, no matter how hard they tried to hide them.

The women in Langley's group were gazing at her as Langley brought her over. Like Langley, they all had a slightly greedy look, though none displayed even an ounce of extra fat. They had all probably been at a splicer's today, having their bodies refined to perfection for the party.

"Everyone," said Langley, "this is Parthenia, the very special young woman I was telling you about."

"Lovely to meet you, Parthenia," said a woman whose hair rose up from her head in a perfect spiral. "Effy, move along, dear," she said to another woman sitting on the sofa. "Make room for Parthenia."

Effy shifted across the sofa, creating space for one more person. Parthenia sank down, a sudden desire to escape overwhelming her. She wanted to sink right into the furniture and away from these predatory women. The spiral-haired woman handed her a bowl containing iced treats. The bowl itself was also icy, refrigerated by the table it had been sitting on.

"Try one," the woman said. "They're delicious." She was staring at her intensely, almost angrily, though Parthenia couldn't figure out why. It was the first time they'd met. She took a treat and ate it, grateful that it melted and slipped down her throat easily. Her mouth was as dry as a bone.

"I have very big plans in store for Parthenia," Langley said. "Very big. We're going to work closely together, aren't we, my dear? I imagine she'll become like a daughter to me."

Parthenia coughed.

"How exciting," Effy said. "Parthenia, I heard you only just arrived on Ostillon. What do you think of the place so far?"

"Oh, it seems nice." It was all she could think to say. Most of her time on Ostillon had been spent running and hiding. It wasn't like she'd taken a tour of the place.

"I love it here," Effy enthused, continuing as if she hadn't heard what Parthenia had said. "It's so quaint! So many ancient customs are still alive. Like hunting. Have any of you been hunting?" she asked the group generally.

The spiral-haired woman rolled her eyes. "We've all been hunting, as you know perfectly well. Personally, I didn't care for it. Riding those animals—what are they called? Horses, I believe —it left me unable to even walk. I had to have deep muscle therapy from my splicer to feel normal again.”

“Mmm… Deep muscle therapy from your splicer,” said a dark-haired woman who hadn’t spoken before. “Now that’s something I wouldn’t say no to.”

“Er, excuse me,” Langley said. “We have a young lady present, don’t forget.”

“Oh don’t be silly,” the dark-haired woman said, “I’m sure she knows a thing or two about what I mean.”

Parthenia sank deeper into her seat.

“Mother,” a voice said.

She looked up to see a lanky young man standing to one side of the group of women. Her chest tightened as she recognized him. He’d been in her suite the previous night when Carina had tried to rescue her.

“Reyes,” Langley said. “I’m so glad you’ve come down to join us this time.”

“As Parthenia’s here, I thought I should,” Reyes replied. “She’ll get bored talking to all you old folk.”

This brought cries of outrage from the women. “Huh, *old*,” Effy huffed.

“He’s just teasing you,” said Langley. “But he has a point. Reyes, why don’t you take Parthenia for a walk? It’s getting stuffy in here and, yes, we old folk are very boring.”

Reyes held out his hand to Parthenia and she felt obliged to take it. He helped her up then led her to the open double doors at the back of the room.

Outside, the air was cool and refreshing. She had been riddled with tension but she felt some of it slip away, despite the fact that Langley’s son had tried to grab Carina before she escaped.

"You were upstairs in my room last night," Parthenia said. "My sister seemed to know you."

"Yeah, I spent some time with Carina over the last few days. She's a cool person but she's misguided."

"How is she misguided?"

"She only sees the bad in everything. Mother tried to persuade her to help the Dirksen cause but she wouldn't. I tried to point out that what we're doing is for the good over the long term. But Carina was too short-sighted to see it."

"Are the Dirksens doing things for the good?" She'd never really understood what it was that the Sherrerrs did. All she'd known about were the meetings Father had taken her to, when he'd given her detailed instructions on what he wanted her to do. Beyond that, Sherrerr business was a mystery to her.

"Absolutely. We've made enormous improvements to Ostillon since arriving here. It was a backward place before. Really primitive. But now it's thriving." He turned to her. "That's the kind of thing you'd be helping us do if you worked with us."

Thirty-Nine

Carina had been working for the labor agency for three days and she still hadn't seen Asha. No one could tell her why the woman hadn't turned up for work. At first, she hadn't been too worried. She wanted to work until the boss at the Mech Battle company arranged a fight for her so she could earn money to bet on herself. But she also had good reasons for wanting to reconnect with Asha.

She had expected to meet a cool reception at the agency because Asha had told her she would pull strings so Carina couldn't work there. But the agency receptionist barely seemed to remember her.

At the end of her third day of work, Carina decided that if she couldn't see Asha there, she would just have to go to her apartment, even if that did mean facing the vile Cavin. She had only been to Asha's home once. It was deep within the warren of cheap, rundown blocks in the heart of the city. She lost her way several times before finally finding the street too narrow for hover vehicles. After she passed the noodle soup shop with its child server, she knew she was in the right place.

She pressed the security panel next to Asha's door three or four times and was on the verge of leaving when the door opened a crack.

"Tammy?"

"Asha, I... What happened to you?"

Though Asha was looking out through a narrow space, it was easy to see her face was purple with bruises.

"Oh, I had an accident."

Carina's heart sank. "Let me guess. Your face had an accidental encounter with Cavin's fist. Where is he? Is he here?"

"He's here, but he's asleep."

"Let me in. I want to speak with him."

"No, I don't want that. I can figure this out by myself."

"You know what?" said Carina. "You're right. I'd love nothing more than to come in there and bash Cavin's brains out for you, but I know that wouldn't do any good. You *do* need to figure this out by yourself. But I really want to speak to him. I need him for something."

"Oh, okay. I guess you can come in then."

Inside Asha's apartment everything was in disarray. It looked as if a major fight had taken place, or maybe the mess had only resulted from Asha trying to escape her no-good boyfriend. Asha hadn't been in to work because she was too beat up or perhaps because Cavin had decided to prevent her. If the latter were the case, as soon as they ran out of money the ban on Asha working would be lifted. The idea of Cavin himself working was likely unthinkable to either of them. Carina had known many similar couples and families in the slum settlement where she'd grown up.

Cavin looked like part of the general mess. He was lying on the sofa, one leg and one arm hanging down, snoring. It was an unusual time of day for a nap. She wondered if he was drugged up. If he was that would make him difficult to talk to, but on the other hand, it would mean she'd come to the right person.

She pulled the sofa out from the wall. Cavin didn't stir. She went around the back and lifted up the sofa, tipping him onto the floor. She could have just pulled him off but she didn't want to get her hands dirty.

"Arghhh," he exclaimed, waking up. "Asha, what the hell are you.... Oh, it's you."

Carina was standing behind the sofa. "I need weapons and a fast hover vehicle. Something like a star racer but a little bigger."

He wiped drool from his mouth. "Yeah, okay. So what does that have to do with me?"

"You know someone who can get them for me."

"Huh. No, I don't," Cavin replied, sitting up and rubbing his messy hair.

"Then you know someone who knows someone."

"What if I do? Why should I help you? My arm still hurts, you know."

"Because I'll pay you a—small—percentage of the cost."

He looked as though his ears had pricked up. But then he said, "Pay me with what? You don't have that kind of money or you wouldn't have been working with Asha."

"I think she might," Asha said. She'd been standing in the corner watching the interaction between Carina and her boyfriend. She walked over to him and handed him their interface. Carina could see the screen, which displayed a Mech Battle advertisement. To her dismay, she saw herself being touted as a new challenger for the fight taking place tomorrow night.

When the boss had agreed to let her take part, he'd made her stand with legs apart and pressing her fists to her hips while he took photographs. She had thought they were just publicity images to be displayed in the stadium, not across the planetary networks. She'd been stupid, she now realized. The only saving grace was that the manager had given her a mask to wear for *a sense of mystery*. Her stage name would be Dark Avenger and she would be fighting on behalf of Pyreco.

Although her face wasn't visible in the advertisement anyone who knew her would guess it was her—anyone including Castiel, Langley, and Reyes. And the latter two had a love of the Mech Battles. They were bound to see her, and then they would know exactly where she would be tomorrow night. But there was nothing she could do about it. She had to go ahead with her plan or she would never be able to rescue Parthenia.

Cavin was looking from the screen to her and back again. "You're right, Asha. It is her. And look at the odds!"

Betting on the fight had already started. As an unknown newcomer, the bookies were offering odds of twenty to one for her to win her first battle and a hundred to one if she won the tournament.

Cavin said, "So this is where you're planning on getting your money? Ha! You and every other idiot before you. You'll be lucky if you come out of it intact."

"That isn't your call. I only need you to put me in touch with someone who has the stuff I want. Look, I'll pay you even if I don't make a deal, okay?"

Asha's boyfriend fingered his stubble. "All right. But you pay me up front."

"No. After the fight. I'm betting everything I have on myself."

"No way. You'll lose and then you won't have anything."

"I'm not going to lose."

"Of course you are. What do you know about fighting?"

"More than you think. Did you say your arm still hurt?"

Cavin rubbed the aforementioned arm. He waved dismissively and sat down. "Okay. Come back later tonight. Give me three hours to set something up. I'll try, but I'm not promising anything. And these people are gonna say no anyway. Then I'll be in trouble for wasting their time. So you better come through with the cash."

"She will, hon," said Asha. "I can get her some work. She'll pay you back." She gave Carina a tiny apologetic smile.

Carina sighed.

FORTY

When Carina returned to Asha and Cavin's apartment later that night, Cavin directed her to another spot where she was to meet the people who could supply her with what she needed. After some bickering over how much and when she should pay Cavin for his service, she set out again. It was already late, and she was grateful that Bryce was around to look after the twins and Darius while she was gone.

Cavin had told her to go to the rooftop of a derelict apartment block a couple of streets away and wait there. When she arrived at the building, she saw that although signs were posted stating the place was condemned and dangerous to enter, squatters had moved in. The low beams of portable lamps and flickers of firelight shone from the windows, occasionally dimming as figures passed across the sources of light.

Carina wasn't afraid of people who lived like this, mostly due to the fact that she had once been in a similar situation herself, but she wished she had a weapon of some kind. If anyone threatened her, flashing a weapon would quickly dissuade them from further action. She didn't want to waste time fighting. It might make her late for her appointment. But she had no weapon, only a flask of elixir.

She passed through the doorless entrance. The elevators were not only not working, they were absent. The open doors revealed dark, gaping shafts. She went to the stairs and began to climb. On her way up, she sidestepped piles of trash and jumped over prone bodies that she hoped were only sleeping. She was reminded of the new block she and Asha had helped to clean before the decorators arrived. This place was quite the contrast.

When she reached the top, she found the fire door to the roof was swinging off one broken hinge. She tugged at it until it fully broke away, then laid it flat on the rooftop. If she needed to leave the impending meeting fast, she didn't want to be struggling to get past the remains of a door.

The rooftop was empty. No exact time had been set for the meeting, so Carina was forced to wait and hope the dealers in illegal arms would actually turn up. She was entirely unknown to them and had no ready cash, so their main incentive would probably be curiosity.

She went to the edge and gazed down to the ground about twenty-five stories below. If her prospective associates decided to drop her off the roof, she doubted she would be able to Cast Transport before she hit the ground. And if she did manage it, would her velocity continue with her to the new location? She didn't know and she didn't want to find out.

The city was quietening down, though the spaceport in the distance remained busy with the fast-moving lights of shuttles taking off and landing. As she watched the brilliantly colored spots, she realized that one—no, two—were heading in her direction. She watched them for several moments to make sure she was correct, and then ran over to the stairwell entrance and stood behind it to avoid being baked in the heat of the shuttles landing.

Sounds of engine noise grew louder while she waited. The noise grew so loud she had to cover her ears, and then the engines cut out. When she heard the shuttle doors opening, she stepped from her refuge, slowly and cautiously. Spooking the kind of people she was meeting was never wise.

Only one person seemed to be in charge, she was relieved to see. The woman sauntered forward in front of her subordinates: two males and a female. All wore floor-length coats made of some kind of animal skin. Its patterning was intricate and beautiful, though it would have looked better on the animals. The boss and her lackeys were also heavily jeweled. They wore tight gem-studded collars of a subtly glowing metal and hand ornaments that could double as knuckledusters.

Cavin did indeed know people who knew people. Carina swallowed, aware of how comparatively unimpressive she looked.

The boss seemed to think so too, from the way she was looking her up and down, the expression on her face souring. Cavin had probably been forced to talk Carina up as a prospective business associate before the black market weapons trader would agree to meet her. Now the woman was experiencing a considerable letdown.

Deciding it would be better not to give her time to conclude she had nothing to gain from the meeting, Carina opened the bargaining process without preamble. She stated her laundry list of proposed purchases, which included as many weapons and explosive devices as she and Bryce could carry as well as a vehicle that would seat six. "I'd prefer space-ready, but a fast hover vehicle would do if that's all you can manage."

The boss hadn't spoken a word while she talked. Silence fell, and after a moment the woman looked over her shoulder at the others and gave a slight shake of her head. She turned to leave.

"I can pay a lot," Carina blurted. She fingered the flask of elixir in her pocket.

The woman faced her again. "That's what I was waiting to hear. How much?"

When Carina named a figure, the woman laughed. Then she stopped and said, "You are joking, right?"

"I can go higher. What would you say is a fair price?"

"Four times what you said. That might be a good place to start for the weapons. It'll be more for the vehicle. And I want half up front."

The deal was impossible for her to fulfill. Winning the tournament and the bets she placed on herself would only give her half of what the woman wanted. "I'm not sure. I have to figure out if I'll have enough."

"I'll take less if you pay it all now."

That would have been an incredibly stupid thing to do. If Carina gave over any money she would be certain to never see the woman again. She seemed to think she was an idiot.

"I need time to think about it."

"One minute."

"I'm going to take a drink," said Carina, knowing that pulling something out of her pocket suddenly might elicit an undesirable, deadly response from the lackeys. As she'd predicted, everyone tensed up.

"Wait," said the boss. She beckoned one of her subordinates and nodded toward her. The man walked up to Carina and patted her over. He quickly found the elixir flask and pulled it out. He opened it, sniffed the contents, and wrinkled his nose.

"Just some weird tea," he said to his boss, pushing the flask into her hands before returning to his side of the divide.

Not hearing any further objections, she swallowed a mouthful of elixir. She returned the flask to her pocket, and then rubbed her forehead as if thinking. While her hand covered her face, she closed her eyes. It was a struggle to Cast Enthrall while under pressure, knowing that all her plans and hopes rode on her Cast succeeding, but eventually she managed it.

She wasn't home free, however. She had only Enthralled the boss. She might have managed to affect more of those present but that would have diluted the Cast so it wasn't as long lasting. She needed the boss to be Enthralled for long enough to make the arrangements. Then she would be unlikely to back out, even if she couldn't remember why she had agreed to the deal.

"I can't pay it all now," Carina said, "or even part of it. In fact, I can only pay you half of what you want when I receive the goods, but I can…" She needed something that sounded at least a little convincing to the others or they would think their boss had gone mad. "I can work for you. Afterward."

The man who had searched her started sniggering.

"Okay," the woman said.

The man abruptly stopped laughing and stared at his boss. He then stared at his colleagues, who also seemed to not quite believe what they'd just heard. The man looked as though he wanted to say something, but he kept quiet.

"Thanks," Carina said. "I appreciate it." She explained where and when she wanted the weapons and vehicle, which would be after she'd won the tournament. If she won the tournament. If she didn't, she would have to lie very low indeed, assuming Castiel didn't kidnap her.

FORTY-ONE

"Come on," said Reyes. "You'll love it. I promise." He pushed the visor into Parthenia's hands.

She looked up into the young man's happy, eager face. Reyes had barely left her alone over the last few days, but Parthenia hadn't really minded. His nearly constant company meant that Castiel had little opportunity to be alone with her, and she was grateful for that, even if Reyes' attention was overwhelming at times.

"What do we have to do?" she asked. "I don't think I understand."

"Come outside and put on the visor. The game will make more sense to you then."

Parthenia stepped through the open doors that led to the lawn. It was a beautiful day, and not for the first time, she felt a little guilty about enjoying the luxury of beautiful surroundings and fine living while her siblings were probably scraping by somewhere. Although 'enjoying' was perhaps too strong a word to describe her feelings about her captivity. She was confused and conflicted. Langley and Reyes constantly talked to her about all the good she could do with her powers, but they had also accepted Castiel into their midst. He was cruel and vicious, and Parthenia couldn't understand why they tolerated him.

"Put it on," Reyes urged.

She pushed the band down over her head and lowered the visor. The pleasant gardens were transformed into an industrial scene. She was inside an old, abandoned factory. Machines towered over her and high above a defective fan spun, its clunk-clunk-clunk echoing.

"There are code words for weapons," Reyes said. "You just have to think of them and they'll appear. You can think of shields too, but you have to bend down to the ground and raise them up or they won't appear. To see the list, think the word 'menu'."

"Oh, I understand now. Ferne and Oriana were asking for a system like this for ages, but Father would never allow it. So it's a kind of battle?"

"That's right. It's more fun with more people, but we can still have a good game with only two of us. We can go wherever we want on the estate. The game will expand into new areas. Do you get it now? Do you want to play?"

She wasn't very keen on the idea. She didn't much like games that involved fighting. She preferred games that tested your wits. But agreeing to play with Reyes would mean a few more hours that Castiel wouldn't bother her. "Okay. I'll need a little time to figure out what everything means."

"Sure. Let's walk down to the grove. We won't be disturbed there and it'll give you a while to read the menu."

As they walked away from the house Reyes took her hand, which felt a bit weird, but she didn't protest. She was disoriented by walking in the new setting and trying to read the list that hovered before her in mid-air. The game modified her sense of touch as well as sight and hearing. Although she knew she was walking on grass, her feet felt as though they were hitting hard, bare metal. Even her sense of smell was affected, she realized. The warm, fresh, clean air she'd been breathing a moment ago seemed to have been replaced by a dusty, acrid atmosphere.

She was beginning to find the list of weapons bewildering. Before she'd read half of it she'd forgotten what was at the top. And she didn't know what many of the words meant. "What's a lightknife?"

"It's an energy beam about as long as your forearm," Reyes replied. "Great for close fighting. If someone has you in a clinch, think *lightknife* and slip it between their ribs. It's high-powered, though, so you run out of energy if you use it for more than a few seconds. That's one for emergencies."

The idea of slipping anything between someone's ribs sounded horrific, even if it was only make-believe. She was beginning to regret her decision. She glanced at Reyes, wondering how he would take it if she backed out, and jumped as she caught sight of him. In the game, he was wearing heavy armor topped by a helmet shaped like a bird of prey.

He turned and said, "What do you think? Cool, huh?"

"Am I wearing something like that?"

"You're wearing the default costume. I customized mine myself. Switch to overview and you'll see."

She thought 'overview' and immediately saw the factory from a high viewpoint. Two figures were walking through it. One was Reyes, with his bird-like helmet, and the other was a woman wearing less heavy or stylized armor. She hardly recognized herself. Instead, she was reminded of Carina. Her heart felt heavy at the memory of her sister. She'd said she would come back but that had been days ago.

"Nearly there," Reyes said.

The game represented the trees of the grove on the Dirksen

estate as pillars that rose from the factory floor to the vaulted ceiling. Where the ground was uneven, the game had made the floor broken and pitted. They reached the pillars and walked in among them.

"Are you ready?" Reyes asked.

"Not really. I know some of the words, but I don't understand exactly what we're supposed to be doing."

"That's easy. We fight each other."

"That's all we have to do?"

"Basically. If you die, you lose. Then we start again. Shall we make it the best out of five? We can use the pillars as cover."

What had given Reyes the idea she would like the game, she had no clue. She had a feeling it was going to be over very quickly, after she'd been killed five times. "Hmm... Okay."

"We can start from opposite ends of the grove and work our way in. What do you say?"

"All right then. I'll wait here. You go to the other side."

"Okay." Reyes set off through the pillars.

She thought 'arm rocket' and the weapon appeared on her wrist while its specs rose in her vision. Was it the right choice? She didn't know, but it was one of the few names she could understand.

While she was trying to decide if she should pick something else, Reyes reappeared from between the pillars. She raised her arm rocket to fire at him, but he lifted his hands. "Don't shoot," he said, laughing.

When he'd returned to her side, he continued, "You don't much like this game, do you?"

"No, not really."

He lifted his helmet and reached out to remove hers too. Suddenly, she was back in the grounds of the Dirksen estate. The air smelled fresh and earthy under the trees and the dappled sunlight was warm.

Reyes Dirksen was smiling down at her. "Sorry. I should have been more considerate. I thought you might like to fight. All my friends love it. But you aren't like that, are you?"

"I guess not." She wanted to tell him more. She wanted to tell him how she'd been brought up to be ladylike, and that her father had despised the idea of any of his children doing anything as rough and uncouth as fighting. But revealing even that much about her past felt wrong.

"Shall we take a walk through the trees then, as we're here?" Reyes asked. Without waiting for an answer, he took Parthenia's hand and set off.

As she'd already denied him the chance to play his game she thought it would be churlish to protest, so she went with him, dangling her visor in her other hand.

"This is my favorite part of the estate," said Reyes. "When I was younger, if I wanted to hide from my mother I would come here. I would sometimes spend hours up a tree watching the servants searching for me."

She smiled. Though his mother was holding her captive, she couldn't help herself from empathizing with him. Their upbringings had been similar. Belonging to a powerful clan brought privilege and comfort—extravagance, in fact—but it had its downsides.

"It's so hot," Reyes said. "Let's stop here in the shade for a moment."

She wondered at this proposal. The day wasn't particularly hot. Reyes led her under overhanging boughs to the hushed, shaded interior around a tree's thick trunk.

"I wanted to tell you, Parthenia," said Reyes. "I'm so glad you came into my life. I like you a lot."

She stiffened. How should she respond? If she rejected him outright, what might he or his mother do? "Well, I like you too," she said. She was about to qualify her statement, but Reyes was too fast. He swooped in for a kiss. She swerved out of the way.

"What's wrong?" Reyes exclaimed. "You just said you liked me."

"Not like that."

"Why? Why not?" His fists were clenched and his face was turning red with anger.

She didn't know what to say. Whatever she said—*because your mother is holding me against my will and you think that's okay* was what sprang to mind—would only anger him further.

She pushed through the branches and out into the grove.

"Don't run away from me," Reyes shouted. "Come back here."

She ran through the grove, dodging trees, heading toward the mansion. It felt strange to be heading to her prison as a place of refuge. But what else could she do? She was trapped. When would Carina come?

FORTY-TWO

Carina lifted the giant main pincers of her mech and lowered them, testing them to their fullest extent. In response, a light appeared in her head-up display. Check. She tested the secondary pincers. Check. She turned in a circle, testing the maneuverability of the legs. Heavy thunks resounded and her visual displayed 360 degrees of the rear part of the stadium, where the mechs and their tech teams waited for the battle to start.

From her position, she couldn't see her opponent but she could hear him or her going through the same checks. It was as she'd thought when she'd seen her first Mech Battle: the operators put the machines through thorough checks before entering the arena. The moves they went through in front of the crowd before engaging in the fight were only for show.

This gave her an idea. If she acted on it she would never be allowed to participate in another battle but that didn't matter. She only needed to win this one. The black market arms dealer would be waiting for her after the show, ready with the weapons and everything else she needed, provided she had her prize money and winnings. Bryce had bet everything they'd earned over the previous days.

"Tammy," the mech manager's voice sounded over Carina's comm. "All set? Everything okay?"

"Yeah, everything's working fine."

"I can see that. I'm asking about you."

"Oh, er... I'm good. Looking forward to it."

The man—who went by his old stage name of The Stomper—had been nervous about giving her a chance, but excitement had overtaken his nerves as the betting on the battle mounted up. His ploy of selling her as a mysterious young newcomer had worked. Her masked image had been displayed on all the entertainment channels, and the manager had even scored an interview on a late-night show, where he'd made up a bunch of nonsense to intrigue the audience. She had caught a glimpse of the show before she'd turned it off in disgust. He'd told the interviewer it was a grudge match: that her family had once worked for Spearcorps, who were sponsoring the opposing team, but they'd all been laid off and were now on the streets.

"Man," The Stomper had said, "the Dark Avenger really hates Spearcorps. It makes her mad just to hear the name."

The audience most likely knew it was all untrue but they didn't care. Believing in the fantasy was fun and a distraction from the slow crippling of their autonomy and freedom by the Dirksens.

The resulting increased interest had worked in her favor. The stadium was sold out.

"Great," said The Stomper. "Try to last as long as you can out there. Give them a good show. If the fight's over in a couple of minutes we'll get complaints."

She rolled her eyes. "Thanks for the vote of confidence."

"I'm just saying..."

Ignoring him, she rechecked the mech's weapons. They were limited due to the safety factor. If a mech hurt an audience member, the company would receive more than complaints.

Each of her main pincers converted to massive hammers, and huge spikes could spring out from the mech's knees. Short-range grapples fired from the machine's midriff in case she wanted to hold the other mech at close quarters and her pincers were gone. She figured in that scenario she could hit it with her—the mech's —head. Her secondary pincers doubled as drills.

She had to give The Stomper some credit: the mech she was fighting in was one of the least beat up he had to choose from. Though the fact only emphasized his lack of faith in her.

An ear-piercing jangle sounded. One minute to go. The noise of the crowd permeated even through her solid surroundings. Somewhere out there, Castiel was probably waiting. Would he try to Transport her out from her mech the minute he saw her? It would be a difficult Cast, even for an experienced mage. She would barely be visible through the narrow slits in the control center, and Castiel would have to Cast at some distance.

Nevertheless, the possibility was her greatest danger, so with great misgiving she'd asked Bryce to bring the twins and Darius along to the battle. Without their help, she would never be able to Repulse Castiel's Casts. She would be too busy fighting. Her siblings would have their work cut out for them tonight, and they would need to remain hidden from Castiel, though he would know they were here somewhere.

"You're on in ten," The Stomper said. "Good luck, Tammy."

"Thanks."

She gripped the controls and focused. She had only one goal:

win five fights. She had to trust her siblings to do their work or she would find herself back on the Dirksen estate and Parthenia would remain captive.

The gigantic doors in front of her split down the middle and swung inward. A roar went up. Her display blinked and darkened in response to the brilliant lights shining from the pit. Across the stadium, she could see another set of doors opening and her opponent standing in shadow, light reflecting softly from dull metal.

The other mech took a step, beginning its walk into the stadium.

She waited.

"Go in now," said The Stomper.

She didn't reply.

"Move, Tammy."

The other mech was inside the pit and was beginning its performance of pretending to check its systems.

"Tammy," The Stomper yelled. "What the hell are you waiting for? Get in there!"

Watching the mech, she waited a little longer. The noise of the crowd was rapidly fading, degenerating to confused babbles.

The Stomper shouted, "If you don't move now, so help me I'll—"

She ran through the doors. "Ran" was a strong word to describe the lumbering gait of the giant mech from a standing start, but she pushed the machine to its extreme speed. She only had one chance and she had to get it right.

The other mech didn't even notice her coming. She slammed into it, knocking it off its feet and into the doors, which had only just closed. The mech bounced against the wall, splintering the rock-hard surface, and slid to the ground.

The crowd went crazy.

Disregarding the ear-splitting howls and whoops, she let her momentum carry her over to the prone mech. The Stomper was bellowing something but she ignored him too. After raising her pincers and simultaneously turning them into hammers, she brought them down with maximum force on the hip junctions of the opposing mech. They were perhaps the toughest parts but she had the perfect shot. If she damaged them, the mech wouldn't be able to move and the fight would be over.

But her opponent wasn't going to give up easily. Projectiles on thick metal ropes shot out and pierced her mech's midriff. The pointed end of one protruded into her cab. A damage report appeared in her display. She sent her secondary pincers to sever the ropes while she struck again at her opponent's hips. Her plan seemed to be working. The mech was trying to stand but its legs were moving oddly.

The secondary pincers couldn't cut the ropes. They couldn't even make a dent. It didn't matter. She brought her hammers down for a third time. The shock of the impact jolted her. She also registered a blow to her legs. The other mech was attacking her with its pincers.

She was convinced the third impact on the mech's hips had done the job. She backed up to move out of reach. She needed her mech to last her through four more battles. The ropes that attached her to the other mech held fast, however, and she found herself dragging it across the floor of the pit. Her mech's systems complained about the additional weight. Another blow struck her legs.

She didn't know what to do. She had no way to cut the ropes but if she didn't move out of range of the other mech hers would soon suffer a lot of damage. Why hadn't they called the fight? Her opponent was incapacitated. She'd clearly won.

She backed up some more. This time, the tension on the ropes tore them from their mooring on the opposing mech. The sudden release caused her to overbalance. Her machine tumbled down.

The horn sounded. The fight was finally called.

Four more to go.

Forty-Three

Parthenia hated the noise of the crowd and she wasn't remotely interested in Mech Battles. Two giant machines fighting each other wasn't a spectacle she relished. A sharp, pulsing headache was irritating her but other than that, she was utterly bored.

Castiel seemed to be finding something about her amusing. Every time he snuck a sidelong glance at her, he smirked. Her brother's enjoyment of her misery wasn't a new phenomenon by any means, but Parthenia suspected there was something else underlying his amusement. She refused to gratify him further by asking what he found funny, however, so she resigned herself to remaining in the dark.

He probably had a nasty plan to execute later on. She only hoped it wasn't going to be aimed at poor Nahla, who had suffered from his spite several times over the past few days. Castiel insisted on using her as a subject on which to practice his Casting skills. He Enthralled her to do stupid, embarrassing, and even dangerous things. When he'd made her walk around the entire estate naked, so that every servant, guard, and gardener saw her, even Langley had been appalled and asked him to stop.

This had resulted in a stand-off of a kind. Langley saw herself as the head of the household with the final say on everything that happened beneath her roof. It wasn't an unreasonable claim, or at least to everyone except Castiel. Langley had gently admonished him and suggested that, if he had to use a living person for his experiments, to choose one of the servants and not his own sister.

Castiel had been furious, though she suspected she was the only one who truly understood the depths of his anger. He'd mastered himself—that time. He'd stalked away, not responding to Langley at all. But Parthenia wondered what would happen the next time the two clashed. Langley Dirksen seemed to think that Casting was similar to performing magic tricks. She didn't understand what an immoral mage could do. She had no idea, for example, of the Split Cast that had killed Father.

Parthenia wondered if she should warn Langley but she doubted the woman would listen. She would only think she was trying to undermine Castiel in the hope that she might Cast and escape. And Reyes hadn't spoken to her since she'd rejected him in the grove, which was a good thing. He'd shown his true colors when he was angry that she wouldn't kiss him. Parthenia realized he'd been manipulating her all along. It would be extremely convenient for the Dirksens to have a mage in the family.

From the corner of her eye, she noticed Castiel sip from a bottle. He was Casting, and as far as she knew it was for the third or fourth time this evening, but why? She scanned the stadium. She couldn't see anything her brother might want to influence. Unless he was only trying to affect the outcome of the battle. That was possible. Langley was betting furiously.

A roar went up so loud Parthenia winced and covered her ears. Her head felt like it was going to burst. She wished she could have just a sip of elixir to Cast Heal on herself but Castiel would never allow it. He would think she wanted it to Transport herself far away, which of course she would.

The battle below was over. The winning mech was leaving the pit and techs were entering from the other side to remove the loser. The crowd was quietening as people began to leave their seats and move around during the interval.

"Well, well, well," Castiel said, "our half-sister's quite the fighter, isn't she?"

Through the pounding of her head, Parthenia took a moment to register what her brother had said. Even then, she didn't guess right away what he was referring to. "What do you mean?"

"Carina, you idiot," Castiel sneered. "How dumb are you? I can't believe you haven't noticed her image displayed all over the stadium. She just won that battle."

Her mouth fell open as she gazed up at the figure of a woman wearing a mask flashing on the display board. It *was* Carina. How had she missed it?

"Of course," Castiel continued, "she's a pretty good mage too, though not as good as me. When she's under my control I'll be sure to make use of all her talents."

Parthenia shot a look at her brother. Did his statement mean what it seemed to imply? Castiel's expression was neutral and far-gazing, lost in dreams of power and control. Parthenia imagined what would be the outcome if her brother tried to force himself on Carina. If he were lucky, he might leave the encounter intact. She sniggered.

Castiel heard. He spun to face her. "What's so funny?" he demanded. "You think you can get away with laughing at me? I'll... I'll...."

Langley placed a hand gently on his shoulder. She was sitting behind him. "It wouldn't be wise to do anything rash in front of all these people, Castiel. Please consider the Dirksen reputation."

He shrugged her off and scowled. After a moment, he leaned close to Parthenia and spoke into her ear. "That bitch might think she has a hold over me, but I'm only tolerating her until I find my feet. I'm going to rule the Dirksen clan, and after I've crushed the Sherrerrs into dust, I'm going to rule this entire sector. People complain about the two clans, but they don't know the meaning of suffering. They won't know what's hit them when I'm in charge. They'll look back on these days like they were paradise. So you better watch out, Parthenia. You better not laugh at me again. I won't forget it. I'll make you pay, and there won't be anyone who can stop me."

Castiel's words chilled her. Though she knew what her brother was capable of, hearing him state his intentions out loud was horrifying. And he could do it, she realized. He could do everything he wanted to because he was a mage.

The second battle was about to start. The doors the mechs entered through were opening. Castiel took a swig of elixir. She gasped. *That* was what he was doing! He was trying to Transport Carina out of her mech. Castiel closed his eyes. She wanted to do something, but what? If she knocked him to distract him, he would only ask Harmon to take her outside. She would have lost her chance. She had to do something effective and long-lasting.

As she dithered Castiel must have made his Cast, for he opened his eyes and muttered something that she couldn't hear over the noise of the crowd. The mechs below had entered into battle. He stood up and searched the stadium with his gaze, then he turned and spoke to Langley.

Her eyebrows lifted in response to his comment. She beckoned Harmon and told him the news, and he in turn spoke into his comm.

Though she loathed speaking to Castiel, Parthenia had a feeling that whatever it was he'd realized, it was pertinent information. She shouted over the crowd, "What is it Castiel? Has Carina left?"

"Ha! No. You guessed I was trying to Transport her? Well, you'll be delighted to hear our dear siblings are here somewhere. They've stupidly revealed themselves by attempting to Repulse my Casts. I thought I noticed something odd going on earlier. Now I'm convinced of it. So it looks as though I have all my little birds in one trap. Very convenient." He gave her a ghoulish smile.

She turned from him in disgust. She hated the thought of being related to him. More than that, she hated how powerless she felt. She couldn't bear the thought of all her sisters and brothers being under his control, and his plans for the future sounded monstrous. But what could she do? She was just one person and she couldn't even fight.

Below her, the mechs were battling hard. Carina seemed to be winning but Parthenia found it hard to tell. She wondered why her sister had decided to take part. It was very strange, especially since it had led to Castiel discovering her. And now it looked like the Dirksen thugs were roaming the crowds looking for their siblings too.

If Castiel succeeded in capturing their remaining family they would be back to a life of servitude—possibly a worse one than they'd endured under Father. Their Mother had been there to protect them to an extent, but Castiel had no one to moderate his behavior.

Parthenia watched Carina fight, wishing she was as strong and brave as her sister. Castiel sipped from his elixir again and closed his eyes. He was entirely unafraid of her, she realized. He was comfortably certain she would sit next to him passively and do nothing to stop him.

A mighty crash resounded below as the mechs collided. Then another crash sounded, though this one was more like thunder and it came from outside the stadium. After a short, confused pause, the crowd returned to their shouts and chanting.

Parthenia's heart was racing. The scenario of the future that was playing out in her mind terrified her. She couldn't let it happen. She just couldn't. Even if she didn't manage to save herself, she had to do something to save her brothers and sisters. She had to make a gesture, no matter how insignificant.

A deafening boom sounded and echoed through the stadium. Again, the noise hadn't come from the mechs. The crowd grew quieter as they tried to understand what was happening. Castiel was also puzzled. He peered around, his bottle of elixir in his hand.

She took her chance. She grabbed it. Castiel registered a moment of shock before trying to snatch it back. He was too late. She threw the bottle down so hard it smashed. The elixir soaked into the floor. Castiel looked up at her, white with rage.

She didn't care. She'd made her gesture. Now what else could she do?

FORTY-FOUR

The third battle of the evening was turning out to be Carina's hardest yet. It wasn't surprising. Her mech had taken considerable damage. The techs had done their best to patch up the machine over the interval but nearly half the display wasn't lit and neither of her secondary pincers were working. Also, the first mech she'd faced had pummeled one of her legs so much it didn't function properly and was slowing her down.

For close-quarters fighting, that didn't matter too much—it wasn't like she could run away from her opponent—but Carina needed as much of her mech as possible to be working if she were to survive to the final round.

One thing to be thankful for was that her mage siblings were doing a good job of deflecting Castiel's Casts. Though she could hardly see any of the crowd, Carina knew her brother had to be here. She hoped her brothers and sister would be able to keep up their efforts all night, and that Langley's thugs wouldn't find them. Bryce had assured her they would be hard to discover in the packed stadium, but that didn't stop her from worrying.

A pincer gripped her mech's head. *Damn.* She'd allowed herself to become distracted. Carina turned on the spot, twisting out of the grip, though the scraping and rending noises this caused were painful to her ears. Her remaining systems were still intact so the damage was probably surface-only.

When fighting, it paid to vary your technique. Her current opponent would have watched her previous battles in order to attempt to predict what she might do. Carina had already used up her one chance at surprising the opposition by foregoing custom and launching straight into an attack—a move The Stomper had severely admonished her for. He'd said she'd nearly forfeited the match, except the officials couldn't find anything in the rule book to say she couldn't do that.

In her second battle, she'd bypassed obvious moves once again. She hadn't even attempted to hit her opponent. Instead, she'd run straight into him, chest to chest, grappled him, and drilled into his knees with her transformed secondary pincers. That had been what had ruined the pincers, though it had won her the fight.

This time, she needed something new. While she was thinking, she smashed into her opponent. At the same time, a crash sounded outside that hadn't come from the collision. She was puzzled. She'd thought she'd heard loud noises in her previous fight—and they had to be exceptionally loud for her to hear them over everything else. She'd thought a massive thunderstorm was on its way, but the latest sound hadn't been thunder.

A bang exploded above her. Carina felt the shockwave in her bones. Her head-up display flashed and disappeared. Her mech had received a colossal blow to the head. The system might reboot and kick in again but for now she was working blind.

In one way, it was frustrating. In another, it was liberating. She had learned the ropes of hand-to-hand fighting long ago.

With her computer system out, her mech was just an extension of her.

She peered through the slit and spotted the looming shadow of her opponent, who was gearing up for another strike. She spun away on her good leg, turned 360 degrees, and flailed both her main pincers into her opponent's side. The other mech had missed her entirely when she moved and was raising itself again.

The concussion vibrated through her cabin, but she hadn't managed to hit hard enough to knock down her opponent. She would have to resort to a tactic she'd been hoping to save for the final battle. It was a desperate measure that would result in more damage to her mech but she couldn't think of anything else.

She activated the circular saw in her mech's head. At least, she hoped she activated it because her display wasn't telling her. Then she heard a satisfying buzz over the screams of the crowd. The onlookers clearly knew what she intended and loved the spectacle.

Carina drove into her opponent. She wouldn't be able to get a good swing at him this way, but she hoped to saw into his mech and mess up his systems so badly he couldn't operate. The opposing mech controller had two options: try to get away or also activate his saw.

The noise of buzzing and grinding redoubled. Her opponent had chosen the latter option, which was bad news but hopefully worse news for the other mech. She had a few seconds' head start. Now it was just a waiting game. She tried to pummel him as well, despite the constraints of the confined space.

A whistling sound pierced the air, quickly followed by the roar of an explosion. The excited screams of the crowd turned to shrieks of horror. Carina leaned forward to see out of the narrow view hole but all that was visible was the blank metal of the other mech. What was going on? That last thing she'd heard had sounded like—

"We're under attack! We're being attacked!"

It was the other mech operator shouting at her.

Of course! That was the source of the other explosions: the Sherrerrs had launched their takeover of Ostillon. A crackling fizz filled the stadium and light flared into her cabin. Wails and shouts were coming from the crowd. She could imagine the panic and rush to leave. She hoped Bryce and the kids weren't hurt and Bryce could get them all out safely. But what should she do?

Her saw was still operating and her opponent was yelling for her to turn it off. She tried but the saw didn't respond. "I can't," she called out. "My system's down. Nothing's working."

The other mech moved away. Without the counterpressure, her mech began to fall. She hit the ground face down and dangled in her safety straps. The saw in her mech's head continued to grind away.

She couldn't see a thing. All her viewing slits were coated in the dust her saw was throwing up in showers. The sounds from outside were a jumble of panicked voices punctuated by the bombardment of the Sherrerr forces. The techs who were responsible for her machine would be running for their lives. She was on her own.

She unfastened her straps one by one, gradually lowering herself to the front of her chamber, which was now the floor. She crawled up the side to the door and punched the exit button. Predictably, the door remained closed. It would run on the same system as the rest of the mech. If she'd been trapped in there after a fight, the techs would have their own way of opening it. Now, she didn't know how she was going to get out.

Carina began to search around in the near darkness. There had to be a manual release mechanism somewhere. The Stomper hadn't bothered to show her what to do in an emergency, but it didn't make any sense to leave the operator with no way of getting out by themselves.

Her fingers probed the bumpy surfaces. As she searched, the realization hit that her entire plan had fallen apart. She wouldn't win her prize or her bets, and the arms dealer wouldn't be waiting for her with the stuff she needed.

Parthenia would remain trapped on the Dirksen estate—only now she would be moved somewhere else, perhaps to another planet as the Dirksens fled Ostillon.

Dammit. Her heart ached for her sister. She couldn't bear the thought of her being held captive by Castiel, a clone of his father. With an entire galactic sector to search, how would she ever find her?

FORTY-FIVE

The stadium was in utter chaos. Parthenia had guessed her father's clan was attacking Ostillon. She was trying to fight against the flow of the crowd, but it was hopeless. Then she noticed the seating was nearly empty. Everyone was crowding into the aisles. She edged along a row and began climbing over the seats.

She had to reach Carina. Her sister's mech was down and disabled, and she was sure she hadn't seen her sister emerge from it. As she reached for a seat, her hand twinged with pain. She rubbed her knuckles, smiled, and continued on.

All around her the people surged and pushed, heading in the opposite direction. Another hissing, crackling projectile arrived, impacting close by the stadium. Whoever was attacking, they were intent on destroying the city. She had to help Carina out and get her away. The stadium had already received a glancing blow, destroying part of an outer wall. It was only a matter of time before the place would be razed to rubble.

Parthenia wished she could shout to her sister to reassure her that someone was coming but she would never be heard over the noise. There was also the chance that one of Langley's guards might notice her and recapture her. She hoped they would be fleeing the stadium too or helping Langley and Reyes to safety. Perhaps they were carrying Castiel out with them. She smiled again.

She'd reached the lowest tier of seating, at the very edge of the pit. Now she was here, however, she couldn't see any way down. The drop was too deep to jump. If she had elixir she could Transport in, but she had none. She ran around the edge. It was deserted except for jumbles of coats and other belongings left behind by the fleeing spectators.

There had to be a way into the pit. Why couldn't she find it? She noticed a dark, empty exit between the seats. Seeing no other option, she ran through and down the stairs at the end of the passage. The noises from outside grew fainter as she descended, following each turn of the stairs and ignoring the doors at each landing. The air became cool and moist. She was definitely heading into the depths of the stadium.

Finally, the stairs came to an end. She pushed open a set of double doors. She had reached the pit. Up close, the two mechs looked even more enormous than they had from above. The center of the standing one was open, its operator gone. The prone mech—Carina's—was still working. The saw in its head was gouging a deep trough in the sand and throwing up a cloud of dust.

She ran over to Carina's mech. She could barely make head or tail of the thing but she guessed Carina had to be somewhere in its center. The dust was choking her. She lifted her shirt over her nose and squinted to keep it out of her eyes. When she arrived at the belly of the mech, she banged on its side. "Carina! Can you hear me?" Her fist striking the metal made no sound, or at least nothing she could hear over the whine of the saw, the still-noisy crowd, and the regular explosions of air-to-ground fire.

"Carina," she shouted at the top of her voice before subsiding into a fit of coughing. Surely there had to be a way to see inside the mech? She wiped dust from her face and stepped closer to the spinning saw. A ridge ran up the side of the machine where a bank of dust had built up.

She pulled her sleeve over her hand and wiped the ridge clean. It was the edge of a narrow slit. She peered through it but she could only see darkness. She put her mouth to the slit. "Carina! Are you in there?"

Then she turned her head and placed her ear against the gap. Did she hear an answer? She thought so. She moved her head to call inside again, but she saw a pair of eyes looking out at her.

"Carina," she cried in happiness. Four fingers poked through the slit. Parthenia grabbed them. "How can I get you out?" she shouted.

Her sister's reply was faint. "I don't know. Can you see anything? Like a manual override?"

She couldn't even see the exit to the machine, let alone the mechanism to open it. She asked her sister where she should be looking. When she'd finally found the spot and cleared away the dust to search the area, she still couldn't find anything to open the hatch. She returned to the slit to tell Carina the bad news.

As she was walking around the giant machine, part of the stadium exploded. Debris began to rain down. Her ears were ringing. She put her arms over her head for protection and continued to return to Carina. She called to her sister through the gap. The four fingers reappeared and she grasped them. "I couldn't find it," she yelled, though her voice sounded faint. "I don't know how to get you out."

If Carina replied, she didn't hear her. She held on to her

sister's fingers and sank down to the ground. She wanted so much to help her but she didn't know what else to do. She couldn't get inside the machine or move it. The stadium was being steadily demolished and Carina was trapped. How could she save her sister?

As she held Carina's fingers, she rubbed away the tears that were mixing with dust on her face. She had finally stood up for herself when she'd gotten away from Castiel. But it wasn't enough. It didn't matter how brave she was if she couldn't help the people she loved.

————

Parthenia had resigned herself to staying with Carina no matter what happened. She couldn't leave her sister here to die trapped inside an ugly mechanical monster. When they'd been together on *Nightfall*, it would have been much easier for Carina to escape if she'd been alone, but she'd risked her life to take all her family with her—even Castiel, though he didn't appreciate it. She could never abandon her now.

Another explosion resounded. As she looked up to see what part of the stadium had been hit, she saw figures running out to her from one of the entrances to the pit. She cringed. So Langley had left behind some guards to find her. Parthenia had thought they must have all left.

But then she noticed through the dust and gloom that three of the figures were shorter than they should be. One of them was very short. Her heart nearly burst with joy.

"Darius," she yelled. She leapt up and ran to the little boy, scooping him into her arms. Oriana and Ferne grabbed her, jumping up and down with happiness.

"Wait," Darius said, struggling. "I have to get Carina out."

"Can you?" she asked as she put him down. "Have you got some elixir?"

The fourth figure walked up. She was shocked to see Carina's friend, Bryce.

"We've got some left, but not a lot," he said, handing a bottle to Darius. "Do your work, kid."

Clutching the bottle in his little hand, Darius ran over to the mech. He reached up to Carina's fingers. In another moment, their sister was out of the machine and standing next to him. As the two embraced, Parthenia burst into tears again. "I can't believe it. We finally did it. We're finally together again." As she spoke, however, she realized that wasn't exactly true.

"Come on," Carina shouted as she began to run.

Everyone sprinted with her to one of the sets of massive mech entrance doors. One of the doors remained ajar, and they slipped through it to the backstage area. The noise of the bombing faded somewhat. Carina led them through the workshop areas and offices until they emerged from the building into the parking lot.

The vehicles that remained were wrecked and in places the ground was cratered.

"We need to Transport somewhere," said Carina, "but I don't know where we'll be safe from the Sherrerr attack."

They jogged across the lot while they thought about what they should do.

"You should thank Darius," Bryce said to Parthenia. "All the time you were in the pit Dirksen guards were spotting you and coming in to get you. Darius Transported them away."

"His Casts are so powerful," Oriana broke in. "He's been moving them to the other side of the planet so they couldn't quickly return in a hover vehicle."

"He must have Transported about thirty of them," Ferne exclaimed.

"I was worried that Castiel would Cast you out of there when the bombardment started," Bryce said.

She laughed. "Well, he wouldn't have been able to for a while. I knocked him out!"

"You did what?" Bryce asked.

"I broke his elixir bottle, and then I punched him. Like this." She made a fist and swung forcefully into the air. "I really hurt my hand, but I don't care. It was fantastic. His eyes rolled back and he keeled over. He was out cold. And then, when I looked around, the bodyguard, Harmon, was gone, and everyone was distracted by the bombing, so I jumped over the edge of the box and into the crowd below."

"But what about when Castiel comes around?" Oriana asked. "Won't he be able to Locate you? He must have something you were in contact with."

"I don't think so. I made a point of washing everything I wore or used every night and I was careful to always clean out my hairbrush. He might think he has something he can use, but he doesn't."

"I know," said Carina, spinning around. "We should go to the forest. The Sherrerrs won't bother attacking that. They'll target inhabited areas and tactical sites."

"But wait," Parthenia said. "We're forgetting Nahla. We have to get her, Carina. We can't leave her there with that monster."

"You mean go back to Langley Dirksen's estate?" Carina looked troubled. "I feel sorry for Nahla too, but do you really think she wants to leave Castiel? She seems to adore him."

"Not any more. Not since he learned to Cast. He's been behaving terribly toward her. It reminds me of how Father used to treat Mother. I'm sure she hates him now. She's just too frightened to show it. We have to help her. Even if she isn't a mage she's still one of us."

"Parthenia," Carina said sadly. "I hear you. But it's too dangerous for any of us to go there. We would have to search to find her and someone would be sure to spot us."

"Not if we know exactly where she is," said Parthenia. She pulled out a handkerchief. "It's hers. She was using it the other day when she had a cold."

"Oh, er..." Carina wrinkled her nose and took the handkerchief, pinching it between her thumb and forefinger. "Okay. That could work. Let's Transport to the forest first."

Forty-Six

Carina appeared in a dark room. All she could hear was the sound of someone breathing, deeply and regularly, as if asleep. As her eyes became accustomed to the darkness, she realized with relief she was in the right place. She also realized that Castiel was an idiot. No one else was here except little Nahla, fast asleep in bed. Her brother hadn't imagined anyone would bother to take her from him. He probably thought everyone else held her in the same low regard as he did.

Langley's mansion didn't seem to have been attacked by the Sherrerrs yet, which was odd. If her suspicion that the woman she'd spotted was one of their spies, the Sherrerrs definitely knew exactly where the estate was and that a high-ranking Dirksen lived here. Well, it wasn't a puzzle she needed to figure out. She hoped to leave the Sherrerr/Dirksen struggle for power behind as soon as she could.

The elixir was down to its last dregs. After she Transported Nahla and herself out they would only have a little left. They would have to find a way to make some more, which might be challenging in a burnt forest. Never mind. Saving the little girl was absolutely worth it.

In two steps, she was beside her bed. Kneeling down, she took Nahla's hand where it lay on the blanket, then swallowed some elixir. She Cast.

They appeared in the forest. Nahla's eyes opened and she sat bolt upright in surprise.

"Yay! Carina's back," Darius yelled. "She got Nahla."

The children ran over to their sister and started making a fuss of her. They began to explain to the shocked girl where she was and what had happened.

"Wait," Carina said. "We have to check Nahla and Parthenia for tracers. Darius, here's the last of the elixir. I'm pretty sure you'll be able to sense them if they're there. Do you want to do it?"

Her brother took the bottle and set to work. After checking both his sisters for the devices he declared confidently that he'd found them. In a matter of moments, he had also removed them without causing any harm. Ferne set off to scatter the tracers over a wide area before the family moved on.

Relieved they were finally free of the Dirksens, Carina walked over to Bryce where he was leaning against the burned remains of a tree. He hugged her and wrapped his arms around her waist. She rested her head on his chest. She was exhausted. Three mech fights had tired her out and the emotional turmoil of the night's events had also drained her.

"It's strange how things turn out, isn't it?" Bryce said. "This wasn't the plan, but you ended up getting Parthenia back anyway, and now you have another member of the family with you."

"Yeah, I hope Parthenia's right about Nahla no longer having any loyalty to Castiel. If she has, she could easily betray us."

"I don't think she will. She's just a little girl."

"Darius is just a little boy, yet he saved me and Parthenia tonight, according to what you say."

"He did. He was amazing."

Carina watched her youngest brother chatting with Nahla, his head of thick, tousled hair bobbing around and his arms making expansive gestures. So much mage power in such a little body. She wondered what he would be capable of when he grew up.

"So, what now?" Bryce asked.

"We have to find a way to go offplanet. If the Sherrerrs' attack is successful and they find Castiel they'll be looking for us too. I want to get everyone as far from both the clans as I can." She was about to tell Bryce about her desire to find Earth when Parthenia walked up to them.

"Thank you for rescuing Nahla. You won't regret it. She's so happy to be away from him."

"I'm glad she's away from him too," Carina said. "I hope she recovers from his maltreatment."

"I think she will," said Parthenia. "We're all better since leaving the Sherrerrs, even though things have been so hard. But I wanted to ask you, what are we going to do now?"

"I was wondering the same," said Bryce.

"Because we have to do something to stop Castiel," Parthenia continued.

Carina made a noise of disgust. "Is he really any of our business any longer? Let the Dirksens have him, or the Sherrerrs, or whoever else wants him."

"But no one else can stop him but us," Parthenia protested. "You should have heard what he was telling me tonight. He plans on taking over the Dirksens and then the Sherrerrs and then whoever else might stand in his way until the entire sector is under his control. Can you imagine how things would be if a mage like Castiel were in charge?"

Carina wanted to disagree with her sister. She wanted nothing more to do with Castiel. But she knew exactly what Parthenia meant and she knew her sister was right. A heaviness settled over her heart as she realized her work wasn't over. She couldn't take her sisters and brothers and escape to somewhere safe. She would have to find a way to defeat the son of an evil father.

"Okay," she said. "I get it. We have to do something, but I don't know what. The truth is, I don't know what I'm dealing with in Castiel. I don't know why his mage abilities developed so late, the same as I don't know why Darius picks up on everyone's emotions and can throw thirty grown men and women halfway around a planet without breaking a sweat."

"But I thought you knew all about mages," Parthenia said.

"Not at all. My grandmother died when I was quite young. Though she might have told me a lot I must have forgotten half of it. I don't even know how Ma and Dad managed to meet when mages are so isolated and secretive."

"Oh, I know that," exclaimed Parthenia. "Mother told me she'd been married before and that she'd met her first husband at a festival...somewhere. I can't remember right now but it'll come back to me if I think about it. She swore me to secrecy, of course, so Father wouldn't find out what I knew."

"Really?" said Carina. It was a lead if only a small one.

"Weren't you saying there was some information about mages in that religion's holy book?" Bryce asked.

"Yes," Carina said uncertainly, "though I had to read between the lines."

"Well, that's a start, isn't it?"

"I guess so."

Parthenia returned to the group of children, who were laughing and chatting as if they hadn't a care in the world. It was hard to believe what they'd each endured recently. If the boys and girls had been at home or in a park, no one could have guessed the trials they had been subjected to over the previous days.

Yet they were under the stars in the remains of a forest fire, the sky flashing and booms pulsing from the Sherrerr bombardment in the distance. They had no food or water or anywhere to sleep, and they had a challenging time ahead, striving to prevent their malevolent brother from achieving his bid for ultimate power.

Carina hoped with all her heart that, whatever happened, her little family would come out the other side unscathed.

CARINA'S STORY CONTINUES IN ...

WILDFIRE & STEEL

Sign up to my reader group for a free copy of the *Star Mage Saga* prequel, *Daughter of Discord*, discounts on new releases, review crew invitations and other interesting stuff:

https://jjgreenauthor.com/free-books/

www.ingramcontent.com/pod-product-compliance
Lightning Source LLC
Chambersburg PA
CBHW070554170726
48291CB00003B/617